THE GENE-POOL BOY
A Novel
By
MIKE SUTTON
Copyright 2024, All Rights Reserved

Copyright © 2024 Mike Sutton.
All rights reserved.

No part of this book may be reproduced, stored, or transmitted by any means—whether auditory, graphic, mechanical, or electronic—without written permission of both publisher and author, except in the case of brief excerpts used in critical articles and reviews. The unauthorized reproduction of any part of this work is illegal and is punishable by law.

Library of Congress Control Number: 202492506
ISBN: Paperback 9798302985408
All are registered to:
War Zone Press, LLC
11074 SW 73RD Circle
Ocala, FL 34476-8964
https://www.WarZonePress.com
Cover art by Peter Liu, 47SCAPES, LLC.

SCAPES

Inquiry emails should be sent to Staff@WarZonePress.com.

Because of the dynamic nature of the internet, any web addresses or links in this book may have changed since publication and may no longer be valid.

This is a work of fiction. Names, characters, places, and incidents either are the product of the author's imagination or are used fictitiously. Any resemblance to actual persons, living or dead, business establishments, events, or locales is entirely coincidental. The views expressed in this work are solely those of the author and do not reflect the views of the hosting website or any other commercial entity or person except the author.

TABLE OF CONTENTS

PROLOGUE	1
PART I	2
One	3
Two	4
Three	6
Four	8
Five	12
Six	16
Seven	18
Eight	22
Nine	27
PART II	30
Ten	31
Eleven	35
Twelve	38
Thirteen	42
Fourteen	47
Fifteen	50
Sixteen	52
Seventeen	59
PART III	66
Eighteen	67
Nineteen	70
Twenty	74
Twenty-one	83
PART IV	86
Twenty-two	87
Twenty-three	92
Twenty-four	95
Twenty-five	98
Twenty-six	103
Twenty-seven	107
Twenty-eight	113
Twenty-nine	116
Thirty	120
Thirty-one	123
PART V	126
Thirty-two	127
Thirty-three	132
Thirty-four	135

Thirty-five	142
Thirty-six	145
Thirty-seven	150
Thirty-eight	160
Thirty-nine	165
Forty	168
Forty-one	171
Forty-two	175
Forty-three	181
Forty-four	185
Forty-five	190
Forty-six	194
Forty-seven	198
Forty-eight	202
Forty-nine	205
Fifty	208
EPILOGUE	212
GLOSSARY	214
ACKNOWLEDGEMENTS	217
ABOUT THE AUTHOR	219

AUTHOR'S NOTE

In my previous novels, except for *No Survivors*, I complained that the research took far longer than the writing. Using Google and Google Maps was a significant step forward. However, ChatGPT, one of the artificial intelligence engines now available, made an incredible difference. Some of the most esoteric facts were available to me in milliseconds.

As with any technical tale, acronyms abound. I have tried to spell them out at least once within the text, except for those encountered in everyday usage. As a reader's aid, a complete list of acronyms is listed alphabetically at the end of the work.

I hope you find *The Gene Pool Boy* entertaining.

Mike Sutton
Mike@MKSutton.com
Saturday, November 16, 2024

FOR:
JOSEPH ANTHONY COSTANTINI

PROLOGUE

On January 20, 2020, in Everett, Snohomish County, Washington State, Patient Zero of the COVID-19 pandemic was diagnosed.

※ ※ ※

According to the Center for Disease Control, as of October 29, 2024, 1,216,744 Americans have died from the disease.

※ ※ ※

On May 25, 2020, George Floyd died in Minneapolis, MN.

PART I
"I'd rather be a white cop delivering the keynote address at a BLM convention . . . "

ONE

Cool, dry air inside her apartment embraced Ginger McGuire. Her escape from Baltimore's heat and humidity was complete one day after the summer solstice. What did the already scorching June heat portend for *August*?

Ginger set her red leather tote bag and a handful of mail on the glass-topped table inside her front door, then dropped her keys into a blue porcelain bowl next to the tote. After removing her white KN-95 face mask, she ran her fingers through her short, blond hair. She retrieved her mail and ambled toward her tiny kitchen, glancing through another day of junk mail. One small but somewhat heavy, tan cardboard envelope's return address surprised her. Mail from Perfect Perfume—her late father's employer—seemed odd seven months after his death.

She laid the other mail on the counter next to the sink. Lifting the envelope toward her face, Ginger pulled the tongue of the tear strip. The end of the envelope popped open,

emitting a soft "*psst*."

TWO

The desk phone intercom beeped. Hunter Morgan turned from the window of Last Resort Investigations office in Baltimore's Legg Mason Tower.

"There's a William Daugherty from WLAB, channel 2, on the phone. He says he knows you," Jeannie Staron announced. "Naturally, I'm suspicious of anyone from the media, knowing your *hate-hate* relationship with them."

Morgan chuckled, sitting down behind his desk. "Well, in this case, he does. Put him through, please."

"Copy that."

A moment later, the phone rang. "Billy Daugherty, how are ya?"

Daugherty's gravelly, Georgia-accented voice sounded tired for this early in the day.

"I've been better, man."

"Yeah? What's up?"

"One of my people is missing. I called the Baltimore Police Department. They won't look into it until she's been missing for twenty-four hours."

"That's standard Baltimore Police procedure, Billy. But with China virus running rampant, they're struggling to keep their workforce at minimum levels like everyone else."

"Who are we talking about?"

"Ginger McGuire. She's my 6 AM anchor. She didn't show up this morning, and we can't reach her."

"When's the last time she was seen?"

"Friday, after her usual time slot. She was here until about 2 PM."

"There's something *bad* wrong, Hunter. I know this kid, and she'd miss her parents' funeral before a broadcast. Would you reach out to your contacts and ask them to at least do a welfare check?"

"I'll do that, Billy, though it may not be immediate. What's her address?"

▶◀ ▶◀ ▶◀

Morgan's call to an old friend responsible for BPD's dispatch—aka KGA— accelerated the request for a "welfare check" considerably. Harper Lowe, a grizzled veteran of the *war* in Baltimore and a paratrooper in

Vietnam, was a man who didn't suffer fools at *all* . . . much less easily. The fact that the request came from the local media didn't hurt.

"KGA to 1C42."

"1C42 standing by," Patrolman Liam O'Leary responded.

"1C42, KGA has a request for a welfare check for a Ginger McGuire at Gallery Tower, 111 West Centre Street, apartment 6-J, as in John. The caller is a station manager from WLAB TV, who reports having had no contact since Friday. A maintenance man will meet you at the location."

"Copy that."

THREE

Residents of swank Inner Harbor apartment complexes were confident their building's controlled access parking garage protected its high-end vehicles.

Pity those poor souls who use street parking.

Cletis Monroe operated on the principle: "Invent the perfect mouse trap; soon, someone will create a smarter mouse."

Of course, inside information always raises a rodent's IQ.

Tonight, his target was a mid-price range Maserati *Quattroporte*—four doors—in stunning *blu emozione* metallic.

His TikTok subscription provided several excellent videos on defeating the vehicle's security system without leaving a mark on the doors or damaging the instrument panel.

Cletis pressed a few keys on his iPhone keyboard, unlocking the driver's side door. Once seated, a few more clicks started the *Quattroporte*. He enjoyed the muscular 580 hp 3.8L V8 engine rumble for a few seconds, then drove toward the garage door. A quick press of the opener on the sun visor lifted the massive steel door to the angular ramp.

The hundred-forty-two-thousand-dollar Maserati drove up to the street, turning left on International Drive. Within seconds, he took the traffic circle's third exit onto President Street, and the *Quattroporte* disappeared into Baltimore's steamy night.

⋈ ⋈ ⋈

Clarence Judge sat down at his basement desk in Olney, Maryland, on St. Florence Terrace in the Hallowell community. Janet had left a stack of mail there before leaving for her four-to-midnight ER shift at Olney's MedStar Montgomery Medical Center— where Clarence constantly feared for his wife's safety as contagion swept the nation.

Sorting through the stack of mostly junk and a few bills, the air traffic controller came across a tan cardboard envelope from the hospital where his mother had died two months earlier.

What's this? Clarence thought, picking it up. He pulled the small tongue, opening it. "*Psst*"

Betty Samuels' day had been terrifying, frustrating, and *very* worrisome. After more blood tests, CT scans, and MRIs to diagnose the cause of husband Anthony's failing liver, the medical profession *still* had no answer. As if his *morbus hepatis* weren't enough, the nagging fear of Anthony contracting COVID roamed her thoughts.

The hour-long drive home to Westminster from St. Joseph's Hospital in Towson west-bound on Baltimore's 695 beltway had become a nightmare. A tractor-trailer had swerved into her lane to avoid God only knew what, hitting her beloved Honda Accord. The trucker braked quickly, allowing Betty's car to spin in front of the tractor, which then broadsided her. The second impact spun her again into the left-most lane, now facing the oncoming traffic. The trucker didn't stop.

Miraculously, she slid to a dead stop without being struck head-on. Now, as drivers tried to get around her in the heavy traffic, many took the opportunity to display their middle fingers and shout obscenities. But not one stopped to see if she needed medical attention.

Finally, a Maryland State resource officer pulled over behind her. He knocked on the driver's window, startling Betty out of her daze. The officer called an ambulance and a tow-truck. He then took her license, registration, and insurance cards to give to a state trooper who would respond to the scene. He wrote down all the information necessary for the trooper to complete the accident report. Finally, he watched the ambulance depart, carrying Betty to the hospital.

Ninety minutes later, a state trooper found her in the emergency room. He returned her license, registration, insurance card, and his completed accident report. Before departing, he complimented the state resource officer for his thoroughness and assistance. "That guy made my report a breeze, ma'am. He's a true professional."

After a friend drove Betty home, she discovered a dead refrigerator freezer with its just-stocked small fortune in meat.

She looked through the mail with a glass of merlot on the end table and her feet on an ottoman. Her dear departed father had been one of the dying breed of warehouse workers. Caught between automation and artificial intelligence technologies, "order pickers" were becoming rarer than honest politicians.

So, the small, brown cardboard envelope from his last employer, DEN Logistics, came as a curious arrival.

"*Psst*"

FOUR

On the sixth floor of 111 West Centre Street, the maintenance man's gaggle of keys rattled as he twisted the master in apartment 6-J's lock. He swung the door inward and jerked backward into the BPD patrolman O'Leary behind him. "*¡Jesus Cristo! ¿Qué ese olor?*"

O'Leary steadied the man and stepped around him. "Stay out here."

Large eyes looked out over the man's surgical facemask. "*You no worry! I not go in!*"

Breathing through his mouth, O'Leary noted no signs of forced entry. He stepped into the lighted apartment cautiously. "*Baltimore Police*! Anyone home?" His loud voice got no response. The lights were on in a short hallway and kitchen a few steps away.

"*Hello*! Ms. *McGuire*?"

Advancing, O'Leary, a five-year BPD veteran, moved to the kitchen door. Ginger McGuire's crumpled body lay between a small island and the kitchen sink, a wedge heel a few inches away from her bare left foot. Her blue pantsuit seemed undisturbed. Ginger lay on her right side, her arm extended as if reaching for a brown object near her hand.

Ginger's body showed no signs of trauma or foul play.

O'Leary could see a fine, off-white powder on the island's countertop. *Cocaine*?

The patrolman keyed his microphone. "KGA, 142, I have an unattended death, DOA, an apparent overdose at this location. Requesting you notify 2100, Office of the Chief Medical Examiner, and a crime lab unit. Also, advise 140."

⋈||⋈ ⋈||⋈ ⋈||⋈

The sector sergeant—aka 140—heard the call and responded. "KGA, 140 requests a lateral with 142."

"KGA: go ahead, 140."

"140 to 142. Need additional units? Any witnesses need transport to 2100?" The original BPD 2100 phone extension for homicide had always identified that unit. O'Leary responded. "142. Negative on units and witnesses."

"140. Stand by for 2100, OCME and crime unit."
"142. Copy."

⋈||⋈ ⋈||⋈ ⋈||⋈

Fifteen-point-eight-two miles southwest of St. Florence Terrace—by crow—Franklin Judge, an up-and-coming IBM systems analyst, pushed open the front door of his McLean, Virginia, home. The soft rustle of paper sliding behind it accompanied the edge of a white envelope, making an appearance. *Got to replace that weather stripping*, he thought for the umpteenth time.

Inside, he bent and collected his mail—mostly junk except for a small brown cardboard envelope.

⋈||⋈ ⋈||⋈ ⋈||⋈

While O'Leary waited for the crime scene unit and office of the Chief Medical
Examiner's staff to arrive, he began looking for the victim's identification. He pulled a pair of X-large, powder-free, black Nitrile disposable gloves from a small pouch on his duty belt. The post-George Floyd defunding insanity, cost-cutting, and COVID-19 supply chain issues forced O'Leary to buy Nitrile gloves since the department never seemed to have any XLs. The fact that they were Raven's seemed entirely appropriate for the BPD.

He started with the most obvious—a large, red tote on a table near the front door. From it, he removed an HP ProBook notebook and Ginger's wallet. Flipping open the notebook,
O'Leary discovered a greeting card envelope. He pulled out a flowery Hallmark birthday card, opened it, noting the date a week before, and signed, "I love you, Baby. Mom."

Looking back at the envelope's return address, it had come from Mrs. Lucrecia G. McGuire in Towson.

My next call. God! I hate Next of Kin notifications! 'Mrs. McGuire, I'm very sorry to have to inform you . . .'

⋈||⋈ ⋈||⋈ ⋈||⋈

It took over two hours for a crime unit to arrive. COVID-19 had taken its toll on the BPD's rank and file in three ways: by infecting numerous staff members; the city requiring all employees to be vaccinated; requiring those refusing inoculation to show proof of a negative COVID test weekly. The mandate meant those who refused to get the "jab," as the President called it, lost time when being tested. Finally, the Baltimore Department of Human Resources made the weekly testing option even more unattractive with the following statement: "Per the protocol: A positive test result keeps you off the job for at least 10 days and you have to use your own paid time off to cover the absence." Detective Bill Wilson arrived a few minutes later. "What have we got, O'Leary?" he said, slipping on Nitrile gloves.

"Looks like another OD, Detective."

"Do we have an ID?"

"Ginger McGuire. She's a TV personality on WLAB. I found her mother's address in the tote bag near the door," O'Leary responded, handing Wilson the birthday card.

Wilson noted the address and handed it to a crime technician. "Bag this."

Wilson pointed at the object near Ginger's outstretched hand and directed the technician, "Get your pictures of that, then hand it to me."

Though Ginger's head position did not give Wilson a full-on view of her face, he felt an odd pang of recognition.

The technician's Canon digital camera clicked from several angles before she handed the object to Wilson.

It felt oddly heavy in his hand. A fine wire ran from the inside of the open-end flap back into the envelope. Wilson upended it. Nothing came out.

The detective pulled a small LED flashlight from his jacket pocket and pushed its orange end switch. Inside, the wire—with something small attached to its other end—lay near a silver tube. *What the hell?*

Wilson handed the envelope back to the technician. "Bag this. Then mark it and treat it as fragile."

"Yes, Detective."

Wilson turned back to O'Leary. "Okay, what else?"

"I haven't seen drug paraphernalia anywhere. The medicine cabinet contents are vanilla. The strongest thing there is Tylenol."

"Okay. Start a canvass of the other apartments on this floor. She's clearly been dead for some time. Check with the maintenance man for video surveillance. If there is, get a copy of the last seventy-two hours.

"Before you leave, mark the front door," Wilson directed, referring to standard yellow crime scene tape.

"Sure thing. You want me to do the NOK?" O'Leary asked.

Wilson shook his head. "No. I'll handle it. I'll want to ask the mother some questions. A piss-poor time to do so, though."

Turning to leave, O'Leary said, "That's why they pay you the big bucks, Detective. See ya."

⋈ ⋈ ⋈

Wilson walked through the apartment with a lab technician, occasionally directing her to photograph or record a specific item or location. Once completed, evidence collection began. The scene suggested a drug overdose, but with no evidence of foul play or forced entry, the process wrapped up relatively quickly for a questionable death. As the crime scene techs packed up, two OCME attendants arrived with a collapsible gurney and heavy-duty plastic body bag.

They carefully rolled Ginger's body onto her back, then arranged her arms and legs before placing her body into the bag.

The sound of a body bag's zipper closing always struck Wilson. *The sound of finality!*

Mike Sutton - 11

FIVE

Caroline McGuire—Ginger's grandmother—sat in her daughter's living room, her face in her hands, sobbing quietly.

Kim McGuire stared ahead blankly. "A drug overdose? That can't be," she said quietly. "My daughter isn't involved in drugs. She never *has* been. *God*! She doesn't even . . . never even *smoked*."

"I'm very sorry for your loss, Mrs. McGuire," Detective Wilson said. "We'll do everything we can to find out what happened. Is there anyone I can call to come and be with you and your mother?"

"No. There's just the two of us . . . *now*!" Kim McGuire waved at her mother, then sobbed quietly into a white handkerchief.

Wilson hesitated momentarily, then asked, "Did Ginger have any siblings?"

"No. She's an only child."

"And your husband?"

"Roger lost his battle with cancer earlier this year."

"I'm sorry, Mrs. McGuire."

Wilson took a business card from a gold container and held it out. "This is my card, ma'am. If you need anything, my personal cell phone number is on it. Don't hesitate to call me. I'll be in touch as we know more. Do you have any questions before I go?"

Kim McGuire lifted her head and shook it weakly. Her soft "No" was barely audible.

"All right, I'll show myself out."

ᴅᴎᴅᴀ ᴅᴎᴅᴀ ᴅᴎᴅᴀ

Similar calls, responses, and conclusions occurred in Olney and Westminster Maryland, and McLean, Virginia.

ᴅᴎᴅᴀ ᴅᴎᴅᴀ ᴅᴎᴅᴀ

"Hunter, I have Harper Lowe on the line for you."

"Put him through, Jeannie. Thanks."

Morgan picked up the handset. "What's going on, you old war horse?"

"Livin' the dream, Brother. Another day in paradise.

"Sorry to be the bearer of bad news, but your WLAB reporter was found dead in her apartment. She OD'd."

"*Really?*"

"Roger that. Another Baltimore success story," Lowe said sarcastically.

"Wow. That didn't sound like the person my buddy called about. She sounded like someone on the way to the top."

"Yeah. We've both seen shooting stars *detour* into the ditch, Morgan."

"Yeah. Who caught the case?"

"Let me look."

Morgan heard rustling papers.

"Bill Wilson. I know him from the VFW. He's a former member of Uncle Sam's *Misguided* Children. He's no *Defective Dipstick*. Bill's got a good in-house reputation.

He'll *work* the case."

"Have you got a number for him?"

"I think so. Hang on."

In the background, Morgan heard, "Hey, Diana! What's Detective Wilson's cell number?"

After a moment, a woman's voice said something indistinguishable.

Lowe repeated the number, and Morgan entered it into his iPhone's contact list.

"Sorry, I didn't have something better to report."

"Thanks, Harper. Give my best to Mary Ann."

"WILCO."

※※※ ※※※ ※※※

"That's pure *bullshit*, Hunter," Billy Daugherty growled.

"Hey, don't shoot the messenger," Morgan responded quietly.

"Sorry, man. It's just that I know Ginger. She's a total *straight* arrow. Didn't even drink at the Christmas party or company picnic. She wouldn't jeopardize a potential network-level career on *nose* candy."

"Billy let's wait for the crime lab and OCME's reports. What I just told you is based solely on what BPD saw at the scene, nothing scientific.

"I have the detective's number. I'll reach out to him."

※※※ ※※※ ※※※

When Anthony Samuels, a former Lead Bomb Technician for the BPD, hadn't heard from Betty for a day and a half, he called a fellow BPD retiree to check on her.

Paul Goodman arrived at the Samuels' home shortly after 9 PM, finding the kitchen door slightly open. Pushing it and stepping into the kitchen, he called, "Betty?" The beginnings of death's stench embraced him immediately.

Though retired, Goodman's investigatory experience kicked in.

Back out! Don't disturb the scene.

On the tiny porch, he opened his Samsung Android phone. Although Westminster had a police force, he dialed the Carroll County Sheriff's Office in Westminster. It might get some noses out of joint, but the sheriff had more resources and experience.

Within minutes, flashing blue lights illuminated the Samuels' home.

Two hours and twenty-seven minutes later, the Carroll County Coroner's Office removed Betty's body.

As they did, Goodman left for St. Joseph's Hospital . . . to break Anthony's heart.

▶◀ ▶◀ ▶◀

Bill Wilson's sister had two primary missions in life. First, the care and feeding of her husband and four-year-old son, Evan. Getting her single brother a suitable partner— preferably a spouse—came in second by a nose.

Dana Van Wyk often invited Bill to dinner. Frequently, he found a single, attractive, additional guest when he arrived. Tonight was no exception.

Demi Chatterley smiled when introduced, extending her hand. "Nice to meet you, Bill. Dana tells me you're a detective."

"I am."

"What kind?"

"I'm with the Homicide Division."

"Oh, *my*! That sounds exciting."

"It has its moments, Demi," Bill responded, already turned off.

Dana spoke up from the nearby kitchen, sensing her brother's southbound attitude.

"What cases are you working on now, Bill? Can you tell us about any?"

"I caught the WLAB anchor case."

Dana turned quickly. "*Who?*"

"Ginger McGuire."

"*No!*" Dana covered her mouth with a hand and an oven mitt. "*How?*" Bill looked at his sister quizzically. "You *know* her?"

"Yes! *You know her*! She's Evan's godmother. You *met* her at his christening."

"Oh, yeah," Bill responded weakly.

"She's my *Sigma Lambda Gamma* sorority sister from Barnard! I just had lunch with her two weeks ago. What *happened* to her?"

Before Bill could respond, Dana continued. "*Wait*! If *you're* investigating the case, she was *murdered*! *How?*"

"I can't go into the details, Sis. You know that." "You can't tell your own family how she died?"

"No."

Dana glared at her brother. "Well, can you tell me if her *mother knows*?"

"She does. I did the notification myself."

"*Oh, that poor woman*! She lost her husband to pancreatic cancer recently. Ginger told me how hard the adjustment has been for her mom and grandmother.

"Please, Bill, how did she die?"

"Fentanyl overdose."

Dana responded immediately. "*THAT'S NOT FUCKING POSSIBLE!*"

The outburst turned Evan's attention away from a toy truck. "Mommy, You said a *bad word*."

The oven mitt covered Dana's mouth again.

SIX

An officer arrived on the St. Florence Terrace scene within a few minutes of Janet Judge's highly emotional 911 call to the Montgomery County Maryland Police Department. The COVID-19 issues facing Baltimore City and Carroll County hampered the state's OCME and the local county's crime unit response. The early morning police activity prompted a close neighborhood friend's offer to let Janet Judge wait in her living room during the delay.

The lack of any drugs, user paraphernalia, or history of Clarence's or Franklin's recreational drug use mimicked the Baltimore and Westminster scenes. One piece of collected evidence mirrored the other locations exactly.

Nothing connected the Southern Maryland and Northern Virginia siblings' cases. Nor did either jurisdiction know that theirs was not the *first*.

⋈⋈ ⋈⋈ ⋈⋈

The call to Detective Wilson went straight to voicemail. Morgan briefly described his Harper Lowe connection and why he was calling.

Within an hour, Jeannie announced Wilson. Morgan answered.

"Detective Wilson, thanks for returning my call."

"Sure. What can I do for you?"

"I'm retired BPD, homicide and bomb squad . . ."

"Yeah, I know who you are, Mr. Morgan. And I know about Last Resort Investigations. You said you had something on one of my cases."

"Just Hunter. No need for mister.

"I just wanted to give you some information about Ginger McGuire."

"What's that?"

"Her boss is an old friend of mine. He insists that she'd *never* use drugs."

"My time at the scene suggests something different. Non-drug use claims and *innocent* convicts. The numbers are about equal."

"Yes, Detective, that's true. But in *both* cases, *some* are valid. That's why we started LRI. I'm just asking that you keep an open mind in this case."

"I do with all my cases. Anything else?" Wilson responded with a slight air of irritation.

"That's what Harper Lowe told me."

"Yeah? You know Lowe from the Force?"

"Yes, and he's a fellow Vietnam Vet.

"Look, I know the OCME, the crime unit, and you are facing a lot of China Virus challenges. I just want you to know that LRI has an outstanding lab and coroner on staff.

If we can be of any assist . . ."

"Let me stop you right there. I'd rather be a white cop delivering the keynote address at a BLM convention than color outside the BPD's evidence protocols. So, thanks, but *no thanks*."

Three short beeps told Morgan the call had ended. *Well, that seemed to go pretty well.*

▶◀ ▶◀ ▶◀

Cletis Monroe had boosted dozens of high-end wheels, but this Porsche Panamera Turbo S, with a 5.3L EcoTec3 V8 and 8-speed *Doppelkupplung*—dual-clutch—transmission, had to be among the *sweetest*! With all the bells and whistles options, it cost more than POTUS made in a year.

If not for ruining Cletis' *perfect* record of delivering *every* order without fail, he would have kept it for himself.

▶◀ ▶◀ ▶◀

A simple observation most people wouldn't think twice about eroded into a chasm between the Judge families, not due to any difference between the siblings but rather their wives. Janet Judge could turn a perceived snub into an irreparable offense.

Early in their marriage, she and Clarence attended a dinner party at the McLean Judges' home. Janet brought a deep-dish apple pie from a well-known Olney bakery. After dinner, Amanda Judge tasted it, wrinkled her nose, and said, "Oh, my! This is *tart*!" Another female guest agreed.

Those observations lit the fuse. To Janet Judge, an unimaginable embarrassment had just occurred.

During the half-hour drive home, Clarence—no stranger to Janet's overreactions— white-knuckled the steering wheel to keep his mouth shut.

For six years since the death of their mother, there had been no communication between the Judge households.

So, when Janet saw Franklin Judge's name on the Caller ID screen, she put the cordless phone back in its charging base.

SEVEN

With COVID-19 killing thousands of Americans daily, the strain on many municipal organizations nationwide became immense. Counter-intuitively, the pandemic aided the BPD's Department Forensic Laboratory Section—aka crime lab. Their turn-around times improved. With the courts shut down, forensic staff members weren't wasting hours or days waiting to testify. Second, staff members' productivity working from home improved due to fewer workplace interruptions.

Detective Wilson generally had crime scene photos, sketches, and evidence listings in three to five days. Autopsy results in seven to ten. Final drug screening could take a little longer, but not generally much more than two weeks.

Wilson opened and read the Analytical Sciences Branch report less than forty-eight hours after visiting the crime scene. The powder on the kitchen island, surrounding counter space, and floors contained a mixture of *pure* atomized fentanyl and a pharmaceutical-grade propellant residue. The same residue covered Ginger McGuire's face and upper body.

The cardboard envelope had been disassembled and photographed. Its return address said, "Perfect Perfume." Wilson Googled it. The search showed an honest company at the same address as the envelope's return.

An oblong U.S. Postal Service postage label covered the upper right portion of the 4.5" X 3" envelope, with Ginger McGuire's address affixed to its center. The pull tab to open it had been on the envelope's opposite side.

The object Wilson could not see fully at the scene was a small silver compressed gas cartridge marked "16 Grams." The report listed its dimensions as 3.5" long and a diameter of 0.84".

What appeared to be a small valve had been attached to the cartridge's threaded end.

A closeup photo showed a thin wire epoxied to the underside of the envelope's tear strip, a tiny red plug at its end.

When initially assembled, the gas cartridge sat, epoxied in place, and confined within small partitions on all sides, preventing lateral movement.

The lab concluded that ripping the tear strip open released a hefty dose of pure fentanyl directly into or near the face of the victim.

Jesus! Talk about hate mail!

⋈ ⋈ ⋈

Had the Judge widows not been Facebook members—Amanda casual, Janet intense— it could have taken months or longer for them to discover the similarities of their husbands' deaths.

The "Six Degrees of Kevin Bacon" concept states that any two people on earth can link through six or fewer acquaintances.

Neither woman would ever consider "friending" the other, but they were now virtually connected through the Bacon theory.

Assuming law enforcement agencies communicated, Amanda took no action. Janet called the Montgomery County Police.

⋈ ⋈ ⋈

At roughly 2,000 feet of elevation, Frostburg, Maryland, is one of the Allegheny Mountains' many jewels. The State University is home to several thousand students and faculty annually.

Associate Professor of Physics Dr. Jerome Phillip Mendelson's record time crossing the tenure track's finish line would be hard to break. His nomination for the Fields Medal ignited an afterburner. While primarily awarded in mathematics, the Fields Medal is among the most prestigious academic commendations. Awarded every four years to mathematicians under 40, Jerome Mendelson had yet to enter his thirties. Although not specifically a physics award, many recipients have significantly contributed to mathematical physics and related fields.

Today, Jerome's mail included a brown cardboard envelope.

⋈ ⋈ ⋈

Janet Judge's call to the Montgomery County Maryland Police received no significant scrutiny. Two brothers OD'ing hardly reverberated the peculiarity gong. The lead on a detective's desk disappeared quickly beneath other objects.

⋈ ⋈ ⋈

Bill Wilson contacted Robert Rich, a friend and recently retired Analytical Sciences Branch technician.

"Bob, Bill Wilson. How are you and Donna doing?"

"Getting ready to leave the People's Republic of Maryland and move to Florida. How 'bout you?"

"Not that lucky. Not yet, anyway.

"So, I've got an odd piece of evidence I need some insight on." Wilson described his case and the evidence photos he'd just received. "Can I shoot this picture over and get your thoughts on it?" "Yeah. Fire away, Bill." "Okay, just emailed it. "So, where in Florida?"

"Central, Ocala. Northwest of Orlando, northeast of Tampa, southwest of Jacksonville. About an hour from the Atlantic and Gulf coasts."

"Hurricanes?"

"Always a possibility. But, at least the fifty miles of land between us and the water will help to reduce their impact."

"Okay, got your email. Let me open it up."

Rich was silent for several seconds, then said, "Wow! That's novel for sure.

"So, a WLAB reporter got this mailed to her at the station?"

"No, at home."

"And Perfect Perfume is an actual company in Baltimore?"

"Yup."

"Any connection to the victim?"

"Not that I know of yet. What I'm really interested in is this gas cartridge. The lab results showed pure atomized fentanyl and pharmaceutical-grade nitrogen propellant. It covered her face and chest area.

"I don't have the autopsy or tox results yet, but I'm sure she OD'd. Your thoughts, Bob?"

"Well, the CDC says two milligrams of fentanyl can be deadly. So, assuming you could load sixteen grams in the cartridge, that would be eight thousand times a lethal dose. Talk about *overkill*!"

"Yeah. A relatively painless way to go, I guess. Anything else?"

"Nobody's buying these envelopes in bulk on the internet, Bill, unless Amazon has opened a store on the dark web. You're looking at a *very* sophisticated stealth-killing device."

"What's the *dark web*, and how do I access it, Bob?"

"I don't think you want to dip your toes into those waters, Bill. Your best bet is going through the department's open-source or digital forensic unit. Those guys are pros."

"Do you have any contacts there?"

"Yeah, I know a guy . . ."

⋈⋈ ⋈⋈ ⋈⋈

LRI's VP of Forensics, Mark Proffitt, answered his desk phone. "Yes, boss? How can

I be of assistance?"

"How do you always know it's me?" Morgan asked with a chuckle. "My phone is set up to flash the word 'alert' when you call."

"Clearly, you've had too much time on your hands. Let me fix that.

"Do you still have any contacts in BPD's Forensic Science Division?"

"Yeah, a couple of dinosaurs are left from my time there. What do you need?"

"Did you read my email about the Ginger McGuire case?"

"I did. See what you can find out about it."

"Copy that."

Mike Sutton - 21

⋈⋈ ⋈⋈ ⋈⋈

Bill Wilson admired the view of Baltimore's Inner Harbor from the fourteenth floor of the Legg Mason Tower. Perfect Perfume CEO's spacious office testified to the company's success. Their attractive, fifty-ish, blonde leader sat behind a massive oak desk. A nearly complete, floor-to-ceiling glass wall offered a postcard view of the city behind her.

Using a magnifying glass, the office manager studied a picture of the front of the envelope mailed to Ginger McGuire. Shaking her head, the woman handed the image back to Wilson.

"This didn't come from us, Detective. That's not our postal account code."

"How about the name 'McGuire'?"

"We had a Roger McGuire," the CEO answered. "He was our VP of marketing."

"Was?"

"Yes. Roger died of cancer six or seven months ago." "Who was his next of kin?" Wilson asked.

"Kimberly McGuire," the CEO answered quickly.

"A resident of Mount Vernon?"

"Yes."

⋈⋈ ⋈⋈ ⋈⋈

In the elevator vestibule, Bill Wilson pushed the down arrow. A soft chime sounded behind him. He turned to see a green downward arrow above an already-opening door. A tall, well-dressed man stood at the car's rear, reading a document. He looked up as Wilson entered.

"Morning."

Wilson nodded, but didn't speak.

The door closed, and the car began to descend.

"You on the job?" the man asked.

"Yeah. Based on that suit, you're not," Wilson observed, looking over his shoulder.

"No, I put in my papers years ago and started a business—Last Resort Investigations."

The man extended his right hand. "I'm Hunter Morgan." Wilson turned and shook hands. His eyes showed surprise.

Morgan smiled. "Your voice is familiar. Have we met before?"

"No."

After a moment of hesitation, Morgan said, "No, we haven't. But we spoke on the

phone recently . . . Detective Wilson."

EIGHT

Dr. Mendelson's absence from a morning class and inability to reach him kicked off a welfare check by the campus police force. The discovery of his body caused notification to the Frostburg Police Department and the Allegheny County Sheriff's Office; neither had dedicated homicide departments. The Maryland State Police Cumberland Barrack "C" was next in the jurisdictional parade, capable of in-depth homicide investigation. Within two hours, MSP investigators were examining the scene.

✂︎✂︎✂︎

Mark Proffitt stood in front of Morgan's desk. "The toxicology report just came back. Ms. McGuire died of an *involuntary* fentanyl OD, boss. That's my term, not the
OCME's."

"*Involuntary*? She was collateral damage?"

"Negative. She was the object of a *very* sophisticated hit."

Proffitt relayed what he'd learned from the crime lab about the scene and evidence collected.

"Atomized *fentanyl*? I didn't know that was possible, Mark."

"It is, and the massive dose she received could have easily killed *thousands* of people. "I wonder if she was working on a story someone didn't want on the air."

Morgan shook his head. "She was the early morning news anchor. Daugherty didn't mention anything about investigative reporting.

"*Shit*! This puts me in a *bad spot*."

"Why?"

"Because I should pass that information onto Billy Daugherty. But doing so could impede the investigation. Billy'll want to pursue this because someone *murdered* a member of his staff. Beyond that . . . 'If it *bleeds*, it *leads*.' WLAB will be all over the story like slick on a banana peel.

"The BPD will ask questions about unauthorized leaks of crime lab information, which could get traced to you and LRI."

Proffitt shook his head. "What are you going to do, boss?"

"Stew on it for a while."

⋈⫿⋈ ⋈⫿⋈ ⋈⫿⋈

Neither Frostburg nor the county constabularies would have significant involvement in investigating Dr. Mendelson's demise. However, a recent police department addition would provide a vital link.

Maryland's Police Correctional Training Commission trains police and correctional officers for law enforcement jurisdictions without discrete police academies.

Rookie officer Peter Farler, a newly minted MPCTC graduate assigned to secure the scene, stood over the victim's body. Nearby, a small cardboard envelope lay on the floor. Its torn side exposed an object reflecting light from a nearby table lamp.

Farler bent to look closer and saw "16" printed on it. He knew better than to touch or move it, but a photograph couldn't do any damage. He used his iPhone's flash feature to record several closeups from various angles.

⋈⫿⋈ ⋈⫿⋈ ⋈⫿⋈

Bill Wilson sat in Kimberly McGuire's living room.

"Ma'am, I know it's difficult, especially at a time like this, but can you tell me about your husband's death, please? I understand he died from pancreatic cancer."

"He did. How did you know that?"

"My sister told me. She was Ginger's college sorority sister."

"Dana? Dana Wilson is your sister?"

"Yes, ma'am."

"Yes. Roger, like most victims, wasn't diagnosed until far too late."

⋈⫿⋈ ⋈⫿⋈ ⋈⫿⋈

The Maryland Coordination and Analysis Center is federally funded but managed by the Maryland State Police. Staffed by agents from the state's major state law enforcement jurisdictions, MCAC shares information and coordinates efforts, focusing on intelligence gathering, analysis, and dissemination of information to fight crime.

Following the OCME's release of Ginger McGuire's autopsy and antemortem toxicology results, a posting appeared describing the case and mentioning the gas cylinder in detail. Even so, the notification of Janet Judge's call concerning her brother-in-law went into the case file—with barely a glance—on a Montgomery County detective's desk.

⋈⫿⋈ ⋈⫿⋈ ⋈⫿⋈

At Baltimore Washington International's Thurgood Marshall Airport, Cletis Monroe settled into an American Airlines first-class seat beside his current squeeze. Like the many other women he'd made the acquaintance of, she brought traffic to a screeching halt.

The stress of his *second* job needed medication, and Nevis Island's Four Seasons Resort offered the perfect luxurious prescription. Part of the Federation of Saint Kitts and Nevis—a two-island Eastern Caribbean nation—Nevis is situated southeast of Puerto Rico and directly west of Antigua and Barbuda.

⋈⋈⋈ ⋈⋈⋈ ⋈⋈⋈

Homicide Detective Julie Stephens's reputation for blunt and scorching sarcasm earned her the nickname "Julicifer" within the Montgomery County, Maryland Police Department. She considered the devil's comparison an honor.

The 5'2" veteran of nineteen years on the job could handle herself well in difficult situations. Dozens of strapping men could testify to Julie's masterful application of Pressure Point Control Tactics. She taught women's self-defense courses twice a week that included a hefty dose of PPCT.

Divorced with daughters thirteen and sixteen, Julie didn't have much time for romantic relationships, due in no part to a lack of offers. The only men not interested in her green-eyed, blonde, girl-next-door beauty with a *very* well-sculpted figure were either gay or navigated using a white cane.

Julie was about to move past the Baltimore OD MCAC item when the term "media" caught her attention. Reading the item in full jogged her memory of a recent lunch conversation. An MCPD crime lab tech mentioned a cylinder in a recent case. *Where was that?*

Julie dialed the tech's extension.

"It was in Olney, Julicifer. *Peculiar* case."

Julie got the case number and then searched the system for it. The file's last entry noted a call from the victim's wife indicating the OD of her brother-in-law in McLean, Virginia.

The assigned detective—a soon-to-be-retired "coaster"—looked up as Julie approached his desk. "Oh, my! A visitor from the dark side. To what do I owe the *displeasure*, Julicifer?"

Julie ignored his comment. "You have the Olney OD case. The victim's wife called about her brother-in-law dying the same way in Virginia."

"Yeah, what about it?" "I'll take it off your hands."

"Why would I give it to you?"

Julie smiled. "You've been retired in place ever since I became a detective. And, if you ever did *give* a fuck about a case, a *mop* looked like a *machete* compared to *your* investigative skills! So, lighten your caseload and make your retirement legitimate."

With a mumbled "*Fuck you*, Julicifer," he handed over the file without PPCT inducement.

⋈⋈⋈ ⋈⋈⋈ ⋈⋈⋈

For over twenty years, Joe Costa ran the BPD's gambit from patrol to SWAT and, finally, the bomb squad. Upon retirement, he became an LRI partner.

When the State of Maryland approached him years later to manage the police section of the Maryland Police Correctional Training Commission, it was time to move on to his greatest love—teaching. Joe's forty-plus years of experience, exceptional instructional ability, and attention to detail created life-saving lectures and demonstrations for countless police officers. Joe loved *this* job above all others!

Though it seemed trivial to some, he presented a valuable parting gift to each graduating class—his cell phone number.

Thus, a young Frostburg patrol officer dialed Joe, shared photos, and asked for an opinion on the odd evidence.

Joe never rode the bus to Assumptionville. He said, "Let me look into this and get back to you, Officer Farler."

⋈⋈⋈ ⋈⋈⋈ ⋈⋈⋈

Julie Stephens interviewed Janet Judge. The grieving widow could think of no one hostile to her husband. The meeting also netted Amanda Judge's name, address, and phone number in McLean.

She then contacted the Fairfax County Police Department, requested a copy of their investigation, and arranged an FCPD escort to Amanda's home for an interview.

The similarities between the Montgomery County case and Ginger McGuire's OD immediately alarmed Julie. Both involved items received through the USPS, meaning the FBI and/or U.S. Postal Inspectors would soon "big-foot" her case.

Like most local law enforcement members, Julie wasn't happy being swatted aside by federal agencies. So, although it might cause Fairfax County *agita*, she drove to the Waggaman Circle address *sans* escort.

Amanda, like Janet, could offer no reason for her spouse's murder. Franklin had not shown *any* indication of substance abuse, be it drugs or alcohol.

As Julie walked toward Amanda's front door to leave, she said casually, "Your sister-in-law mentioned the death of Clarence and Franklin's father."

"Yes," Amanda replied, "pancreatic cancer less than a year ago."

⋈⋈⋈ ⋈⋈⋈ ⋈⋈⋈

Dozens of Google searches did little to help Bill Wilson understand the dark web. The more he read, the less he understood. However, numerous warnings describing the pitfalls of delving into cyberspace's underworld made him *very* hesitant to use a BPD computer, and in no way did he intend to expose his own iMac desktop.

His reading included discussions on "black" and "white hats," the latter being hackers working to counter the nefarious actions of their evil opposites.

Like Julie Stephens, Wilson knew the USPS' delivery of Ginger's death device would soon end his investigation. Federal usurpation would be a small and welcome caseload reduction for some detectives, but not Wilson. If a gene sequence for tenacity exists on a DNA helix, Wilson's was abnormally prominent. He intended to work this case regardless of federal involvement.

It was time to call Bob Rich's *guy* in the open-source unit.

NINE

When Joe Costa pulled the latest Maryland Coordination and Analysis Center Report, he discovered two cases strikingly similar to Dr. Mendelson's in Frostburg.

Within minutes, he called Morgan. "Have you been following the WLAB reporter case?"

"Yeah. Ginger McGuire's boss called me to see if I could speed up a welfare check on her. Now, I've got my ass in a crack."

Morgan explained his Daugherty dilemma.

"Sounds like *no* action is the best choice right now," Costa suggested. "The woman won't be any less dead if you tell him the truth. And things may work out, so you don't have to say anything."

"Yes, but I'm going to feel very guilty not being honest with him."

"If you have been with him so far, let that suffice until something changes—good or bad," Costa suggested. "Anyway, two other cases look identical based on an MCAC report I just read. One in Olney, the other in Frostburg."

"*What*?"

"Yup, same MO. Cardboard envelopes, gas cylinders, and massive aerosol fentanyl delivery." "Any connection to the other victims, Joe?"

"Not at the time the report was released. I'm going to do some digging and see what I turn up. I'll pass on anything I find to Proffitt and CC you."

"Okay. Let me know if you want us to get involved *officially*.

"Jesus, Ted Kaczynski's mail bombs reigned terror from the '70s to the mid-90s, killing three. This new nut-job tied Ted's record in less than two weeks."

⋈||⋈ ⋈||⋈ ⋈||⋈

Julie Stephens reviewed the Virginia case file and accompanying evidence photos.

The return address label on the envelope read "George Washington University Hospital." That clicked something in her memory.

She quickly turned to the Olney, MD case envelope photos—"George Washington University Hospital."

⋈||⋈ ⋈||⋈ ⋈||⋈

"Open-source unit, Detective Poulin."

Bill Wilson introduced himself and explained the reason for his call. After a short discussion, Roger Poulin asked for the evidence photos.

Wilson sent them, and soon, Poulin acknowledged their receipt.

"Let me look into this. I'll get back to you, Wilson."

⋈||⋈ ⋈||⋈ ⋈||⋈

Janet Judge answered Julie's call on the second ring.

"Hello?"

"Mrs. Judge, Detective Stephens. Did your husband have any connection with the George Washington University Hospital?" "No."

"None at all?"

"Not that I know of."

Sounding deflated, Julie said, "Oh. Okay . . . "

"His father died there. But Clarence was never a *patient*."

"Cause of death?"

"Pancreatic cancer."

⋈||⋈ ⋈||⋈ ⋈||⋈

At 100 Edison Park Drive, Gaithersburg, Maryland, Julie Stephens walked from her car toward the MCPD headquarters office. Even the day's scorching heat and humidity couldn't dampen the cold shiver running down her spine. Active serial murders across multiple jurisdictions needed coordinated *local* investigations.

Back at her desk, after referencing the Baltimore case report, Julie dialed the BPD homicide division, asking for Detective Wilson.

Incredibly, he answered.

Wilson knew about the Olney murder, but not Virginia's victim. At this point, neither knew of Dr. Mendelson's case in Frostburg.

"What was the return address on your victim's envelope?" Julie asked.

"Her father's former employer, Perfect Perfume."

"Did pancreatic cancer kill McGuire's father?"

"Yes, ma'am."

"*Please*, just Julie. I feel old enough without being a *ma'am*."

"Okay, I'm Bill." "Got ya.

"The Judge brothers' father too, at GW University Hospital. The return addresses are on both their envelopes. So, what will you do when the feds steamroll in, Bill?"

"I'll keep working the case on my own time if necessary."

"Why?"

"It's personal. Ginger McGuire was my nephew's godmother.

"Are you just going to turn your case over?"

"Nope."

"Why?"

"Because I'm a stubborn bitch who finishes what she starts.

"We can share information as we get it, if you like."

"Fine with me. I'm pursuing these fentanyl-loaded cylinders and the envelopes they came in with our open-source unit. One of my lab rat buddies says they may be available on the dark web.

"Are you an internet geek, Julie?"

"I'm still learning to navigate on the *lit* web."

"Okay, I'll see what I can find out and get back to you."

They ended the call by agreeing to use only private cell phones for future communications and non-departmental email for evidence updates.

PART II
"The *effluent* just hit the fan."

TEN

"It's a package deal. The buyer won't take the Bentley without the Bugatti Chiron Super Sport. Only ten were produced, and one is en route to an American. So, hide the Bentley until it arrives, and we can fill the order."

Cletis Monroe's hand seemed ready to crush his iPhone. "What th' fuck do you mean *hide it*?"

Nevis Island's remaining benefits evaporated like peanuts before pigeons.

"*You fuckin' ordered it*! *YOU hide it!*"

The woman's silky voice instantly turned tungsten-hard.

"You've made a *lot* of money through our association. If you want to *continue* . . . hide

 . . . the . . . *fucking* . . . *Bentley!*"

Cletis knew *that* tone. Rumors of gruesome results for those ignoring it cooled his objections as if a virtual, icy Gatorade challenge bathed them.

"Okay, Cindy," he responded meekly. "But what's with the Bentley Continental GT? It wouldn't make a decent down payment on a nearly four-million-dollar Bugatti."

"I have no idea, Cletis. The client is one of the wealthiest men in the world. His people called with the order and stipulated its parameters."

"Why doesn't he just buy the Bugatti outright?"

"Cletis, this *ends* Q and A. Bugatti *only made ten*. The client didn't *win* the Bugatti *lottery*. *Hide* the Bentley. I'll be in touch."

The soft beep in Cletis' ear said Cindy had left the building.

⋈|⋈ ⋈|⋈ ⋈|⋈

The formation of a federal inter-jurisdictional task force immediately drew bureaucratic blood. The FBI baited by the murders; the ATF assaulted the drug's summit; the USPS used postage stickers wielded by their Postal Inspection Service as shields against being bullied out of investigative glory.

The three agencies would descend on the BPD, OCME, MCAC, MSP, and Fairfax County's equivalent's organizations, shutting down the local investigations faster than a Tesla in Antarctica. Within twenty-four hours, the Baltimore City, Montgomery County, Maryland State Police, and Fairfax County cases would be snared in the federal web.

⋈ ⋈ ⋈

Command, staff, and supervisors—especially the first-line detective, patrol, and specialized unit leaders—were informed of federal investigative assumptions and the task force's contact information in each jurisdiction. The OCME staff were advised to notify the feds of any questionable deaths or ODs fitting the cases' pattern.

Bill Wilson and Julie Stephens discussed the directives, agreeing to strain their elasticity.

⋈ ⋈ ⋈

Knowing of the federal annexation of his and Julie Stephens' cases, Bill Wilson assumed others had been as well. But he called Roger Poulin in the open-source unit, hoping to glean some last-minute information via the back door.

"Roger, Bill Wilson. I hadn't heard from you in a while and wanted to know if anything turned up in your searches."

"I can't talk to you, Detective."

"Look, Roger. I know the feds have circled the wagons around my case, but I'm . . . " "Bill! *I can't **talk** to you*," Poulin whispered, almost frantically, before ending the call.

Wilson looked at his phone as if it held a secret about why Poulin sounded so anxious. Interdepartmental cooperation didn't typically shut down when a federal agency assumed case control.

If he wanted to pursue the case, he'd have to find a source outside the BPD. Only one came to mind.

*Maybe Google can find the best recipe for **crow**.*

⋈ ⋈ ⋈

Cletis Monroe adjusted the powder blue Bentley Continental GT convertible's auto dimming rearview mirror before carefully backing the car into a 10' X 20' climate-controlled storage space. He wore no gloves. Anger at having to babysit the vehicle had overridden his standard precautions. He wiped down the steering wheel and gear shift before carefully opening the door to avoid hitting the wall.

Still simmering at the thought of covering its cost, he rolled the overhead door down and locked it. Walking toward the exit gate, he ordered an Uber.

⋈ ⋈ ⋈

"Hunter, I have a BPD Detective Wilson on the phone for you," Jeannie Staron announced.

Morgan smiled inwardly. *I wonder how his BLM keynote went.*

"Put him through."

"Good morning, Detective. What can I do for you?"

"We never had this conversation. Agreed, Mr. Morgan?"

"Yes, sir. No need for formality here. Hunter will do fine."

"Okay, I'm Bill. Two other cases match the McGuire case to a tee," Wilson said.

"In Olney and Frostburg?"

"Frostburg?"

"Yes. A university professor. What two are you talking about?"

"Olney and McLean, Virginia."

"Oh! Didn't know about McLean. I guess we learned something from each other."

"Yeah, speaking of learning, that's why I'm calling. What do you know about the envelopes these devices are coming in?"

"Nothing other than they're similar," Morgan answered.

"They're not 'similar'—they are identical and unique. What's your cell number? I'll send ya a couple of pics."

Morgan gave Wilson the number, and a few seconds later, his iPhone beeped.

Morgan reviewed the photos, noting the similarity to Joe Costa's shared set. "Look, Bill, in full disclosure, yours aren't the first time I've seen these envelopes. One of my former partners sent me pics of the device used in the Frostburg case. "Odd looking and clearly designed to deliver a deadly cargo."

"Exactly. I've done dozens of Google searches and can't find anything remotely close to these available commercially. A former member of MCAC suggested they might be available on the dark web. From what I've read, you need a miner's light and a mine detector before venturing onto *that* cyberspace off-ramp. My kit bag has neither. Can your techies do these searches?"

"Can't MCAC help you out there?"

"I've been down that road, Hunter. Called a guy in their open-source unit. I sent him the photos I just sent you and asked him to see what he could find on the dark side. I just called him again. He freaked out. *Whispered* he couldn't talk to me and hung up.

"There's a federal task force cocktail of abbreviations working the cases now. I think someone put the fear of God into the crime lab folks about keeping the lid on any evidence." Morgan chuckled. "I'd love to be a pinstriped suit's lapel pin in *that* sudden death cage match.

"Let me talk to our chief lab rat, Bill, and see what he thinks. What's the best way to reach you?"

Morgan wrote down Wilson's cell number and ended the call.

⋈ ⋈ ⋈

The federal task force status update at 2600 Lord Baltimore Dr, Windsor Mill, MD

21244—the FBI's Baltimore Field Office—had long since lost cordiality. Special Agent in Charge Maddison Mitchell stood at the end of a conference table long enough to land a small aircraft and shouted! "*Everybody SHUT UP!*"

Slowly, the angry discord dwindled to almost total silence.

She looked around the group. "I want one statement from each agency on your current investigative status. Just what you know, *no* speculation. There will be *no* interruptions or comments during the update.

"Postal."

"We know each package has been canceled on the Eastern Seaboard. Maryland, PA, New Jersey, Delaware. No biometric data has been recovered. The postage amount on each package is accurate. However, the postage labels are printed on an untraceable, counterfeit machine."

"Can you adjust your mail scanning equipment to find and stop future threats?" Mitchell asked.

"We are attempting to do that now."

"Thank you." Mitchell looked at her second-in-command. "FBI."

"We have found no connection between the four victims at this point. None have any criminal history nor do any close family members. All victims are in their late twenties to late thirties. Each received device came from an employer or organization affiliated with a parent. Two victims are brothers.

"The propellent is simple carbon dioxide. We've never seen fentanyl atomized for other than legitimate pharmaceutical uses.

"As Postal said, there is no biometric data in or on any of the packages or cylinders."

"Thank you. ATF."

"The fentanyl is the purest we have ever seen—far higher quality than anything coming across the southern border. The samples from each device are identical. That's it." The postal representative raised her hand.

Mitchell looked at her somewhat sternly. "Yes?"

"Are we going to make a public announcement about this threat?"

"No. Not at this time. We only have four cases. An announcement could cause panic and drive the perp underground."

A quiet voice from the other end of the room asked, "How many dead will it take to *change* your mind?"

⋈||⋈ ⋈||⋈ ⋈||⋈

Morgan walked into Proffitt's office. "How much do you know about the dark web?" Proffitt turned from a large computer monitor.

"I know it's out there and used for nefarious purposes, but I don't have any personal experience with it."

"Look at the pictures I emailed you a few minutes ago. See if you can find anything similar. Okay?"

"Sure," Proffitt said. "Let me talk to a couple of my guys. I'll get back to you."

ELEVEN

Over the next five days, additional cases arose in New Jersey, Pennsylvania, North. Carolina, and Maryland. Maryland's in Gaithersburg caused a call to Montgomery County's 911 dispatch center. Julie Stephens answered the responding patrol's call for an investigator. Waiting for the lab techs and OCME to arrive, she used her cell phone to take numerous photos of the now-familiar cardboard envelope, including its return address. Julie then collected samples of the white powder on and near the female victim.

Back at her desk, Julie ignored her lieutenant's instructions to notify the task force with any additional evidence. She did, however, call Bill Wilson.

"We've got another case down here, Bill."

"Same MO?"

"Exactly. I'm sending you photos I took. I also collected samples of what I'm sure is fentanyl before the lab guys got there."

"Do the feds know yet, Julie?"

"Not from me."

Wilson filled Julie in on his conversation with Morgan and asked if she knew about LRI.

"I've only heard stories second or third hand about their involvement in cases no one else wanted to lay hands on."

"That's what they do. Overturned some ironclad convictions and stopped others cold.

"What are you going to do with the samples you have?"

"I don't have a plan yet, just wanted them for insurance."

"How about sending them to Morgan for analysis? They've got a top-rank lab."

"If I send 'em, there goes the chain of custody. I'll drive them up there tomorrow. Maybe we can meet for lunch."

"Works for me."

Paul Frederick Peterson's Iraq War Purple Heart was his Arlington National Cemetery ante. A who's-who of political and military leaders attended. Few in the assemblage actually knew the man. They *all* knew his wife—Lucille Peterson, the Speaker of the U. S. House of Representatives.

Mr. Peterson's pancreatic cancer battle had been mercifully short—four weeks to the day following his diagnosis.

The Peterson's only child had come as a surprise development with the Speaker nearing her forty-third birthday. Jasmine worked in her mother's Capitol Hill office part time. Her father's death caused an extravagant and intricately planned wedding to be postponed. Now, less than two weeks away, checking and fine-tuning the final details kept Jasmine at home today in Arlington, Virginia.

Near noon, the mail arrived through the front door slot, falling to the hardwood floor with a soft thud.

⋈‖⋈ ⋈‖⋈ ⋈‖⋈

Julie Stephens saw Baltimore's I-695 Beltway as a parallel universe. Near noon, the traffic mirrored DC's I-495 ring for congestion and aggressive driving.

She entered the city's inner harbor area, parking near Mason's Famous Lobster Rolls takeout restaurant on East Pratt Street.

After a short walk, she found Bill Wilson sitting at a table with a cup of coffee and a manila folder.

"Bill. Julie Stephens. How are you?"

Wilson looked up and smiled. "Hungry. How 'bout you?"

"As my Pop says, 'I could eat the south end of a northbound mule.'" Shaking his head, still smiling, Bill replied, "I'm not *that* hungry.

"Take a look at the menu board and tell me what you want. I'll get it while you hold the table."

Julie scanned the choices. "A Lobster BLT Roll and a water." She reached into her purse, "Let me pay for it, please."

"Nope. My turf, my treat. You can buy in Montgomery County." Nodding, Julie closed her purse and sat down.

⋈‖⋈ ⋈‖⋈ ⋈‖⋈

Mark Proffitt sat in Morgan's office. He slid a computer screenshot across the desk. "I think the team found what you're looking for, boss."

Morgan looked down at the first sheet. Several cutaway drawings showed a device identical to the photos from Joe Costa and Detective Wilson.

"Looks like a match to me, Mark. Where do they come from?"

"North Korea by way of China, as best we can tell."

"Loaded with fentanyl?"

"Yes, but you can order the toxin of your choice. Fentanyl, botulism, ricin, you name it."

"Cost?"

"Twenty-five-K apiece."

"Wow. So, this isn't a poor man's crime spree."

"No, sir. The payments are in Bitcoin. Something else that's not a pauper's plaything. It's down a little today, hovering around sixty-nine-five."

"How are they delivered?"

"We don't know. You have to make the payment and have the seller confirm it before you get any delivery information."

Morgan glanced down at the drawings again. "Any way to trace past purchases or buyers, Mark?"

"No, sir. That's what the Dark Web offers. Anonymity for parties on both ends of any transaction."

Bill and Julie had finished their sandwiches when Wilson's phone rang. "Detective Wilson."

"Bill, Hunter Morgan. We have some info on your packages. Are you free to drop by this afternoon?"

"Yeah, I am. I'm near your office. How about we come over now?

"We?"

"Yes. Detective Julie Stephens from Monkey County is with me. She just caught her second fentanyl case."

"Bring her along. Do you know where my office is?"

"Legg Mason Tower."

"Roger that. See ya soon."

TWELVE

Police radio scanners have served news organizations for years. With the advent of the information highway, law enforcement traffic can be monitored far from the scene.

A 911 call from a housekeeper to Arlington County Police in Virginia dispatched a patrol call to the home of Jasmine Peterson—the well-known House Speaker's daughter. Within minutes, indiscrete radio chatter announced the Capitol Police's arrival, and the phrases ". . . drug overdose" and ". . . similar local cases."

A WLAB assistant producer in Baltimore monitored the internet posts, alerting the news department and William Daugherty.

⋈||⋈ ⋈||⋈ ⋈||⋈

Maddison Mitchell hung up her desk phone. An assistant sat facing her.

"Welcome to *Shit City*!" she said, taking a deep breath. "The *effluent* just hit the fan." "What's up, Maddison?" Lonnie Jerry, her second in command, asked.

"The Capitol Police are at the home of the Speaker's daughter. She appears to be victim number nine. Director Courtemanche wants us in his office immediately."

⋈||⋈ ⋈||⋈ ⋈||⋈

Wilson, Stephens, Proffitt, and Morgan sat at his conference table. Photos of evidence from several crime scenes and the dark web drawings littered the surface.

"Hermit Kingdom exports," Julie commented. "Of course, the Chicoms must make a buck off it, too."

"How do you get Bitcoin?" Wilson asked. Morgan looked at Proffitt for an answer.

"I'm no expert, but here's what I've learned. You can buy Bitcoin, Ethereum, or any of the other twenty or so digital currencies available directly from their websites using a credit, debit, or another payment method—Apple Pay, Google Pay, etc. Or you can buy it from a cryptocurrency broker like Coinbase, eToro, or Kraken.

"There are two ways to hold your digital currencies. The first is called 'custodial.' Suppose you buy Bitcoin through a brokerage company. The brokerage maintains the custody of your purchases. If so, you submit requests to the brokerage to make payments on your behalf. Some companies severely limit who you can send payments to.

"The second is 'self-custodial,' which uses an app on your phone. The Bitcoin.com Wallet app, for example. The app lets you download crypto purchases and pay for anything, anytime, without restrictions. An attractive option on the dark web."

◁|▷ ◁|▷ ◁|▷

The Baltimore Mirror's news tip line recorded the following call. "People are being murdered in Maryland and surrounding jurisdictions using fentanyl *bombs* sent through the

USPS. There have been eight deaths so far. The FBI is covering this up."

Senior reporter Dusty Rhodes' executive assistant listened to the message and dashed into his boss' office.

◁|▷ ◁|▷ ◁|▷

After introductions and Julie Stephens' turning over the Gaithersburg murder evidence, Mark Proffitt stood at the whiteboard in Morgan's office, a blue erasable marker in his hand. "Okay, what are the cases' similarities?"

Bill Wilson spoke first. "My vic's father died of pancreatic cancer. The package's return address was his former employer."

Proffitt noted the two facts on the board.

Julie Stephens nodded. "Mine, too. Pancreatic cancer took the Judge brothers' dad. Both their packages' return addresses were GW Hospital, where he died.

"The Gaithersburg case I just caught came from the victim's dead mother's employer.

I haven't determined if cancer killed her, but I will ASAP."

Proffitt updated the board. "Married or single?"

"The Judge boys are hitched," Julie responded. "My new case was single."

"The reporter was single. How about the guy at Frostburg State, Morgan?" Wilson asked.

"Single as well," Morgan answered. "Did any of these vics have kids? The professor did not."

"Not my vic," Wilson said.

"Mine are oh-for-three, which is interesting. Considering the ages, you'd think one of the Judge boys would have had a child or two."

The intercom light flashed on the table's conference phone before Morgan responded.

Jennie Staron announced, "Hunter, I know you don't want to be disturbed, but I have Dusty Rhodes on the line. She says it's urgent. Sounds like she's calling about your meeting's subject."

Morgan looked at the other attendees and raised an index finger to his lips. They nodded understanding.

"Okay, put her through."

Morgan's primary phone line light glowed, accompanied by a soft ringing.

After he pushed the speaker button, he answered. "Hello, Dusty, what's up?"

Dusty said nothing momentarily, then asked, "Why am I on speaker? You're not alone?"

"No, I'm here with Mark Proffitt."

"Oh, okay. Hi, Mark."

"Hello, Dusty."

"We got an anonymous tip line call. Can I play it for you?"

"Sure, go ahead."

"People are being murdered in Maryland and surrounding jurisdictions using fentanyl *bombs* sent through the USPS. There have been eight deaths so far. The FBI is covering it up."

Every eyebrow in Morgan's office moved toward the ceiling.

"I have the caller's phone number. Can you run a trace on it for me?" Dusty asked.

Morgan chuckled. "So, you want to *un*-anonymous your tip line."

"I do in this case, if the feds are keeping the public in the dark. Can you help me out?"

Morgan looked at Proffitt, nodding. "Mark?" "I can look into that, Dusty. What's the number?"

Proffitt repeated it after writing it on the whiteboard.

"Correct," Rhodes said. Then, after several seconds, "Wait a minute. That was too easy. You all know something about this *already*, don't you?"

"FBI coverups are nothing new, Dusty. *You* know that as well as we do."

"Morgan, don't bullshit me. What do you know?"

"You asked us for a favor. Take 'yes' for an answer, Dusty. Mark will get back to you." Morgan pressed the button next to the red light, turning it off.

"*Shit!*"

"What's the problem, boss?"

"When this gets out, I will likely *lose* a good friend."

⋈||⋈ ⋈||⋈ ⋈||⋈

Director Luke Courtemanche surveilled his executive staff on the seventh floor of the FBI's J. Edgar Hoover Headquarters. "Let's cut to the chase. Is the Speaker's daughter the latest in the string of fentanyl deaths you're working?"

Maddison Mitchell nodded. "Yes, sir. Ms. Peterson is the ninth case."

"*So far*," the Director injected.

"Yes, sir."

"Have we established a profile yet?"

Maddison squirmed uncomfortably in her chair before answering. "Yes, sir. A broad profile."

"Let's hear it, Maddison."

"He is likely to exhibit a complex profile, possibly indicating various psychological, social, and behavioral factors."

"He? Women tend to use lethal and less vicious means—guns, knives, and so on. At least fentanyl leaves the body suitable for an open casket."

"Yes, Director. The perp may be a woman. But, men far outnumber women on a serial killer's list."

"True. Please continue, Maddison."

"He or she may be a past or current drug user familiar with opioids in general and fentanyl in particular. The individual's actions show criminal motivations, possibly driven by revenge, power, control, or financial gain.

"The person exhibits manipulative behavior, a lack of empathy, impulsivity, and a disregard for societal norms and legal boundaries.

"Finally, the perp will most likely have a criminal record spanning multiple years and offenses."

"That profile wasn't painted with a fine brush, Maddison. You just used a roller. You need to make it *tack* sharp *very* quickly."

"Yes, Director. We'll do that."

THIRTEEN

Morgan called WLAB's Billy Daugherty after the impromptu meeting ended.

"What's up, Hunter?"

"Billy, I'm here with Mark Proffitt, my lead lab rat. Do you mind if I put you on speaker?"

"No, sir."

Morgan pushed the speaker button. "Okay. I want to bring you up to speed on some developments associated with Ginger McGuire's murder."

"Okay. Shoot."

"It seems she was the first of multiple cases. I know of five in Maryland, one in Virginia, and three in other states. All with the same MO as Ginger's."

"Are you talking about Speaker Peterson's daughter in Virginia?"

The question took Morgan and Proffitt by surprise. "No, I'm talking about Franklin Judge in McLean. The Speaker's daughter . . . ?"

"Yeah. We picked up some police transmissions about activity at Jasmine Peterson's Arlington home. Maybe a drug overdose. Our sister station in DC is on the scene. The Capitol Police and the Northern VA ME are on site, too."

"Didn't the Speaker's husband die recently?" Morgan asked.

"Yeah, pancreatic cancer."

"So did Ginger McGuire's dad, Billy."

"Oh, yeah! You're right."

Morgan didn't have to wait long for the inevitable question.

"Are you telling me all the victims had relatives who died of . . . "

"Yes, those I know about did. Billy, my advice is to be *real* careful with this story. The feds will mount an investigative shit-tsunami if Jasmine Peterson is the ninth vic. And you *know* shit rolls *downhill*."

⋈ ⋈ ⋈

Driving back to MCPD Headquarters in Gaithersburg, Julie Stephens called the latest Maryland victim's husband. His wife had surrendered to pancreatic cancer.

Having shared phone numbers and email addresses before leaving Morgan's office, she quickly called Wilson and then Proffitt with updates.

Once finished, Proffitt recounted Morgan's conversation with Daugherty *vis-à-vis* Jasmine Peterson.

⋈ ⋈ ⋈

"I have the results on Dusty's phone number, boss. You want me to call her?" Proffitt asked.

"No, I'll do it, Mark. I was a little sharp with her when I hung up. "What did you find?"

"It's a burner phone. No way to trace it."

"Oh." Morgan's obvious disappointment wasn't lost on Proffitt.

"There is a scintilla of good news, Hunter."

"What's that?"

"The call bounced off a cell tower less than a tenth of a mile from 2600 Lord Baltimore Drive in Windsor Mill."

"And . . . ?"

"That's across the street from the FBI's Baltimore *Field Office*."

Morgan didn't respond. Instead, he pressed Jeannie Staron's intercom button.

"Yes, sir."

"Do you know if Joe D'Elia is in the building?"

"He was earlier. Do you want me to find him?"

"Please. If so, ask him to come to my office. If not, have him call me."

"Copy that."

⋈ ⋈ ⋈

Joe D'Elia walked into Morgan's office and joined him at the conference table.

Hunter brought the retired Deputy Special Agent in Charge of the FBI's Boston Field Office up to speed on the fentanyl murders.

D'Elia leaned back in his chair, swiveling slightly toward Morgan. "None of these victims have *any* children?"

"We don't know about three of the deaths, but the five in Maryland and one in Virginia do not.

"There may be a ninth in VA. The daughter of Lucille Peterson . . . "

"The Speaker of the House?"

"The very same. It's not confirmed yet, but local law enforcement radio chatter suggests it may be. The Capitol Police are on scene."

D'Elia nodded. "Somebody from the House or Senate is involved. How can I help?" "We know the tip to *The Mirror* came from a burner close to the Baltimore Field Office.

It may be someone associated with the investigation. A task force maybe, Joe?" "Oh, you can bet the *farm* on it. At least the ATF, PIS, and the Bureau.

"If someone has their knickers in a knot about ordering toe-tags in bulk, it's likely not an FBI or ATF agent. They're too much in lockstep. My guess is a Postal Inspection

Service agent. Postal people tend to consider the public as *customers*."

Looking down at a picture of one of the crime scene envelopes, Morgan said, "Joe, can you give me a quick thumbnail PIS profile?"

D'Elia thought for a moment. "Yeah. Probably someone more interested in the human aspect of the case. The comment about a cover-up sounds like he or she wants to go public with the threat to prevent more victims. The Bureau would resist that until forced to issue a warning by public or political pressure."

"If the Speaker's daughter *is* a victim, I'd say the political pressure is already building," Morgan pointed out.

"Amen to that."

"So, let's assume a USPS person called in the tip. Would they *have* a burner or be forced to buy one?"

"PIS agents would have staff dealing with web issues. So, I doubt they'd carry one, unless it were for personal reasons.

"I think that would be an impulsive purchase. Probably somewhere close to the point of the call." "Let's hope so. How would you feel about doing some scut work?"

D'Elia smiled, pointing to his teeth. "These expensive crowns cover the damage scut work did during my early days with the Bureau. I think I can remember how."

⋈ ⋈ ⋈

As Joe D'Elia closed the door, Morgan called Dusty Rhode's cell.

She answered before the first ring ended. "You calling to apologize for being a *dick*, Morgan?"

"Well, with that warm opening, maybe I should just hang up now. Can you be civil for a few minutes? That's a stretch, but see if you can pull it together. Okay?" "So, Proffitt wasn't the *only* person with you. Was he?"

Morgan took a deep breath. "No, Dusty. He wasn't."

"Who else?"

"Two LE members who will remain nameless. Do you want to know your phone number or not?"

"Yes, please," Dusty said grudgingly.

"The number is a burner."

"No surprise there. Anything else?"

"Yeah. It came from outside the FBI's Baltimore Field HQ."

"*No shit*? A fed with a guilty conscious? Okay, anything else you care to share?" Morgan hesitated for several seconds, and Dusty pounced.

"*There is*! You're trying to decide if you should tell me, right?"

"With your instincts, you should have been a cop."

Dusty laughed. "My instincts told me I'm too *smart* to be a cop!"

"There's still a lot of room for *charm* improvement.

"What I'm about to tell you is something you'll probably hear from WLAB's news crew soon. Did you hear about their anchor who died recently?"

"Yeah, along with the rest of Baltimore County. But I don't remember any details being revealed."

"She was murdered, Dusty."

"Then why the silence on the BPD's part?"

Morgan explained the circumstances of Ginger McGuire's death.

"Fuck me, Morgan! This woman was one of the cases the tipster is talking about?"

"Ginger McGuire was the first. There are currently eight confirmed cases. There may be a ninth in Arlington, VA, involving Speaker Peterson's daughter."

"*What*? How do you know *that*?"

Morgan shared his conversation with Billy Daugherty.

"It's not confirmed, but it's a member of Congress or the family of one, since the Capitol Police are there."

"*Christ*! So, give me the names of the victims you know about."

"Dusty, promise me *no* LRI employees will be named in *any* story."

"*Jesus*, Hunter! You have to ask me *that*? Have I *ever* hung anyone at LRI out to dry?"

"No, and let's make sure it stays that way."

Morgan explained the murders' sequence, locations, and victim's names.

"Okay, anything else?"

"Yes. So far as is known, a parent of each victim died of pancreatic cancer recently, including the Speaker's husband." "Holy *shit*!

⋈||⋈ ⋈||⋈ ⋈||⋈

As soon as Morgan ended his call with Dusty, he called Jeannie Staron into his office.

"What's up?" she asked.

Morgan told her about his conversation with D'Elia.

"Get a couple of our in-house investigators to map out all the stores in a one-mile radius of the FBI's Baltimore Field Office that sell disposable cell phones. It's a long shot, but maybe the guy who called the tip into *The Mirror* bought his burner locally. Then give me the list."

"Copy that."

⋈||⋈ ⋈||⋈ ⋈||⋈

At 0200 HRS, in Owings Mills, Maryland, two men dressed in black, including their balaclavas, approached the front door of a modest three-bedroom raised ranch home. Disregarding the blue and white ADT sign near the front steps, one man quietly picked the door's deadbolt.

Inside, one moved silently to the second-floor master bedroom. His hand covered the woman's mouth before she could scream. Down the hall, the second intruder muffled a teenage boy's cry.

In Ellicott City and Columbia, Maryland, the same sequence of events took two more small families hostage.

⋈⋈ ⋈⋈ ⋈⋈

Dusty Rhode's executive assistant compiled the obituaries of the four Maryland and confirmed Virginia victims. None of the "Survived by" lists mentioned children.

FOURTEEN

Joe D'Elia—like most retired FBI agents—received credentials marking his service at the Bureau. These "creds," at first glance, looked very official. Their use to infer official FBI business was considered *very* poor form.

Generally, the sight of the letters "FBI" didn't engender questions, including the word "official." Minimum-wage convenience store employees, some possibly illegal, didn't ask questions at all. So, D'Elia worked the list of thirteen stores selling burner phones close to the FBI Field Office, as if he had just graduated from Quantico. Getting the sales receipts from four establishments took him less than a day—seven buyers over the last seven days. Five credit cards and a cash purchase.

The store manager frowned, looking at the sales report.

D'Elia noticed her expression and asked, "What's the problem?"

"Something's not right. Let me go look at our inventory."

In a few minutes, the woman returned. "We're missing a phone."

D'Elia smiled. "Maybe a cash sale that went into someone's pocket?"

"That's what I'm thinking."

"Okay, I need your surveillance data for the last two weeks."

"We only keep it for seven days. It rolls off after that, one day at a time. I can put it on a DVD."

"That works."

⋈⋈ ⋈⋈ ⋈⋈

Ironically, though, established in 1909 by an Italian—Ettore Bugatti—the automaker is

French, headquartered in Molsheim. Their vehicles are among the world's most expensive.

The Bugatti Chiron Super Sport's 1,578 horsepower, 8.0-liter quad-turbocharged W16 engine, extensive use of carbon fiber materials, and special tires allow it to go from zero to sixty in 2.4 seconds. Starting at just under four million dollars, a Super Sport's prices can increase significantly depending on options.

Bugatti uses trusted logistics companies specializing in handling high-value, delicate cargo, ensuring their luxury vehicles' safe and secure transportation. Multi-million-dollar vehicles aren't transported on tractor-trailers like American, Japanese, and other manufacturers. These four-wheeled jewels move across the sea and land in containers that could make a Triple Crown winner bound for a stud farm jealous.

The vehicles are fitted with protective covers—on the exterior body, wheels, and interior—to prevent damage during handling and transport. Bugattis are securely fastened inside specialized containers that accommodate the car's dimensions and low ground clearance.

Vehicles bound for North America are carefully loaded onto Le Havre or Antwerp ships. Once across the Atlantic, after clearing customs in American ports, transportation to their final destination, directly to customers or authorized Bugatti dealerships, is typically within these enclosed carriers to maintain the vehicle's pristine condition.

High-end, specialized trucking firms equipped with state-of-the-art Global Navigation Satellite System/Real-Time Kinematic Positioning allow Bugatti to track a vehicle's location down to the centimeter. Multi-GNSS/RTK tracking and geo-fencing alert the manufacturer and security company of any route deviations before the final delivery point.

⋈⋈ ⋈⋈⋈ ⋈⋈

"Invent the perfect mousetrap; soon, someone will create a smarter mouse."

Sitting behind the wheel of a white Ford Econoline van in the dark truck stop parking lot, Cletis Moore, typically the epitome of calm, wasn't. He tried distracting himself by imagining the new toys tonight's payday would provide.

The Bugatti Chiron Super Sport's caravan would be here in twenty-seven minutes—a lead and trailing security vehicle sandwiching the truck. Each car carried an armed guard in the front passenger seat. A third armed man rode shotgun in the tractor.

Cletis and six other hijackers knew the trucking company in Baltimore and Bugatti in Molsheim, France, tracked the Super Sport's precise location in real-time with fidelity the U.S. military could only dream of.

Regardless of a car's top-end speed, Cletis knew there were two things it couldn't outrun—a bullet and a radio. Tonight's operation had to be surgically precise.

⋈⋈ ⋈⋈⋈ ⋈⋈

At their Legg Mason Headquarters, it took several hours for a background investigator to review D'Elia's DVD. After watching multiple cell phone transactions based on the sales records, one didn't follow the typical pattern. Usually, a phone was retrieved from the stockroom. The sale rang up and was completed with a credit card or cash. In one instance, the clerk took a woman out of sight to the rear of the store. They returned a few minutes later with what looked like a cell phone box in her hand.

In less than thirty minutes, the investigator revealed the personal information of the five credit card burner sales. The cash transaction took a little longer. Surveillance cameras' relatively high-definition images were the grist for an AI facial recognition mill.

The atypical sale proved the most interesting.

To Morgan's surprise, but not D'Elia's, the purchaser was . . . a Postal Inspection Agent.

"Notice you don't see any cash exchanged," D'Elia said.

Morgan nodded. "No sales record, *ergo* no phone number."

"Bingo, Ringo!"

Standing behind the investigator, D'Elia turned to Morgan, smiling.

Morgan laughed. "Don't gloat, Joe. It's unbecoming." D'Elia chuckled. "I'm not. I have the same question you'd ask a dog chasing a car.

'What are you going to do with it when ya catch it?'"

※ ※ ※

Apex Security's nationwide offices had only one ironclad rule—only Law Enforcement Safety Officer Act-qualified candidates would be considered. LESOA, enacted in 2004, gave current and retired guardians of the Thin Blue Line *federal* authority to carry a firearm in all 50 states, the District of Columbia, Puerto Rico, and all other U.S. possessions, except the Panama Canal Zone. This act negated any *state* requirement for carry permit reciprocity.

Without LESOA's cover, the three-vehicle caravan moving the Bugatti from the Port of Baltimore to Cincinnati, Ohio, would have had to change guards at the Maryland Pennsylvania state lines to meet the Keystone State's requirement that an armed *in-state* security company be used.

Apex employees fell into two categories. Drivers with extensive four or eighteen-wheel evasive maneuver training. Guards from SWAT and Hostage Rescue Teams trained on various handguns, long rifles, and tactics.

All inter-vehicle communications in the approaching Apex caravan employed encrypted walkie-talkies. These hand-held radios used hopping—altering their frequencies during transmission—for additional security.

A former Georgia State Patrol officer—Cletis Monroe's group leader—knew LEOSA's rules and gaps well and planned accordingly.

※ ※ ※

Morgan shook his head. "That's a damn good question, Joe. How do we use this information . . . *legally*?"

D'Elia thought momentarily, then said, "I don't think we do. At least not yet."

FIFTEEN

Approaching I-70's westbound exit 202 at 0310 HRS, the Apex caravan began to slow. At the bottom of the ramp, they turned left onto Ohio-149 South. Three-tenths of a mile later, the tractor-trailer turned left, lumbering into the Pilot Travel Center behind the lead security vehicle. Refueling required the tractor to bear right and travel counterclockwise in a half-circle to align with the diesel fuel pumps. An Econoline van pulled out of a parking space to follow the tractor.

The lead and trail cars turned left toward a cluster of gas pumps and the Pilot store. Only one vehicle occupied a pump. Two cars sat near the store. One's backup lights came on, backing away and departing.

Watching the two black Ford sedans pull into spots near the store, the ex-Georgia Patrol officer keyed his encrypted walkie-talkie and said, "Now!"

⋈ ⋈ ⋈

Inside, a Pilot security guard monitored the storefront cameras. The Ford's drivers and passengers exited their vehicles. Nothing seemed amiss as the four men walked toward the diesel pumps and out of the cameras' fields of view. The woman turned her attention to the in-store activity. At this moment, on a Sunday morning, Pilot hosted more employees than customers.

⋈ ⋈ ⋈

The dash-cam in an empty, idling tractor behind the diesel pumps videoed activity out of the Pilot security systems' sight. Two men exited the Econoline cab, walked to its rear, and opened its double doors.

The sedan drivers and guards arrived, now flanked by two men dressed in black coveralls, their faces covered. After being searched and disarmed, the Apex employees' hands were zip-tied behind them. The dim light in the Econoline cargo compartment silhouetted a fifth hijacker assisting the bound men into the truck.

Finally, the Apex tractor driver and guard arrived behind the Econoline, each flanked by men in black coveralls. Once searched and tied, they joined the other hostages.

With the double door secured, a hijacker entered the driver's side of the van's cab. Its backup lights glowed, and a reverse alarm sounded faintly. With enough clearance, the truck swung around and passed the trailer.

Two people walked to the Apex tractor's cab. Four figures went toward the Ford sedans.

No refueling took place. Within minutes, the convoy crossed back under I-70, continuing north on Ohio-149, avoiding the interstate's license plate readers.

◁▷ ◁▷ ◁▷

The Pilot security guard watched the tractor-trailer pull away from the diesel pumps, followed by the white van.

That's weird. The tractor didn't refuel, and the van can't use diesel.

◁▷ ◁▷ ◁▷

Three suburban school districts received absentee calls as the sun rose over Baltimore.

SIXTEEN

D'Elia beat Morgan and Jeannie Staron to the office, something very few did.

A few minutes later, the two arrived together. Seeing Joe, they glanced at each other in surprise.

"Have you got an apple for the teacher, Joe?" Jeannie asked with a giggle.

"No, I have doughnuts and coffee." D'Elia pointed to a Dunkin' box and a cardboard cup carrier on Jeannie's desk.

"I've changed my mind, Hunter," D'Elia continued before the others could respond.

"About . . . ?" Morgan asked, taking a coffee out of the carrier.

"The dog catching the car."

⋈⋈ ⋈⋈ ⋈⋈

The Baltimore Mirror's daily edition lay on Morgan's desk. The headline read:

"IS THE FBI COVERING FOR A SERIAL KILLER?"

The story outlined the victims' names and the order of their deaths. No public information or social media suggested they knew each other except for the Judge brothers. However, each had recently lost a parent to pancreatic cancer, and none were parents.

"Dusty didn't waste any time, did she?" Morgan said more to himself than Jeannie or D'Elia, standing beside him. "She figured out the lack of offspring."

"Her story made me change my mind," Joe said. "It mentions a call to *The Mirror*'s tip line. It took us less than a day to figure out who called the paper. The Bureau will probably find her even sooner."

Morgan turned to D'Elia. "So, what do you want to do, Joe?" "Reach out to the postal inspector with some advice."

"On *what*," Jeannie asked.

"The 1989 Whistleblower Protection Act. This woman is trying to alert the public to a severe threat. She will have her life ruined if she's not aware of the legal protections afforded her. The WPA may not cover her *derriere* completely, but it can't hurt for her to know about it. And she needs to line up a lawyer, *pronto*.

※ ※ ※

Special Agent in Charge Maddison Mitchell's generally pale face approached fire engine red. "*Someone fucking leaked*!" she said through clenched teeth.

Several task force members shifted nervously in their seats.

"The Director just ripped fifteen years of atta-girls off my career after seeing *The Mirror*'s story."

The lead ATF agent, sitting near Mitchell, said, "And *you* think it came from one of *us*." "*You bet your fucking ass I do!*"

"Are you on *crack*?" the ATF agent asked. "There are nine cases, at the *moment*, in half a dozen local jurisdictions. Cops *talk* to each other. They know about this task force and that the Bureau is running it. You refused to make a statement in the public's interest. We've had four, maybe five, deaths since then.

"If your career is circling the drain, your makeup mirror will reveal the responsible party!"

A flatulent flea would have sounded thunderous in the room.

※ ※ ※

Immediately after the meeting ended, Mitchell took Lonnie Jerry aside.

"Do we have the phone number that called *The Mirror*'s tip line?"

"Negative. *The Mirror* claims the person who called is a source and won't divulge it." "*Get* me the fucking number. *Now*! Go to the FISA Court if you have to."

"Boss, maybe you should let it go for now. The number only allows us to charge Ramos. It doesn't move the case ahead."

"Jerry . . . get . . . me . . . the . . . FUCKING . . . NUMBER!

"Copy that."

※ ※ ※

That evening, WLAB ran a half-hour special on the life and death of Ginger McGuire. Their coverage referenced the *Mirror*'s tip-line story and included brief on-camera interviews with Ginger's mother, Janet Judge, and Dr. Jerome Mendelson's widow. Noting the similarity to the murders' MO and pointing out that none of the victims had children.

※ ※ ※

One-half mile north of I-70 on Ohio Highway 149, the Apex convoy turned left into the Doan Ford dealership's parking lot—the location just inside Apex security's geofence.

The company employed no off-hours security other than motion-detection cameras. An email to the sales department late the previous afternoon contained a virus. The vehicles' arrival left no video record.

A blue Ford F-150 pickup with a custom trailer attached awaited the Bugatti. The model XLT 4X4 with a 5.0 Liter V8 could tow the trailer and Bugatti's 4,323 pounds without straining.

Trailers could easily be found to accommodate the Bugatti's length, width, and height. But its four-point-nine-inch ground clearance required a *very* gently sloped ramp. And the vehicle's GPS tracker presented a problem. With a separate battery, it sent signals continuously when the car wasn't running. The trailer's lead-foil lining solved that issue.

Five hijackers quickly placed long ramps behind the Apex trailer to remove the Bugatti. Cletis and the seventh hijack member watched the Econoline van prisoners.

Cletis stayed in the shadows as much as possible. Even so, at one point, a voice in the van asked, "Don't I know you, man?"

"*Shut the fuck up,* asshole!" another Apex employee snapped. "You tryin' to get us killed?

"He don't *know* you, brother! *None of us* do!"

Like an Indy 500 pit crew, the precision transfer would have made A. J. Foyt proud.

Once unloaded, the tractor-trailer and two hijackers departed the dealership for I-70 West to give the illusion of normalcy. Two additional hijackers in the Ford XLT turned left out of Doan's parking lot onto Ohio 149 North, towing the silver trailer. Another left put them on Highway 40 West in less than three-tenths of a mile. Five miles later, the Econoline entered I-40 West, headed for an Indianapolis suburb.

Doan Ford's Body Shop has a small 25' X 20' storage building on its northwest side. One of the three remaining hijackers picked the building's lock. The six Apex employees were left inside bound and gagged to be discovered on Monday morning,

Two of the remaining hijackers each drove a Ford sedan, speeding west on I-70 to catch up with the Apex tractor-trailer.

The Econoline van—Cletis Moore at the wheel—returned to I-70, turning east toward Baltimore. East of Somerset, PA, he turned south on U.S. Highway 219 for a short respite from the monotonous interstate. Nearly 25 miles later, he entered I-68 East.

⋈⋈ ⋈⋈ ⋈⋈

In Apex's Baltimore Security control room, the movement of the Bugatti went unnoticed by the sound-asleep agent monitoring the convoy's progress. By the time she awoke, other routine updates had pushed the vehicle and GPS alerts off the monitor.

⋈⋈ ⋈⋈ ⋈⋈

Before being assigned to the Fentanyl Murder Task Force, Special Agent Postal Inspector Althea Ramos spent most of her time at Baltimore's main office at 900 East Fayette Street.

Catching up on her "day job's" work, Ramos looked up when a counter agent knocked at her door.

"Althea, there's an FBI agent here to see you." Ramos could see Joe D'Elia behind the agent.

"Send him in."

As D'Elia entered the office, he thanked the counter agent and turned to Ramos. "Actually, I'm *retired*. I was the Deputy Special Agent in Charge in Boston."

Holding out his hand, "Joe D'Elia. I'm with Last Resort Investigations now."

Ramos' eyes seemed to widen slightly. "Oh? Then why are you here?"

"Hopefully to give you some valuable advice."

"Because . . . ?"

"Because you purchased a burner phone and used it to make a call to *The Baltimore Mirror*'s tip line about the FBI covering up the fentanyl murders."

Now Ramos' eyes widened significantly. Her brown skin seemed to darken slightly.

"*I did no such thing!*"

"Ms. Ramos. Paying cash for the phone was smart. Buying it under the table so there is no transaction record—brilliant. But making the call a stone's throw from the FBI Field Office wasn't. Your excellent facial image on the store's security camera and a voice

comparison of yours and the tipsters will get you crucified faster than Jesus."

※ ※ ※

An attorney from the DOJ's National Security Division applied for a FISA warrant on behalf of the FBI, requesting permission to monitor and/or physically search *The Mirror*'s phone records for information related to foreign intelligence.

※ ※ ※

The Mirror's Health Section lay open on Dusty Rhode's desk. A picture of Dr. Pasquale Santini sat above an article on his innovative use of stem cell injections to help promote healing and repair damaged tissue in the shoulder joint.

Opening the contacts on her iPhone, Dusty searched for Pat's name, then dialed his cell phone.

"Pat Santini."

"Doc, it's Dusty Rhodes. Have you got a minute?"

"Sure, what's up?"

After giving a brief synopsis of the fentanyl case, she concluded, "So, the odd thing is, *all* of the victims had a parent who died of pancreatic cancer. And *none* of them had any children."

"Wow, Dusty! That *is weird*."

"Any thoughts?"

"The only things that come to mind are drug trials. Go to ClinicalTrials.gov. You can search for past, current, and future trials in the recruiting phase by searching for pancreatic cancer."

"Can you hang on a minute while I do a quick search?"

"Go ahead."

A Clinicaltrials.gov pancreatic search returned a list of over 700 trials. Showing results for: Pancreatic Cancer | Within 200 miles of Baltimore Metropolitan Area

NCT02993731

A Study of Napabucasin Plus Nab-Paclitaxel With Gemcitabine in Adult Patients With

Metastatic Pancreatic Adenocarcinoma

Conditions

Carcinoma, Pancreatic Ductal

Locations

Washington, District of Columbia, United States

Baltimore, Maryland, United States

Hershey, Pennsylvania, United States

Newark, Delaware, United States Show 267 more locations

COMPLETED

NCT00714701

Screening for Early Pancreatic Neoplasia (Cancer of the Pancreas Screening or CAPS4 Study)

Conditions

Early Pancreatic Neoplasia

Familial Pancreatic Neoplasia

Locations

Baltimore, Maryland, United States

COMPLETED WITH RESULTS

NCT01673334

Evaluation of EUS-Guided 22 Gauge Core Biopsy Versus Fine-needle Aspiration for Suspected Pancreatic Neoplasms

Conditions

Pancreatic Tumor

Locations

Charlottesville, Virginia, United States

WITHDRAWN

NCT02534246

Head-to-Head Comparison of Two Needles EUS Guided FNB

Conditions

Pancreatic Tumor

Locations
Hershey, Pennsylvania, United States
RECRUITING

. . .

"*Christ*, Pat! There are *hundreds*. How would we ever get through all of these?"

Dr. Santini laughed. "Or . . . you could ask a family member which trial their loved one participated in."

"Why didn't I think of that? Apparently, I'm not as bright as some people think I am. Great, Pat! Thank you!" "My pleasure."

"Tell Philomena I said 'Hey!'"

"You bet, Dusty."

⋈||⋈ ⋈||⋈ ⋈||⋈

Joe D'Elia watched Althea Ramos sag in her chair, seemingly ready to burst into tears. "*Oh, my God*," she whispered. "*What have I done?*"

"Ms. Ramos, the first thing you have to do is line up a lawyer." D'Elia pulled a folded sheet of paper from inside his blue sports jacket. He opened it and laid it on Ramos' desk.

"These attorneys specialize in whistleblower cases. Call their offices. Find out who can see you the soonest. If you can't get an appointment in the next few days, see if you can sign a retainer agreement with one.

"My firm found you in less than a day. I don't mean to scare you, but the FBI will be here soon. Take a few days off to get your affairs in order as much as possible. That will also avoid the embarrassment of being arrested here.

"When you're arrested, say *absolutely nothing*. *Do not* answer *any* questions.

"*Insist* on having your, or *any* lawyer, present during all interrogations.

"The agents will try to scare you with threats of life in prison and hundreds of thousands of dollars in fines. Don't get me wrong, they will have serious charges to file against you, but there are always plea bargains.

"Get rid of the phone you bought. If you don't have it, the Bureau will be able to prove you purchased a phone but not the phone that made the call.

"Voice analysis is not an exact science. They may not be able to show a high likelihood that your voice and *The Mirror*'s recording are the same person. Your lawyer will want an independent voice analysis done in any event.

"Finally, continue your work on the task force until you're arrested. It may buy you some time, and being inside the investigation could provide valuable insight." Ramos looked stunned, bordering on catatonic.

D'Elia had planned for that, producing another sheet and placing it on her desk.

"Ms. Ramos, this is a list of everything I just said. Keep it with you and follow the steps in order. My personal cell number and email address are listed at the bottom.

"Do you have any questions?"

Ramos lifted her head slowly, tears dripping off her cheeks onto a white blouse.

"Am I going to jail?"

"It's too soon to know. Follow my instructions to at least minimize the chances."

"Can you be my lawyer?"

⋈⋈ ⋈⋈ ⋈⋈

Lonnie Jerry stuck his head in Maddison Mitchell's office. "We got our warrant and should have the tip line's number by close of business today, boss."

SEVENTEEN

I-68 Eastbound crosses over Little Tonoloway Creek near Hancock, Maryland. The highway's elevation there is 820 feet. A poor place to fall asleep at the wheel.

A white Econoline van drifted gradually from the right lane onto the highway's shoulder and a gently sloped, grassy bank adjacent. Its angle increased quickly for the next tenth of a mile. The angle neared fifty degrees just before a deep ravine's protective guardrail.

No trailing nor oncoming vehicles witnessed the Econoline avoid the guardrail and barrel-roll into dark treetops.

※ ※ ※

Dusty's EA made phone calls to relatives of several fentanyl victims without success. The first three refused to speak to anyone from the press. The fourth wouldn't answer questions because the drug company required participants *and* family members to sign non-disclosure agreements.

Dusty texted Pat Santini.

"Are NDAs for family members standard in drug trials?" "No. Extremely uncommon. I only know of two."

※ ※ ※

Early Monday morning, a Silver Spring carpet company reported its white Ford Econoline van stolen to MCPD's Emergency Communications Center, aka 911. The County's southeast area was consistently auto thieves' favorite target location. A bit more job security for the MCPD's Auto Crimes Enforcement Section—ACES.

※ ※ ※

Apex Security headquarters received a frantic call from the leader of the Bugatti convoy reporting the hijacking. The corporate jet departed BWI less than an hour later to return the team for debriefing. Although less than twelve hours had passed, the police in Ellicott City, Baltimore, and Howard Counties were notified of the break-ins and hostage-taking. Subsequent investigations found no valuable biometric evidence.

※ ※ ※

The multi-agency federal task force met just after 0830 HRS in the FBI's Baltimore office with a *new* lead ATF member.

Per Joe D'Elia's prediction, the Bureau quickly connected the dots on *The Mirror*'s caller location, adding a final nail in the insider source coffin. However, assuming the caller previously possessed the burner phone, an immediate search for a local vendor did not follow. The FBI's bureaucratic approach resulted in a much broader net being cast.

The Federal Trade Commission regulates cell phones in the U.S., but contracts with the North American Numbering Plan Administrator to assign the phone numbers. Numbers are given to wireless providers from the available North American Numbering Plan pool in the vendors' designated area codes and exchanges.

The number *The Mirror's* tip line recorded had initially been issued to Verizon Wireless. However, the vendor had no user information, indicating the phone's likely refurbishment—wiping all user data. Verizon's prepaid cell phones, either new or refurbished, are sold by several vendors and third-party resellers, adding to the complexity of the investigation.

Althea Ramos tried desperately to hide her anxiety in task force meetings. Fortunately, few of the discussions touched on USPS issues.

After several days without progress, the investigation's focus finally narrowed to local purchases—two miles from the FBI Field Office—yielding nineteen stores. Lonnie Jerry assigned a relatively young agent to canvass the vendors.

Assuming the buyer would not make a purchase close to the field office, the agent began with the stores on the outer search perimeter. Anxious to please Jerry, the agent got credit card sales receipts *and* surveillance video of *all* buyers.

Eight days after Ramos' departure, the young FBI agent arrived at her purchase point.

※ ※ ※

Richard Schutz—then a captain—served in Vietnam's Mekong Delta with Hunter Morgan. After the Vietcong raided the Vinh Chau team house, taking American POWs, Shutz and Morgan were members of the team sent to recover them. Now the principal owner of Apex Security, Schutz mounted another *recovery* effort . . . for the Bugatti.

Decades after Vietnam, the two veterans stumbled onto each other in Columbia, Maryland, raising awareness and money for homeless veterans.

Schutz, desperate to avoid a four-million-dollar-plus loss, had an even greater exposure—Apex's reputation. Publicity of the theft would mortally wound the company.

He suspected an inside job, starting with the operator who hadn't noticed the Bugatti's GPS signals and the geofence warning. Outside assistance would circumvent any employees' attempt to subvert the investigation. Only one company came to mind.

⋈ ⋈ ⋈

Althea Ramos dialed the number on the bottom of the sheet Joe D'Elia left her. The call went to his voicemail.

Her brief message didn't sound distraught.

⋈ ⋈ ⋈

Morgan returned Schutz's call after the weekly LRI staff meeting.

"Welcome Home, Brother," Schutz said. "I appreciate your getting back to me."

"Welcome Home, Dick. What's up?"

Schutz explained the Bugatti situation and his concern about internal involvement.

"I can't let this get into the press, Hunter. It will ruin me and put a lot of people out of work. Can you have your team assist with the vehicle's recovery and cover my ass in the process?"

⋈ ⋈ ⋈

"Althea Ramos."

"Joe D'Elia, returning your call. Are you all right?"

"I may be more than that, Mr. D'Elia."

"Yeah? How so?"

"The FBI hasn't found my cell phone purchase."

"You mean not yet?"

"No. In today's task force meeting, SAIC Maddison Mitchell said they won't expend any more resources looking for the burner phone owner."

"How much time did they spend looking for an owner?" "Over a week, maybe ten days."

D'Elia was silent momentarily, then said, "I think I know what happened, Ms. Ramos. And to say you dodged a bullet would be an understatement worthy of the British."

"Let me know if anything changes, please."

⋈ ⋈ ⋈

Callimachus, a Greek poet and scholar born circa 305 BC, is generally credited with first saying, "Set a thief to catch a thief."

The word "erudite" could have had a picture of Roger Graves next to it in the Oxford English Dictionary. LRI's primary motor vehicle theft investigator's transition from a notorious Arizona gang member to a polished law enforcement professional made Roger worthy of the inspirational speaker circuit. A lenient judge and a highly skilled—and expensive—attorney kept Roger from checking into the state's *Gold Star Hotel*. Even Georgia, one of several states with the highest police officer vacancies, wouldn't hire a felon.

Roger advanced quickly in the Atlanta PD's Auto Theft Investigative Unit due to his experience in the Perpetrators' Arizona chapter. Nine years into his career, a machete-wielding carjacker removed his left index, middle, and ring fingers. Though his nondominant hand, the injury left Roger one hundred percent disabled. Workers' Compensation benefits covered most of his medical expenses. The Atlanta PD's retirement system paid him enough to get by, but not by much.

The law enforcement community is more closely knit than most people might expect. When an LRI auto theft investigator retired, Morgan asked her if she could suggest a replacement. While a member of the Augusta PD, she'd worked with Graves on several task forces and knew his story.

Morgan called Roger that day, offering him a job after a Zoom interview.

Today, Roger Graves sat in Dick Schutz's executive conference room. Piles of Apex employees' files covered a long mahogany table. The six members of the Bugatti security team's bank and credit card accounts had already been run by investigators at the LRI offices. None showed any excessive spending or other suspicious traits. Now, the rest of Apex's employees' financials, especially those who missed Bugatti's monitoring anomalies, faced the same scrutiny.

Each of the three guards' cell phone records showed a call from their homes before the hijacking was thought to have taken place. Something too odd to be a coincidence, requiring a thorough investigation.

One employee's banking showed nothing particularly unusual. However, Cletis Monroe's American Airlines Citibank Executive Master Card—annual fee of $450— showed two first-class tickets to and from Nevis Island and a week at the Four Seasons Resort. Hardly a cheap date.

There were a couple of charges from a climate-controlled storage facility—nothing unusual there—many people had more *stuff* than room for it.

And . . . Cletis hadn't been to work since the Bugatti heist.

His supervisor called Cletis' cell phone several times, all of which went straight to voicemail. His mother, Naomi Monroe, had not heard from him in several days.

Roger interviewed the woman who monitored the GPS and geofencing tracking in real-time that night. A single mother of two children—one with extraordinary special needs— could certainly have been prone to corruption. Her finances showed no unusual bank deposits and several credit cards without enough remaining limit to purchase a first-class stamp. Finally, the supervisor responsible for reviewing the GPS and geofencing activity reports the following day reported no issues. Nothing in his financials pointed to corruption.

That left the missing IT employee. Cletis Monroe's work record had several positive reviews, including commendations for innovation and problem-solving.

His AA credit card payments were about double the required monthly minimum. At that rate, his expensive vacation might rack up more in interest costs than the initial flights and hotel stay.

※ ※ ※

Dusty Rhodes and her EA tried to persuade a victim's loved one to break their silence. Each drug trial participant's next of kin feared severe penalties for violating the NDA.

At her wit's end and about to call *The Mirror*'s legal counsel for advice, her phone rang.

"Dusty, Pat Santini. Got a minute?"

"I've always got time for you, Doc."

Santini chuckled. "I was going through some old emails and came across something that might be interesting.

"One of my patients, who later died of pancreatic cancer, participated in an early detection test study of the disease several years ago. It was one of half a dozen over a decade by the same company. All were withdrawn due to poor results. Ironically, their CEO became a pancreatic loser's statistic six months ago."

"What company is this?" Dusty asked, not convinced Pat's information had value.

"*Was*, not is. Airmed Pharmaceuticals. It was privately held and filed for Chapter Seven bankruptcy two years ago.

"Anyway, I don't know if that's useful, just a thought." "Thanks, Pat. I appreciate the call."

※ ※ ※

Despite its being covered in the media, the Joint Federal Taskforce, with an abundance of investigative experience and resources, hadn't gleaned that none of the victims had children.

※ ※ ※

The group, mired in investigative do-loops, seemingly meandered from one theory to another. The House Speaker's calls to FBI Director Courtemanche were getting more frequent and caustic.

SAIC Maddison Mitchell knew her time to produce results was in the single-digit day range. Then, like a divine investigative manna-MRE, a miracle arrived.

※ ※ ※

Roger Graves interviewed the three Apex convoy guards separately. Their stories were nearly identical. Two armed men invaded each of their homes outside of Baltimore. Wives were told to call their husbands. A masked man took the phone once the call reached the intended party. The guards were to force the convoy off I-70 at exit 202 for the Pilot Service Center. There, they would be met by hijackers. A failure to comply or any resistance would result in the death of the guards' family members. Each man said his caller indicated the other guards received the exact instructions.

Finally, family members were told any report to the police of their being held hostage for twelve hours would result in the death of the husband.

▶◀▶◀ ▶◀▶◀ ▶◀▶◀

A purple 2022 Dodge Charger SRT Hellcat traveled south on State Road 97—Queen Street—in Littlestown, Pennsylvania. The state's tinting statute required that side front, back, and rear windows allow more than 70% light in, ensuring visibility and safety on the road. Other than the windshield, the Charger's tinting obfuscated its interior.

State Trooper Angelo Resato, traveling in the opposite direction, saw the Charger turn right onto Boyer Street, providing a good view of the tinting infraction. Stopping for oncoming traffic to pass, Resato turned left, then followed the Dodge. Accelerating, he lit the light bar and gave the siren two quick blasts.

Without using a turn signal, the Dodge swerved toward the curb, then hit and rode up onto it, stopping opposite the Mason-Dixon Line Firearms company.

Trooper Resato called in his car stop location and activity and exited his vehicle. Approaching the Dodge's driver-side rear, the front passenger window lowered. A white cloud escaped like a scene from Cheech and Chong's classic *Up In Smoke*.

Resato rapped on the driver's window with his Penn State class ring.

The window lowered a few inches. A young white man, wearing mirrored sunglasses, glanced up at the trooper. "Yes, sir. What can I do for you?" "Put the window down full. Do you know why I stopped you?"

Lowering the window, the driver said, "No, sir."

"Your windows are tinted one hundred percent. The law requires no more than thirty percent tint on all side and rear windows.

"I need your license, registration, and insurance card, please."

"Sure thing, officer."

With great effort, the driver pulled a wallet from a rear pants pocket, fumbling through it and producing a Maryland license. He handed it blindly out the window as he leaned to his right, opening the glove box.

Resato bent over to see an attractive young woman in the passenger seat, smiling at him blithely.

The driver pulled a white envelope from the glove compartment and produced Carrol County, MD, registration and State Farm Insurance cards. Resato took the cards and the license. "Sit tight, Mr. Wahl."

"Yes, sir."

In the patrol car, he ran a check for wants and warrants on the driver—who had neither. Resato walked back to the Dodge.

"Mr. Wahl, do you have a medical marijuana card?"

"No, officer. It's legal now."

"In Maryland. You're in Pennsylvania. Step out of the car, Mr. Wahl." Wahl looked at his companion and whispered something inaudible.

"*Step out of the vehicle*, Mr. Wahl."

Wahl turned back toward Trooper Resato, shaking his head. He unbuckled his seatbelt, opened the door, and stood up.

"I'm placing you under arrest for driving while impaired. Turn around and put your hands on the vehicle's roof, Mr. Wahl."

Shaking his head again, Wahl complied.

Resato moved Wahl's left hand off the roof and behind his back, handcuffing it. He then repeated the process with the right hand.

"Step to your right, Mr. Wahl." Wahl started to move left.

"Your *right*."

The prisoner stepped right.

With his hand firmly on the handcuffs, Trooper Resato leaned down and looked at the passenger. "*Stay where you are*."

The Trooper moved Wahl to the patrol car, placing him in the driver's side rear seat. Once secured, he walked to the passenger side of the Dodge.

"Step out of the car, please."

The woman unbuckled her seat belt, swung the door open, and lost her balance. With her hand in the grass, she looked up at Resato. "Oops!"

The trooper held out his hand. The woman took it and got out with her left hand on the door. Standing unsteadily, she giggled.

"Thank you, officer."

"What's your name, miss?"

"Donna."

"Your full name, please." "Danamarie Samuels."

"Let me see your ID, please."

"I don't have one with me," she said and laughed again.

"How old are you, miss?

"Almost nineteen."

"Ms. Samuels, I'm arresting you for public intoxication."

Once his second prisoner occupied the cruiser's passenger-side back seat, Resato—with his dash and body cam still recording—searched and inventoried the Dodge. Finally, he used a business-size card with printing to test the window's tinting. Raising the driver's window a quarter of the way, Resato held the card on the inside, with the printing toward the street. His body cam recorded none of the card's printing being visible.

PART III
"She says that like it'd be a *bad* thing."

EIGHTEEN

Since Mrs. McGuire was the closest geographically, Dusty Rhodes took one more run at Ginger's mother—face-to-face this time.

Sitting in Kim's beautifully decorated Mount Vernon living room, the reporter had mentally declared defeat. She rose from a light grey Christopher Knight Home Nicole Fabric Settee and extended her hand to Kim, holding a business card. "Mrs. McGuire, if you change your mind, please give me a call."

Smiling, Kim took the card, glancing at it briefly before setting it on the coffee table.

As her hostess rose, Dusty remembered the last conversation with Pat Santini. "Does the name Airmed Pharmaceuticals mean anything to you?"

Kim McGuire's head snapped up, mouth agape. "*I never said that name!*"

The movement startled the reporter. Taking a step back, Dusty saw fear in the woman's eyes. "That's *it*! *Airmed* ran the trial your husband participated in."

"*I never . . . told . . . you that!*"

"No, you didn't, Mrs. McGuire. Even if you *had*, I've *never* revealed a source."

※ ※ ※

Trooper Resato's search of the Dodge in Littlestown uncovered over two pounds of marijuana. The weed didn't garner much attention compared to nearly half a kilogram of pure fentanyl powder, two canisters of nitrous oxide—aka laughing gas—and twenty-four small silver compressed gas cartridges marked "16 Grams."

The State Police Troop H commander, being well aware of the fentanyl murders' MO, notified the FBI's Harrisburg Field Office across town. Within minutes, the Bureau snatched the evidence faster than a pickpocket could take a Saint Mark's Square wallet.

※ ※ ※

Dusty Rhodes rushed back to her office, calling her executive assistant on the way.

"Ophelia, I think Airmed Pharmaceuticals ran the drug trials all these patients were participants in. Start digging up everything you can find."

"Mrs. McGuire told you that?"

"Not in so many words, and we'll never link her to this information. Understand?" "Yes, ma'am."

☒☒☒ ☒☒☒ ☒☒☒

The federal task force met ninety minutes after Trooper Resato's arrests. The Zoom call between the Harrisburg and Baltimore Field Offices reviewed the evidence, particularly the fentanyl and gas cylinders.

A deep dive into William H. Wahl's history showed a variety of small-time crimes: disorderly conduct, underage drinking, reckless driving, noise violations, and possession of drug paraphernalia. Nothing remotely akin to possession with intent to distribute at the low end and nine counts of murder in the first, which the fentanyl and gas cylinders suggested. A federal warrant to search Wahl's Westminster, Maryland apartment netted another pound of marijuana, over two hundred fentanyl pills, and more nitrous oxide, but none of the delivery envelopes.

Several days had passed without another victim since Jasmine Peterson's murder. The lack of a final evidentiary envelope rivet in Mr. Wahl's case was attributed to being . . . "out of stock."

Maddison Mitchell asked Lonnie Jerry to wrap up the meeting while she called Director Courtemanche personally with the fantastic news.

"*Amazing* work, Maddison. I never had any doubt you'd pull it off."

His words were practically orgasmic. "*Thank you*, Director."

☒☒☒ ☒☒☒ ☒☒☒

As soon as she could safely, Althea Ramos called Joe D'Elia about the break in the case.

"Does this Wahl guy have a long rap sheet?"

"No. Just a bunch of nickel-and-dime misdemeanors."

"So, this guy goes from a low Single-A crime league to the Majors like some kind of criminal *savant*? I'm not buying *that*."

"SAIC Mitchell is under tremendous pressure, Mr. D'Elia."

"I'm sure she is. But if she's wrong, her short fall from grace will have an epic career ending impact."

☒☒☒ ☒☒☒ ☒☒☒

D'Elia quickly passed Ramos' update onto Morgan.

Within minutes, Jeannie Staron announced a call from Dusty Rhodes.

"Ms. Rhodes, what can I do for you?" "*My*, so formal."

"Can you do me a huge favor?"

"I'll give you the standard answer. 'It depends.'"

"The other day, I called you, and you said you were with Proffitt. Later, you said there were two members of law enforcement there with you too."

"Yes."

"Did they have cases similar to the Ginger McGuire murder?"

"They did."

"Can you give me their names?"

"Why do you want them?"

"I mentioned Airmed Pharmaceuticals to Kim McGuire today. She . . . "

Morgan interrupted. "Airmed, you mean like a *medevac*?"

"No. Ophelia, my EA, found some old information on the web. The short version is that Airmed is the goddess of healing in Irish mythology.

"The company ran several unsuccessful drug trials to find an early detection protocol for pancreatic cancer. They're out of business now, but the trials required family members to sign NDAs with severe penalties if they shared any information about their family members' participation."

"Okay. So, what are you asking, Dusty?"

"For the contact information for the two cops who were with you. I need to try to confirm what I'm sure is true. They could ask the family members of their victims about a connection to Airmed."

"I can't give you their information, Dust . . . " "*Jesus fucking Christ, Morgan, all I'm ask . . .* " "*Hey*! Just hold on. Let me finish. *Will ya*?

"One of them is working the McGuire case. You already know about that one. The other is working two cases in Montgomery County and is in contact with the widow of a third victim in McLean. I'll call the detective to ask if they can get an Airmed confirmation."

Dusty didn't speak for several seconds. "I'm sorry, Hunter. I just get so wrapped up that

I don't . . . "

"I understand. I'll make the call. I'll pass your contact information on. They can call

you directly, if appropriate."

NINETEEN

"Mrs. Judge, I have one quick question. I know you're concerned about violating the drug company's NDA. I'm going to mention the name of a company. Don't say *anything* if it ran the trial your husband participated in. Is that clear?"

"Yes."

"Was the company Airmed Pharmaceuticals?"

After nearly ten seconds of silence, Julie said, "Thank you."

"Thank you."

Silence followed the question when Stephens spoke to the second Judge widow in McLean and the husband of the Gaithersburg victim.

⋈ ⋈ ⋈

Rather than call Dusty Rhodes, Julie reported back to Morgan. After giving him an update, she asked, "Anything new on your end?"

Morgan filled her in on Ramos' call to D'Elia.

"*No shit?*"

"Joe thinks it's too early to break out the Dom Pérignon, based on this Wahl guy's past low-rent exploits. But we'll see." "Have you told Bill Wilson yet?"

"No. Haven't had the chance."

"Mind if I give him a call?"

"Not at all."

⋈ ⋈ ⋈

Director Courtemanche updated the Attorney General and then Speaker Lucille Peterson as soon as SAIC Mitchell's call ended. The Speaker shared the news with her chief of staff. Within minutes, the entire office was abuzz.

With a flash, WTCR—D.C.'s sister station to Baltimore's WLAB—broke into their 4 PM news program.

"We have an unconfirmed report of an arrest in Littlestown, PA. A suspect—thought to be the fentanyl murderer—may be in custody there."

⋈ ⋈ ⋈

Bill Wilson reacted to the Wahl news with D'Elia's skepticism. "That rap sheet sounds more like this guy is a *courier*, not a killer."

"It does," Julie Stephens agreed. "And if so, that's a *lot* of product to move around while stoned. And, some drug czar *ain't* a happy camper. The feds better blanket him with serious security. Especially if his boss thinks he might try to cut a deal."

※ ※ ※

Mrs. Naomi Monroe filed a missing person report with the BPD eight days after Cletis' last phone call.

※ ※ ※

Morgan updated Dusty with Julie Stephens' Airmed confirmation.

※ ※ ※

Western Maryland is rife with camping spots and picturesque hiking trails. Little Tonoloway Creek is a hidden gem near Hancock, a short drive from I-68. The creek offers scenic and peaceful hiking experiences of varying difficulty through lush forests, rocky outcroppings, and crystal-clear waters.

An avid birding couple from Pittsburg stopped for a water break next to the creek. The sounds of the highway in the distance above were a minor distraction. Taking in her surroundings, the woman said to her husband, "John, what's that up *there*?"

"Where?"

Pointing, she said, "The white thing, wedged between the trees and the cliff."

※ ※ ※

William Wahl and his attorney faced Maddison Mitchell and Lonnie Jerry. The interrogations had gone on for hours. At this point, Wahl's only comfort came from the public defender not costing him an appendage.

"Agent Mitchell. There are no more ways for my client to tell you he's innocent of murder."

"*Special Agent in Charge*, Counselor."

"Mr. Wahl, you're in a shitload of trouble. Virginia has the death penalty, and you have not just one but *two* victims in the Commonwealth. And killing the Speaker of the U.S. House of Representatives' daughter will put enough pressure on a prosecutor to make a *diamond*."

※ ※ ※

A *Baltimore Mirror* story ran the following morning, connecting the defunct Airmed Pharmaceuticals to the fentanyl murders. With no corporate offices to contact, Ophelia called the law firm that handled the Chapter 7 filings. The firm refused to comment.

The lone heir to the family fortune—Fitzroy Adam De Burgh—served briefly as CEO between his father's death and the completion of Airmed's corporate failure.

De Burgh's home of record in Centreville, Delaware, had security rivaling the White House. Dusty Rhodes drove there in hopes of getting access in person. The guards were polite but very firm in denying any entrance or information.

A background investigation on De Burgh listed a vanilla history of a professional student: Sidwell Friends School; Bachelor of Science in Economics, concentrating in

Business Analytics from UPenn's Wharton School; a bachelor's, master's and Ph.D. in biochemistry from MIT; and a bachelor's, master's and Ph.D. in pharmacology from Oxford. Whether to prolong his entry into the family business or a legitimate thirst for knowledge at forty-four, Fitzroy drew his first Airmed paycheck.

Young De Burgh's deep admiration and love of his father came first among the background investigation's few personal mentions.

⋈⋈ ⋈⋈ ⋈⋈

Eighty miles southwest of Baltimore, the FBI's Dangerous Goods/Hazardous Materials Response Unit—aka Crime Lab—is located in Quantico, Virginia. The evidence collected from the Dodge made a quick private jet trip from Harrisburg, PA, before William Wahl's interrogation began. By mid-afternoon, the case against him was starting to fall apart.

The fentanyl did not match the purity of samples collected from the crime scenes. Wahl's contraband also contained different chemical structures.

The gas cartridges contained nitrous oxide—aka "laughing gas," used in dentistry as a sedative and analgesic agent and by drug users to get high—rather than carbon dioxide.

⋈⋈ ⋈⋈ ⋈⋈

Extracting the vehicle above the Little Tonoloway Creek took most of three days. The van's final resting position, sixty feet above the valley, wedged between a large tree and the rocky hillside, presented another problem—a large rock outcropping directly above it prevented it from being raised straight to the road.

The tree keeping the van from falling farther into the valley would have to be cut away from the mangled Econoline. A suggestion to simply topple the tree into the valley received an immediate rejection. The Potomac Heritage National Scenic Trail claimed the cleanup would close part of the trail indefinitely and be prohibitively expensive to clean up and remove.

The requirement to keep debris from crashing to the valley floor meant two cranes and a heavy-duty tow truck needed to be in place. With a longer than standard tow truck cable, the wrecker lowered a worker to assess the situation directly.

The man determined the van would fall if the treetop holding it firmly against the hillside were cut without the rear axle being secured first.

With the first crane taking a strain on the van and the second securing the treetop, a courageous worker freed the front of the Econoline. As the treetop rose to the road, the van swung from under the rock outcropping and followed.

※ ※ ※

The task force did not receive the FBI's lab findings well.

The news of William Wahl's arrest had quickly spread from two Atlantic Coast NBC affiliates to the network's nightly national news.

Newspapers from *The New York Times* to *The Belleville Telescope* ran front-page stories above the fold.

Hordes of reporters, podcasters, and bloggers hounded the DOJ's Public Information Office spokesperson for updates. After being peppered with Wahl questions at an unrelated major announcement, the Attorney General gave up and walked away from the podium.

Shortly thereafter, Director Courtemanche occupied a molten seat in the AG's office.

"Who's running the task force, Luke?"

"Maddison Mitchell, sir."

"Okay, move her ass to the most remote field office in Alaska today."

"This isn't her fault, sir. She's done a fine job. If anyone should be demoted, it's me. I called the Speaker with the news prematurely."

"Somebody has to take the bullet."

"Then give me a blindfold and a cigarette."

※ ※ ※

A shattered windshield and side windows allowed birds of prey to disrespect the Econoline van's corpse. The head, missing the left ear, eye, and eyelid, slumped near a deflated, bloody airbag. A macabre smile of teeth and bloody gums showed through a gaping hole in the cheek. Holes in the shirt showed other wounds.

This poor soul would not have an open casket.

TWENTY

Quantico's analysis did not support William Wahl being the fentanyl killer. The massive amount of fentanyl and marijuana provided more than enough evidence to indict him for possession with intent to distribute controlled substances.

Due to overcrowding and logistical issues in the closest federal detention center— Schuylkil Federal Correctional Institution—Mr. Wahl found himself temporarily housed in the Harrisburg jail. Julie Stephens' prediction came true. Guards discovered Wahl shanked in the shower two days later. He was DOA at the hospital.

Fortunately, Danamarie Samuels, the Dodge passenger, only received a warning. Her parents arrived from Westminster by late afternoon to take her home.

※ ※ ※

A recipient of the following day's mail in Wheeling, West Virginia, notched the tenth fentanyl murder statistic.

※ ※ ※

The Maryland driver's license for the Econoline van occupant appeared genuine at first blush. But, the State Police quickly tagged it as a high-quality fake. DMV records revealed the name on it belonged to a deceased WWII veteran, with a false address in the Chesapeake Bay estuary.

His fingerprints and DNA were compared to local, state, and federal databases without a match.

GEDmatch is a valuable database used for genetic genealogical research. In the last decade-plus, law enforcement has used it to create family trees and find relatives of suspects and victims. GEDmatch users can agree to or decline law enforcement's access to their data.

Strict guidelines and legal authorization, such as a warrant or court order, must be in place before GEDmatch data can be accessed and used in a criminal investigation. Ancestry.com and 23andMe also allow access, but with stricter policies.

And so, the Washington County, MD Medical Examiner's Office uploaded a DNA sample to GEDmatch.

⋈||⋈ ⋈||⋈ ⋈||⋈

With the task force back to square one, tempers were on edge. The latest death in WV brought the USPS under Maddison Mitchell's naked, swinging, interrogation lightbulb. "Ms. Ramos, why has the Postal Service not been able to scan for and stop these packages? How tough can it be to put a drug-sniffing dog on a *conveyer belt*?"

"We don't put dogs on conveyers, Special Agent Mitchell.

"The postage meter used on these packages is a clever counterfeit. It uses the valid tracking codes of recently hacked postal customer accounts across the U.S. Our systems recognize these numbers as valid.

"The size and shape of the envelopes are not unique. Tens of thousands may go through any sorting center in a single day. So far as we know, ten have been mailed to date."

⋈||⋈ ⋈||⋈ ⋈||⋈

A bored ATF agent sitting on the opposite side of the room from Ramos absentmindedly dialed the number of *The Mirror*'s tip line burner phone.

A phone rang in Althea Ramos' purse. She reached for it. SAIC Mitchell snapped, "*I said silence your fucking phones!*" *Odd*, the ATF agent thought, ending the call.

The phone stopped ringing as Ramos retrieved it.

The ATF agent pressed the redial button.

The phone in Ramos' hand, visible to Mitchell and the ATF agent, rang again.

The agent shot to his feet. "*There's* your burner phone, Agent Mitchell!"

⋈||⋈ ⋈||⋈ ⋈||⋈

Ophelia studied Fitzroy Adam De Burgh's BI details closely, noting a ten-month gap in its timeline beginning after his father's death.

⋈||⋈ ⋈||⋈ ⋈||⋈

Thanks to LRI's hundreds of investigations over the years, Roger Graves had access to License Plate Reader data from 43 State Police agencies. He began timing the convoy on I-70 Westbound in Ohio between the last LPR before Exit 202 and the first west of Exit 202. A forty-seven-minute gap.

Contacting the Pilot Travel Center's security department, Graves obtained video of the convoy. He sent a copy to LRI's video team for possible enhancement.

Eleven minutes elapsed between the arrival and departure at Pilot. Thirty-six minutes unaccounted for.

Googlemaps.com allowed Graves to determine the distance from Exit 202 to the following western LPR.

Calculating the time for a 2018 Peterbilt 389 tractor with a Cummins X15 engine hauling the Bugatti's 4,683 lbs. to get up to speed after entering I-70 again and trigger the LPR recording—six minutes.

The Apex hostages were left at Doan Ford. No video existed there. But, allowing five minutes for the convoy to get from Pilot to the dealership and back to I-70 still allowed twenty-five minutes to move the Bugatti to another vehicle.

✂ ✂ ✂

A subsequent arrest, search, and inventory of Althea Ramos' handbag found Joe D'Elia's business card.

"*Christ on a pogo stick*! *Fucking* D'Elia!"

Maddison Mitchell glanced at her deputy. "What's up, Lonnie?"

Waving the business card, Jerry said, "I worked for Joe D'Elia a lifetime ago. After he retired, he joined LRI. Working on some unsolved cases in upstate New York, he pulled some shady shit on me to get evidence in another of their investigations."

"What was the other case?"

"You remember when Axel Favre and his family were kidnapped in Switzerland by the Iranians?"

"Who doesn't? Didn't you get a commendation out of that, Lonnie?"

"Yeah, I did. But it could have easily shitcanned my career."

With a satiric smile, Mitchell said, "So, give Mr. D'Elia a call. I'm sure he'd love to catch up with you."

✂ ✂ ✂

Morgan dialed Dusty Rhodes' cell number.

"Rhodes."

"Morgan here. The feds have arrested Althea Ramos, your fentanyl tipster."

"How? We've refused to give them any information."

"They must have gotten a warrant somehow. Ramos had the phone used to make the call in her purse."

"I smell a rat, Morgan. After all, it *is* the FBI."

✂ ✂ ✂

LRI's lab technicians turned the grainy Pilot video into images clear enough to read the plate on a Ford Econoline van following the convoy. Roger Graves assumed it had been stolen and searched the recent auto thefts in surrounding states. The vehicle had been reported in Silver Spring, MD. He passed the information to the MCPD-ACES.

Finding no LPR record of the van continuing west on I-70, Graves believed the thief abandoned it after the hijacking. Scanning police reports in Ohio, Pennsylvania, and Maryland netted a fatal accident in Maryland on I-68 Eastbound in Washington County.

✂ ✂ ✂

Ophelia—an avid Facebook participant—used her social media experience to uncover and "friend" three former Airmed employees. Through conversations and private messages with them, she learned the name of the executive secretary to the father and son CEOs. One Gloria Cosgrove lived in Wilmington, Delaware.

An Airmed Facebook friend said Fitzroy's ninety-day gap had been rumored to be a "sabbatical" at the Brandywine Hospital for Behavioral Health in Wilmington.

◁▷ ◁▷ ◁▷

Dusty Rhodes sat in *The Mirror*'s editor of the health section's office.

"Buzz, have you ever considered doing a story on pharmaceutical companies' efforts to find a cure for pancreatic cancer?"

"No, not that I recall. But it sounds like an interesting idea. Why?"

"I'd rather not say at the moment. But now that I've mentioned it, would it be true to say you're *considering* it?"

"D'Elia."

"Joe, it's Lonnie Jerry."

"Hello, Lonnie! How are you?" "Althea Ramos sends her regards."

"How is Ms. Ramos, Lonnie?"

"So, you admit you know her."

"It's illegal to lie to an FBI agent. I know her. What about it?"

"How do you know her, Joe?"

"*That*, Lonnie, is none of your business."

"You'll change your tune when we indict you on a host of federal charges. Obstruction, false statements, and conspiracy just to start with."

"The Bureau battered and bloodied itself, letting family members of high-ranking politicians skate on crimes no civilian would. No one with half a brain on the seventh floor, especially the Director, will trot out an indictment for a decorated former SAIC of the Boston Field Office. Certainly not for the bullshit charges you just rattled off."

"We'll see, Joe."

⋈ ⋈ ⋈

"Ms. Cosgrove, I'm Dusty Rhodes with *The Baltimore Mirror*. Our paper is considering a story on pharmaceutical companies' efforts to cure pancreatic cancer. I know your former employer, Airmed Pharmaceuticals, tried to create an early diagnostic test for the disease. I was wondering if you have any contact information for Mr. Fitzroy Adam De Burgh.

We'd like to interview him about the difficulties in early testing for the disease."

"I doubt he will speak to you. I understand he is *very* reclusive now."

Dusty rolled the dice. "Has Mr. De Burgh been that way since his time at Brandywine

Hospital?"

Cosgrove didn't answer for several seconds. *Shit*! *Snake eyes*! Dusty thought.

"And well before that," Cosgrove finally answered. "Fitz went downhill after his father's cancer diagnosis and fell apart completely when he died."

"Oh! I'm sorry to hear that.

"Would you mind sharing his phone number, if you have one?"

⋈ ⋈ ⋈

Roger Graves continued his convoy tracking. An abandoned vehicle report from Muskingum County, Ohio, listed the Apex tractor-trailer on a cul-de-sac just North of Orphans Road on CR 726.

Graves saw a blue Ford pickup pulling a silver trailer pass the Apex rig while tracking the Peterbilt west on I-70. The Ford, traveling faster than the tractor, slowed down, then continued slightly ahead of the other truck through a second and third LPR at exit 234— CR 726. Depending on the LPR's spacing, the two vehicles stayed close for three to six miles.

These guys know each other.

D'Elia called Morgan to update him on Lonnie Jerry's call.

"Do you think this will blow back on LRI, Joe?"

"Maybe indirectly. But I doubt it, unless there is some deal-hanging fire for us to work with the DOJ that they could pull the plug on."

"Nothing going on there."

"Like I told Lonnie, the Bureau has created enough stink for a lifetime. Russia Gate, the Parkland School shooting in Florida, school board members threatened by parents, devout Catholics as terrorists, arresting abortion protesters at homes in SWAT gear, mislabeling evidence, lying to the FISA court, and other abuses of authority.

"I don't think the Director wants to shine a light on anything else. Especially something tough to prove."

⋈||⋈ ⋈||⋈ ⋈||⋈

Although Althea Ramos hadn't followed one of D'Elia's critical pieces of advice, she had others—keeping her mouth shut and retaining a lawyer specializing in whistle-blower cases.

At her arraignment, Attorney Elizabeth Pedley argued that the Bureau's case was flimsy in that it had a single piece of evidence. The fact that Mrs. Ramos had the phone used to call *The Mirror*. They had yet to prove that her client *made* the call. With Ramos' lack of any criminal behavior, even traffic violations, and her decades of public service with the USPS, release on her own recognizance could be considered reasonable.

The prosecution objected vehemently, but the judge, seeing no concern of flight risk, agreed to Althea's ROR.

⋈||⋈ ⋈||⋈ ⋈||⋈

Dusty's call to Fitzroy Adam De Burgh went to voicemail.

⋈||⋈ ⋈||⋈ ⋈||⋈

With the Apex Peterbilt accounted for, Graves continued tracking the blue Ford. Two hundred twenty-two miles after the two vehicles separated, the Ford took Exit 73 onto I465 North in Indianapolis, Indiana.

After 12.9 miles, it exited onto Meridian Street, going south.

Graves now tapped into Indianapolis' Street camera network. Turning left onto East 82nd Street and then taking the first right onto Pennsylvania Street—Carmel's prestigious Spring Mill Estates. He did not see the Ford again.

Going to Zillow.com, Graves could see the McMansions in the 8100 block. The property at 8103 North Pennsylvania dwarfed the other large homes. It included a six-car garage.

Googlemaps.com's "street-view" feature provided more details than Zillow's still images.

A Bugatti could feel very at home there.

GEDmatch found a second cousin's partial match to the DNA sample uploaded by the Washington County ME. Emlyn Marie Beaumont lived in Dundalk, Maryland.

"Mr. Morgan, I have some information on the Apex hijacking." "Roger, at this point, there's no need for 'mister.' What have you got?"

"Yes, sir.

"I think Mr. Schutz will find the Bugatti in the 8100 block of East 82nd Street in Indianapolis. Most likely at 8103."

"*Outstanding*, Roger. I'll give him a call. *Thank* you."

On the 7th floor of the J. Edgar Hoover building, Joe D'Elia's prediction proved correct. FBI Director Luke Courtemanche had *no* interest in a spotlight casting another shadow of doubt on the Bureau. His spotless reputation was the primary reason for the president's selection and the Senate's confirmation. This a desperately needed trait for the leader chosen to remove the patina of distrust blanketing the organization.

Dick Schutz breathed a massive sigh of relief hearing Morgan's update.

"*My God*, Morgan. I can't thank you enough!"

"Let's not celebrate too quickly. We think we know where it is. We haven't recovered

it yet."

"Can LRI get it back?"

"No. It's best to work through the Indianapolis PD. I'll give them a call and see what I can do. I know the SWAT commander there. I'm sure he can point me in the right direction.

"More to follow as soon as I have anything."

The Mirror's legal department challenged the legitimacy of the FBI's warrant in federal court, claiming a Fourth Amendment violation of the paper's phone records. A separate motion argued that any evidence collected should not be admissible.

The Washington County Sheriff's Office report of the fatal Econoline van crash mentioned the ME's DNA submission.

HIPAA regulations will probably prevent the ME's office from giving out information on the victim's ID from his DNA. But, what the hell . . .

To Roger Graves's surprise, a call expecting nothing provided surprises.

First, HIPAA does not cover DNA evidence. Second, in record time, GEDmatch had already provided the name of a second cousin living in Dundalk, Maryland.

⋈⋈ ⋈⋈ ⋈⋈

In Morristown, New York, an off-duty River Club Restaurant waitress became the eleventh fentanyl victim.

⋈⋈ ⋈⋈ ⋈⋈

Among the many properties Fitzroy Adam De Burgh owned in the U.S., Europe,

Australia, New Zealand, and Singapore, one stood out to Ophelia in her dogged quest for his information. At just under $8 million— a relative slum compared to the others—Twelve Degrees North, Lance Aux Epines offered more than luxury on the Island of Grenada.

⋈⋈ ⋈⋈ ⋈⋈

Julie Stephens and her academy classmate, Addison Carlson, sat for dinner at the Sin & Grin Mexican Restaurant in Gaithersburg.

After ordering a pitcher of margaritas and two house specials, they caught up on each other's lives as usual.

"Looks like your fentanyl cases are growing, Julie."

"Fortunately, I've still only got two. But I hear the total is up to eleven, with another in New York State."

"How about you? Anything interesting?"

"No, ACES doesn't advertise for crime fighters looking for adventure. We get an occasional carjacking that ends with a DOA. Somebody stole an Econoline and did a swan dive into a gorge from I-68 in Washington County. *That* would have been interesting, watching the local sheriff trying to extract the vehicle."

"Why? Where was it?"

"Pinned between a tree and a cliff. Took days to get it out."

⋈⋈ ⋈⋈ ⋈⋈

Morgan contacted his Indianapolis Metropolitan Police Department SWAT friend. The commander offered to call the head of Indianapolis' Auto Theft/Heist Interdiction Team. As a result of his request, HIT detectives moved quickly, getting a search warrant for 8103 East 82nd Street. Within twelve hours of the Bugatti's recovery, Apex Security had it flown to the buyer in Cincinnati.

⋈⋈ ⋈⋈ ⋈⋈

The DNA relative GEDmatch identified, Monica Rivers, answered her phone.

"Hello."

Graves introduced himself.

"Ms. Rivers, I'm with Last Resort Investigations. We're trying to identify a victim of a traffic accident. The Medical Examiner in Washington County submitted the victim's DNA to a national database. It appears this person is a second or third cousin of yours.

"Do you have family members in the Baltimore area?"

"Yes, quite a few."

"Okay. Your second cousin would be the child of a parent's cousin. Do you know if your mother or father has cousins?"

"My father does. His cousin Naomi."

"Do you know if she has children?"

"I believe she has three sons."

"Do your parents have any other cousins?"

"Not that I know of. Naomi is the only one I've ever heard about."

"Can I get her contact information, please?"

Monica Rivers hesitated momentarily. "I don't know you, Mr. Graves. With all the scamming that goes on today, I'm careful.

"You said you work for Last Resort Investigations. Are they in Baltimore?"

"Yes, ma'am. Would you like their number?"

"No. I'll look it up. I'll have my father call you if they confirm you're an employee. Where can you be reached?"

Roger gave his cell number. "That's very smart, Ms. Rivers. Few people would be as cautious."

Rivers confirmed it was the number calling. "Thank you, Mr. Graves. Goodbye."

TWENTY-ONE

"*Airmed Pharmaceuticals*! We had to learn about them from the fucking *Baltimore Mirror*! None of you *crack* investigators could connect *that* dot?" Maddison Mitchell shook her head in disgust.

"I have to get my daily ass chewing from the Director in three hours. I better know every

Airmed detail, down to what beer the night janitor drinks, or I won't be here tomorrow!"

A voice at the rear of the room whispered, "She says that like it'd be a *bad* thing."

⋈⋈ ⋈⋈ ⋈⋈

Dusty Rhodes had a puzzled look on her face when she asked, "Why Grenada, Ophelia? What's so special there?"

"Beautiful beaches, tropical climate, safety, security, excellent health care. You know, all the things that attract cash-carrying tourists."

"Fitzroy can find all those in Monaco or the Maldive Islands. So, again, why a multimillion-dollar *shack* in Grenada?"

"He can't buy citizenship in Monaco or the Maldives, though. And, here's the biggie, boss. Grenada has *no* extradition treaty with the U.S."

⋈⋈ ⋈⋈ ⋈⋈

Monica Rivers' father called Graves with the phone number for Naomi Monroe.

Speaking to Mrs. Monroe on the phone—without explaining all the details—Roger told her of the GEDmatch information suggesting she might be related to a traffic accident victim. He asked if he could come to her home and collect a DNA sample.

Naomi agreed.

As he left her home, he turned and thanked her.

"I just hope this helps somebody out there wondering. I *know* what that feels like."

"What do you mean, ma'am?"

"I can't get in touch with my youngest, Cletis. I filed a report with the police."

"What kind of work does he do?"

"He does computer stuff. Don't ask me what. He explained it a dozen times without making any sense to me."

"Where does he work?"

⋈⋈ ⋈⋈ ⋈⋈

"Sir, we've indirectly connected all the fentanyl victims to Airmed Pharmaceuticals' drug trials. They're out of business. Have been for several years. Chapter Seven."

"Indirectly? How?"

Maddison Mitchell paused before answering. "Through a story in *The Baltimore Mirror*, sir.

"I know that sounds bad, Director. But . . . " "It *isn't* bad, Maddison. It's *terrible*.

"Can you imagine what the press will say if they find out a *local* newspaper is our *investigative* source?"

"Sir, we've clamped the lid on any press releases from now on for that very reason."

"Yeah, well, good luck with that! It was a tip to *The Mirror* that kicked this hornet's nest *open*."

"Yes, sir. And on that subject. We have the tipster in custody. Althea Ramos, a PIS agent."

"That's small comfort, Maddison. Her call made the Bureau look like we were withholding information at the expense of citizens' safety."

⋈⋈ ⋈⋈ ⋈⋈

Even FedEx couldn't get Naomi Monroe's DNA sample to Washington County's ME as fast as Graves could drive it there. Although, he had little doubt about the Econoline van driver's identity now.

As he drove west on I-70, he called Morgan with the update. They agreed to wait for an ID confirmation before saying anything to Dick Schutz . . . or Mrs. Monroe.

Graves felt he had a duty to do her notification rather than an unknown state or BPD officer . . . if it came to that.

⋈⋈ ⋈⋈ ⋈⋈

Another Montgomery County resident received a fentanyl package. The results mirrored the other eleven cases. Again, Julie Stephens attended the scene before anyone from the task force. After photographing the evidence with her phone, she collected another sample of the powder on and around the victim. As in the other cases, the woman had no children.

On the way to MCPD headquarters in her car, she called Morgan and then Wilson with updates.

While talking to Morgan, he had to take a call from an LRI investigator. As Julie opened her car door at headquarters, her phone rang.

"Julie, Morgan here. Sorry I had to cut you off."

"No worries. Hot case?"

"Yeah. A friend from Vietnam had a *very* expensive car his company shipped for the manufacturer hijacked. The guy who tracked it down in Indianapolis had an update on the identity of one of the thieves who left himself hanging in a gorge on I-68."

"Was it an Econoline van?"

"It was. How do you know that?"

"A friend works in ACES, MCP's auto theft people. It was stolen in Silver Spring.

She told me about the sheriff up there trying to extract it. Apparently not a trivial process." "No, it wasn't. Probably soon to be a case study."

"If you get an ID, let me know. I'll pass it on to her."

Roger Graves walked into his Glen Burnie apartment a few minutes before midnight. Hopefully, Naomi Monroe's DNA comparison to the van victim's would be completed the next day.

Case notes and documents were scattered on his small dining room table/desk—Cletus Monroe's AAdvantage frequent flier report lay on top.

Graves picked it up. An item he'd disregarded two days ago seemed to leap off the page.

PART IV
"A pancreatic cancer *vigilante*."

TWENTY-TWO

"Hunter, I'd like to cast a little bread on the federal waters."

"Like what, Joe?"

"I'd be surprised if the task force had determined that none of the fentanyl victims have children."

"Really?"

"Yes. I'm sure they got wrapped up in the arrest of the kid in PA and took their eye off the ball. Then, when that became nothing more than a good drug bust, they returned to the basics."

"They must be desperate, Joe. Julie Stephens just called in a twelfth victim in Monkey County. A female with no children."

"At this point, they'd take just *desperate* as a great day.

"So, you have no objections?"

"Okay. What do you have in mind?"

✂✂ ✂✂ ✂✂

"Special Agent Jerry."

"Lonnie, Joe."

Jerry didn't speak for several seconds. Finally, "Yeah, and just what can I do for *you*?"

"Nothing. Maybe I can help you this time."

"I won't hold my breath, Joe."

"Well, now that you're up to twelve bodies, do you want to turn down any helpful information?"

"*How* do you know about the latest victim?"

"Because cops talk to each other, Jerry, and they *talk* to LRI." Again, Jerry didn't speak.

"Okay, Lonnie, I'll go if you're not interested.

"*Ciao*."

"*Wait*! What have you got?"

"You already know the victims are all associated with past Airmed trial patients.

Right?"

"Are you fishing, Joe?"

"No, *The Mirror* already pointed everybody in that direction. Then WLAB ran a special that mentioned neither the professor nor their anchor had children."

"We knew that. Nothing special there. So, what's your big scoop?"

"Lonnie, *none* of the *twelve* have any children."

"That's not true. Some do."

"Yeah? Well, LRI can't find birth certificates for any. But, maybe you super sleuths can."

⋈ ⋈ ⋈

The Washington County ME's office called Roger Graves just before 11 AM. The Econoline victim and the DNA sample he delivered the previous day shared a parent-child relationship.

Having seen pictures of the body, Graves wanted to avoid Naomi Monroe having to identify her son. He asked the ME staff member on the call, "Can dental records be used to make the final ID of the body?"

"No, Maryland law requires fingerprints or a government-issued ID."

"Is there anything you can do to clean up his face?"

"No, that would be up to a cosmetology specialist at a funeral home. The face is in rough shape, so I understand your concern for the person making the ID. It's just something the

ME's office can't accommodate. Sorry."

"One last question. Can you release the body to a funeral home before the final ID?" "Yes, but not until they confirm the deceased's identity."

⋈ ⋈ ⋈

"*Shit*!" Maddison Mitchell covered her face with her hands.

After several seconds, she looked at Jerry again. "Can't we uncover *anything* on our own? First, *The Mirror* is our source, and now *LRI*?" "Sorry, Maddison. I'm frustrated too.

"I've got the team confirming what D'Elia said. But, knowing him, that's already been done by LRI."

"So, how does this help us, Lonnie?"

"I don't think it does immediately. It just gives us a finer point on the perp . . . or perps."

⋈ ⋈ ⋈

Roger Graves called Naomi Monroe.

"Ma'am, I have some information about your son, Cletis. Can I come over to talk to you?"

"It's bad news."

"It is. Can I come over?"

"No sense in you wasting time and money comin' to tell me he's dead, Roger. What happened?"

"Yes, ma'am." Graves took a deep breath. "He was driving on I-68 in Western Maryland and went off the road. Probably fell asleep at the wheel.

The van he was driving went into a ravine. Cletis was trapped there for several days before the vehicle was recovered."

"Just tell me this, did he suffer?"

"It doesn't look like it. The medical examiner believes he died instantly on impact."

"What do I need to do?"

"Well . . ."

"Wait a minute. Cletis doesn't have a van. Are you sure it's my Cletis?"

"Yes, ma'am. Your DNA sample says you're his parent."

"What was he doin' way out there in a van?"

Graves wasn't going down the "hijacking" road. "Well, maybe he'd rented it to move something. Helping a friend, maybe."

"Cletis doesn't have many friends here, much less out there. What was he up to?" "Mrs. Monroe, I really can't speculate on that.

"Is one of your other sons nearby who can be with you?"

Naomi ignored the question. "What do I have to do?"

"Someone needs to identify Cletis' body. If one of your sons can, it might be best."

"You don't want me to see him."

"No, Mrs. Monroe. You can have a funeral home identify his body if you have his passport or driver's license."

"Can't they just use the license he had on him?"

"He didn't have it with him. A family member can or a funeral director with an official state-issued document."

"Where do I have to go?"

"He's in the Washington County morgue, ma'am. Sixteen-two-thirty-two Elliott Parkway in Williamsport.

"Can I call one of your sons for you, Mrs. Monroe?"

"No, I'll do it. Thank you for your help, Roger. I appreciate it."

⋈⋈ ⋈⋈ ⋈⋈

After Graves updated Morgan on the ID, Hunter called Dick Schutz and then Julie Stephens.

Julie shared the ID with Addison Carlson, who, out of curiosity, ran a check on Cletis Monroe. She found a ticket issued to him months earlier for an illegal right turn on a red light. The ticket had not been paid, and Cletis had not appeared in court to defend himself.

Addison called Julie with the update.

The homicide detective decided to run a BI on Cletis herself.

⋈⋈ ⋈⋈ ⋈⋈

Roger Graves found Cletis' rented Climate-Smart Self-Storage address via Google— 5910 Moravia Park Drive. Querying the BBB website, the company seemed legitimate with good customer reviews.

When he arrived, an otherwise attractive young woman greeted him, save for the various piercings on her eyebrow, nose, cheek, and lip. Her nametag read "Betsy." Her short dark hair offered a backdrop for blue-pool eyes he could dive into.

"Good morning. How can I help you?"

"Good morning, Betsy," Roger said, introducing himself and presenting his LRI ID card. "I'm investigating the death of one of your clients, Cletis Monroe. Monroe died in a traffic accident several days ago."

"Oh my God! I'm so sorry. How can I help you?"

"Thank you. Yes, passing with a whole life ahead is very sad.

"I know you have a lot of state laws about deceased customers' belongings being turned over to their estates. I don't want to infringe on any of those, but if possible, I'd like to know what he has stored here. Would that be possible?"

"As long as you don't remove anything. I have to go with you,"

⋈ ⋈ ⋈

Joe D'Elia saw Morgan refreshing his coffee in LRI's canteen.

"Hunter, I've got a fentanyl case theory I want to run by you. Do you have time now?"

"I'll make time, Joe. What's up?"

⋈ ⋈ ⋈

Lonnie Jerry stuck his head in the boss' office. "Maddison, D'Elia was right. *None* of the victims have children."

⋈ ⋈ ⋈

A Climate-Smart electric door rose slowly, revealing the nose of the Bentley. Roger stepped to the driver's side, front windshield. Without ever touching the vehicle, he bent and studied the VIN plate. After taking a close-up picture of it, he walked back to Betsy.

He reached into his pocket, retrieved a money clip, removed a fifty-dollar bill, and handed it to her. "That's all I needed. Thank you."

"*Oh my God*! *NO, THANK YOU*!"

⋈ ⋈ ⋈

"Hunter, all the fentanyl victims are children of participants in failed trials of an early diagnostic test for pancreatic cancer.

"None of them have *any* children. *None*."

"All that's true, Joe. Where are you going with this?"

"A pancreatic cancer *vigilante*."

"*What*?"

⋈ ⋈ ⋈

"Ophelia, are you suggesting that Fitzroy is behind the fentanyl murders? That he's some sort of criminal mastermind?"

"No. I'm asking what Grenada offers he can't find in more luxurious surroundings elsewhere."

⋈||⋈ ⋈||⋈ ⋈||⋈

Knowing Cletis Monroe's "second" job, Roger Graves checked stolen vehicle reports in MD, PA, and VA without finding the Bentley's VIN. Expanding to other Eastern Seaboard states—NY, NJ, DE, NC, SC, and FL produced no results. Nor did he find it in the National Crime Information Center's database for other states.

Let's see who had a quarter million to buy it, if it isn't stolen.

⋈||⋈ ⋈||⋈ ⋈||⋈

"Let's test your theory, Joe. Do we know if any of the victims have been diagnosed with pancreatic cancer?"

"No, but . . ."

"And what are the chances that *all* of them have the disease?"

"I'll admit . . ."

"God only knows how many serial killers there've been over the years; call them vigilantes if you like. Their victims range from streetwalkers to venture capitalists. But I don't recall a single case of any bent on killing people who were already sentenced to virtually certain death."

"If you'll just step down from . . ." Morgan's cell phone interrupted D'Elia.

"Yes, Jeannie, what's up?"

"Roger Graves is on the phone. He's trying to finish up the Bugatti case. Do we have access to the National Motor Vehicle Title Information System?" "No, but I know someone who does. Have him text me the VIN."

"Copy that."

⋈||⋈ ⋈||⋈ ⋈||⋈

"Julie, Hunter Morgan here."

"Hey."

"Can you get your ACES friend to run a number in the NMVTIS for me?"

"You bet. What is it?"

TWENTY-THREE

Maddison Mitchell's rumpled clothes, tired, heavy eyes, and sluggish movement suggested she'd had little time away from the office and sleep. Clearly, the woman's stress level approached a breaking point.

"Okay," she said slowly. "Let's start slicing and dicing what we know to be true.

"All twelve victims are a child or children of pancreatic cancer fatalities. Each parent participated in an Airmed Pharmaceuticals study to find an early test for the disease. The now-defunct company went into Chapter Seven several years ago.

"None of the fentanyl package victims have any children. What does that tell us?" The lead ATF agent raised his hand.

"Do you need the restroom? If not, you don't need to raise your hand." Mitchell's normal, aggravated tone seemed muted.

"Do we know if any of the package recipients *have* pancreatic cancer?" Mitchell looked at Lonnie Jerry.

Looking uncomfortable, he said. "We don't know if autopsies were performed. I doubt that a forensic pathologist would look much further for a cause of death beyond massive fentanyl ingestion.

"But, how would anyone know the medical condition of people not involved in the trial?"

"Agent Jerry, get on the phone to the latest victim's law enforcement jurisdiction. Find out if an autopsy was performed. If so, did it include an examination of the pancreas? If not, have the autopsy repeated.

"If there are any other victims not as yet interred, check their autopsy status."

Mitchell pointed to three FBI agents sitting next to Jerry. "Huey, Dewey and Louie, get off your asses and work the phones. I want an answer to these questions by *seventeen hundred today*."

SAIC Maddison Mitchell's last command implied a sizable adrenaline injection.

⋈||⋈ ⋈||⋈ ⋈||⋈

"Hunter, if there's no early test for one of the most deadly forms of cancer, and there *is* a genetic link to the disease, preventing the passage of that link could be seen as *prevention*."

"Yeah, if someone's mind is more twisted than a DNA helix. I think you're *waaaaaaay* out on a very slim limb, Joe."

"Maybe. I'm just thinking outside the box."

Morgan didn't respond for several moments. "I appreciate that, Joe. Give Doc Santini a call and see what he says about the genetics link."

⋈||⋈ ⋈||⋈ ⋈||⋈

"Julie, it's Addison. I ran your VIN. According to NMVTIS, the Bentley wasn't purchased by an individual. Miach Laboratories LLC bought it in twenty-twenty-two.

Delaware issued the title. Hope that helps."

"Thank you! I'll pass it along."

⋈||⋈ ⋈||⋈ ⋈||⋈

"Doctor Santini, I'm Joe D'Elia. Hunter Morgan suggested I call you. I'm an investigator with LRI.

"Can you answer a couple of questions about pancreatic cancer?"

Santini chuckled. "Wow, there's suddenly a lot of interest in *that* subject."

"Really? Who else, Doc?" "A reporter from *The Mirror*.

"What's your question, Joe?"

"Is there a genetic link to the disease?"

"Genetics can play a role in pancreatic cancer's development. But it's not the sole factor. Hereditary genetic mutations, such as in the BRCA2 gene, have been linked to an elevated risk. Most cases are thought to be from a combination of genetic, environmental, and lifestyle factors."

"Does it affect more men or women?"

"The American Cancer Society says approximately fifty-six percent of cases are men. Women account for about forty-four percent. These percentages can vary slightly depending on the population studied and other factors."

"Anything else?"

"A couple more, Doc. You've heard of the fentanyl murder cases?"

"Sure, who hasn't?"

"Would there be any reason for a pathologist conducting an autopsy on a victim exposed to a massive fentanyl dose to examine the pancreas?"

"Well, that's not my field, but I wouldn't think so, unless some other factor pointed to a connection."

"Thank you, Doc. I *really* appreciate your time."

"You got it, bud."

⋈‖⋈ ⋈‖⋈ ⋈‖⋈

None of the fentanyl death autopsy reports mentioned examination of the victim's pancreas.

In light of eleven cases before Marion Kohen's—an Orthodox Jew—and her family's desire to bury her commensurate with her faith, the MC ME waived the need for an autopsy.

Her family quickly and vehemently denied the FBI's request for an exhumation order. Rather than spend time and resources in a legal battle, Lonnie Jerry moved on to other families.

"I think we'll have to drag somebody into court, boss."

"What's the situation?"

"Seven of twelve say no dice. Each family's first question is, 'Why can't someone else do it?'"

"When they hear others have refused our request, they take the same route."

"Tell 'em you can't reveal other peoples' decisions."

"Which is just a longer way to say, 'they said no too.'"

Mitchell nodded. "Yeah. Did any have organs donated, especially the pancreas?"

"No, boss. A drug overdose death would likely contaminate and eliminate any transplant opportunities."

"Okay. Pick a family without solid religious affiliations and find a *friendly* federal judge."

⋈‖⋈ ⋈‖⋈ ⋈‖⋈

Naomi Monroe waited in a car outside the Washington County ME's office. Inside, sons Marcus and Aaron formally identified their younger brother's body.

⋈‖⋈ ⋈‖⋈ ⋈‖⋈

The BI Julie Stephens ran earlier on Cletis Monroe showed nothing more than Addison's mention of an outstanding traffic ticket and missed court appearance.

She decided to Google Miach Laboratories. One of the responses mentioned "Miach" being the brother of "Airmed" in Irish mythology. *That* rang a bell.

⋈‖⋈ ⋈‖⋈ ⋈‖⋈

"Hunter, I've got some info for you on the Bentley."

"Shoot."

"It was purchased by Miach Laboratories, LLC in Delaware in twenty-twenty-two." "That doesn't sound familiar, Julie." "It will.

"Miach was the brother of Airmed in Irish folklore."

"So, a subsidiary."

"Yup."

TWENTY-FOUR

Federal District Judge Matthew M. McLaughlin met Maddison Mitchell's "friendly" requirement. He had a reputation for having all the best qualities expected of a jurist, including . . . exhaustive thoroughness.

"*Amiable* Matt" treated everyone in his court with the same dignity and respect he expected in return. However, his soft-spoken questions could be an iron fist covered in calf's skin.

So, as the United States Court for the District of Maryland came to order at Baltimore's 101 West Lombard Street, in the case of the United States v. Janet Judge, Amiable Matt had more than a few questions.

"All rise."

Judge McLaughlin entered from his chambers and took the bench.

"Please be seated. The court will come to order.

"Introductions. Plaintiff?"

"John Kenyeri for the Department of Justice, Your Honor."

"Thank you, Mr. Kenyeri. The defense?"

"Your Honor, Mary Murphy representing Mrs. Judge."

"Very well. Let's proceed. Mr. Kenyeri, the FBI is seeking an order to exhume Mrs.

Judge's husband's body. Is that correct?"

"Yes, Your Honor."

"For what purpose, sir?"

"I'm sure Your Honor is familiar with the fentanyl murders."

"I am."

"Pursuant to our investigation to determine the person or persons committing these crimes, we need to determine if Mr. Judge had pancreatic cancer." "How will that knowledge benefit your investigation?"

"Your Honor, all the victims are the children of people who died of that disease. This information would help to better understand the perpetrator's motive."

"How many other victims had pancreatic cancer?"

"None that we know of, Your Honor. None of their autopsies examined the pancreas."

"This is the first exhumation you propose to do?"
"Yes, Your Honor."
"How many cases have there been to date, Mr. Kenyeri?"
"Twelve, Your Honor."
"So, let's say I grant your request, you exhume Mrs. Judge's husband, and he shows signs of cancer. That would be eight-and-a-third percent of the total. Hardly an indication of a trend. Would you then want to exhume more bodies?" Kenyeri hesitated.
"Had you not thought of that next step, Counselor?"
"Frankly, Your Honor, our assumption is if one victim had the disease, they all did." "Evel Knievel would envy *that* leap, Mr. Kenyeri. Let me ask something else.
"The first victim of these murders was a newscaster at WLAB. Correct?" "Yes."
"Yet you chose Mrs. Judge's husband to exhume when the first victim's family is geographically much closer. Why is that?"
"Mrs. Judge was a random selection, Your Honor."
"Forgive me, Mr. Kenyeri, but I find that difficult to believe.
"You could have chosen Mrs. Lucille Peterson's husband, but you didn't."
"Your Honor, our investigation is centered in Maryland."
"A federal court in Virginia could have acted in Maryland. I imagine neither the WLAB employee nor the husband of the Speaker of The U.S. House of Representatives were part of your *random* pool of candidates.
"Ms. Pedley, I am ruling in favor of your client. Further, the Department of Justice shall be responsible for all court costs and Mrs. Judge's legal fees, which are to be paid immediately."
Smiling at both parties, Amiable Matt banged his gavel. "We're adjourned."

⋈⋈ ⋈⋈ ⋈⋈

In Morgan's office, Roger Graves looked at his boss, then D'Elia. "So, an expensive vehicle is sitting in the storage space rented by a dead car thief. And it's not on a hot list anywhere. Why would *that* be?"
D'Elia looked at Morgan. "Maybe because reporting it stolen could be more expensive than losing it."
"Meaning what, Joe?" Morgan said.
"Everything points back to Airmed. Their subsidiary bought the Bentley. Their test participants' children are being murdered. Even a blind pig could find that truffle."
"Do you think the feds are pursuing that angle?" Roger asked.
"Maybe, but they don't know about the Bentley connection. They'd be at the former CEO's gate if they had that piece."
"Can we get Bill Wilson to look at the car on the Q-T?"
"Without a warrant, Joe?"

"In general, the Fourth Amendment's protection against unreasonable searches and seizures doesn't apply to dead people. If there's no connection in the Bentley to the murders, the fact that an Airmed subsidiary bought it will just muddy the fed's investigative waters."

Morgan nodded. "I'll run it by Bill and see what he thinks." "Boss, if Wilson decides to check it out, it might be helpful if I go with him."

Dusty Rhode's *Mirror* article outlined Judge McLaughlin's quashing of the DOJ's efforts and pointed out Fitzroy Adam De Burgh's foreign properties, highlighting Grenada's lack of an extradition treaty with the U.S.

Within hours of the story hitting the street and internet, *The Mirror*'s editor received a call from a prominent and influential Washington, D.C. law firm—Gibson, Bender & Shapiro—threatening a slander suit on behalf of De Burgh.

Jefferson Bender, a personal friend of the Attorney General, placed a call asking if the DOJ considered his client a person of interest in the fentanyl murders.

"*Fucking flat-footed AGAIN!*" Maddison Mitchell's rage made her face nearly glow. "*Grenada*, for *Christ's sake*?

"Lonnie, get a search warrant for everything Fitzroy Adam De Burgh owns in the U.S., and *all* Airmed Pharmaceutical's records. *Do not* go to Judge McLaughlin!"

TWENTY-FIVE

When Graves and Wilson walked into Climate-Smart Self-Storage, Betsy smiled broadly. "Mr. Graves, you're back."

"Hello, Betsy." Smiling, Graves pointed toward his companion. "This is BPD Detective Bill Wilson. Can we look at Mr. Monroe's storage space again, please?"

"Certainly. Right this way."

▷||◁ ▷||◁ ▷||◁

Wilson's eyes widened at the sight inside when the door rolled up. "I need to take a look inside of it, Betsy. Okay?"

"You're the police. I don't think I can say *no*," she giggled. Wilson smiled and stepped to the driver's side door, slipping on a pair of Nitrile gloves. Inside, the keys lay on the front seat. Seeing nothing else on the front seats or floors of the Bentley Continental GT, he leaned the driver's seat forward. Nothing in the back, either.

Pressing a button on the driver's door marked "Trunk" released the rear deck's latch. Wilson walked to the car's rear and slowly lifted the deck lid with two fingers. A light illuminated the interior. At the back of the trunk, closest to Wilson, lay a small handle, colored to match the trunk's interior.

A slight popping noise accompanied the lifting of the handle. Wilson then used it to raise the cover over the spare tire and a small hidden compartment for personal items.

Graves joined Wilson.

Though lighted, the spare tire and compartment were in shadows. Roger produced a small LED flashlight and clicked it on.

▷||◁ ▷||◁ ▷||◁

Lonnie Jerry didn't want to ask about probable cause for a search warrant, but as a professional, knew he had to.

"Maddison, do you think we have enough PC to get a warrant?"

"It's the only direction we have to go in, Jerry. Who else would know the family structure of the victims? These can't be random attacks. Not *twelve* times."

⋈||⋈ ⋈||⋈ ⋈||⋈

"That's one of the fentanyl envelopes, Hunter!" The excitement in Wilson's voice was infectious.

"It is. Did you touch it, Bill?"

"I did not. Graves is my witness. We photographed it, closed the trunk, and hightailed it back here." "Good.

"Joe, what's our next step?"

⋈||⋈ ⋈||⋈ ⋈||⋈

Dusty Rhodes sat in Rick Miller's large office, sandwiched between the assistant editor and *The Mirror*'s legal counsel.

The paper's editor, a handsome man in his early fifties, boyish face seemed as stern as the reporter could remember seeing it.

"Rick, they've got nothing to sue over. We haven't accused De Burgh of anything. We reported the facts. He owns a home in Grenada, which has no extradition treaty. Where's the slander?"

"Dusty, Fitzroy is the sole heir to an estate valued at 84 billion dollars. He could *buy* this paper if he wanted to. Or cost us millions in legal fees. That would be *pocket* lint to him."

"Since when does *The Mirror* cower before bullies? Rick, you've backed me when I actually *had* scandalous information on very wealthy people.

"Consider this: *maybe* we're getting close to something De Burgh is *guilty* of."

⋈||⋈ ⋈||⋈ ⋈||⋈

D'Elia, Wilson, and Graves sat at Morgan's conference table.

D'Elia said, "Hunter, we need to give this information to the task force *post haste*. If we don't, the Bureau could gen up charges for aiding, abetting, or obstruction of justice. They might not stick, but do you want to take that chance?"

"Let's give him a call."

Joe produced his cell phone, dialed Jerry's number, and put the call on speaker.

"Special Agent Jerry."

"Lonnie, it's D'Elia. You have a minute?"

"*Barely*. What do you want?"

"To help your fentanyl investigation. I'm here with Hunter Morgan, one of his investigators, Roger Graves, and BPD Detective Bill Wilson."

D'Elia quickly explained LRI's involvement in the Bugatti hijacking. Cletis Monroe's connection to the heist and the discovery of the Bentley. Finally, the discovery of what appeared to be a fentanyl envelope in its trunk.

"Lonnie, the Bentley was purchased in twenty-two by a subsidiary of Airmed Pharmaceuticals in Delaware. There's no record of it being sold or *stolen*."

⋈||⋈ ⋈||⋈ ⋈||⋈

Five FBI Laboratory technicians arrived at the storage facility within ninety minutes via helicopter from Quantico. After securing the scene, they searched the Bentley for blood, hair, fibers, fingerprints, DNA samples, weapons, or other trace evidence. The trunk received the most attention. After photographing and videoing the suspected fentanyl envelope, they removed, documented, and bagged it.

The images were uploaded to Quantico's Lab and distributed to the task force in Baltimore.

⋈||⋈ ⋈||⋈ ⋈||⋈

The Mirror's monitoring of BPD radio traffic picked up chatter about the FBI having sealed off the area around the Climate-Smart Self-Storage on Moravia Park Drive. An unidentified voice asked, "Is this fentanyl thirteen?"

WLAB picked up the transmission also, immediately dispatching a reporter and mobile unit to the scene.

⋈||⋈ ⋈||⋈ ⋈||⋈

Althea Ramos sat in Elizabeth Pedley's Washington, D. C. office. Mrs. Pedley and her husband practiced together, specializing in local, state, and federal whistle-blower defenses.

"Mrs. Ramos, the government's charges against you are serious. But, T.J. and I have discussed your case at length and think we can get them withdrawn or at least greatly reduced." Elizabeth's soft East Texas drawl had a soothing quality—a dose of verbal Valium. "Will I lose my job and pension?"

Elizabeth smiled. "Let's fight one battle at a time, ma'am. I assure you, we'll do everything we can for you."

⋈||⋈ ⋈||⋈ ⋈||⋈

Morgan's cell phone played *Sweet Home Alabama*, indicating a call from someone in his contacts. A glance at the display read "Rhodes, D."

"Hello, Dusty."

"Morgan, I have a straightforward question. I promise not to mention the source. Okay?"

"You can ask. I may not answer. Go ahead."

"How many fentanyl murders have there been?"

"Why do you ask?"

"The FBI's got a storage company on Moravia Park Drive wrapped up in yellow crime scene tape like it's Christmas morning. Some loose-lipped cop asked if it was 'fentanyl thirteen' on the radio. Have there been *twelve* murders?"

⋈||⋈ ⋈||⋈ ⋈||⋈

Maddison Mitchell's broad smile at the Bentley news and its potential evidence disappeared when Luke Courtemanche entered her office.

"Maddison, are you looking at Fitzroy Adam De Burgh as a suspect?"

"We are, sir."

The SAIC updated her boss on the apparent breakthrough.

"I want to search his estate."

The Director rubbed his chin thoughtfully. "Okay, but make sure his attorney, Jefferson

Bender, is there when you do."

"Where's *that* coming from, sir?"

"The AG, Maddison. Make sure you *pussyfoot* through Delaware's peach blossoms."

Infidelitas, Bravitia, Integritas
By Dusty Rhodes

FBI Inspector W.H. Dane Lester created the Bureau's motto—"Fidelity, Bravery, Integrity"—in 1935. The words describe the high moral standards and motivation the FBI expects from its staff. But what if the command chain *executives* don't possess those traits?

The Mirror has learned there have been *twelve* fentanyl murders in the Atlantic Coast states. Readers may recall our tip line received a call last week about the then eight deaths the FBI concealed from the public. Did a lack of earlier warning contribute to four additional *needless* deaths? Should the Bureau's motto become:

"*Infidelity*, Bravery, Integrity?"

The front-page story went on for over three thousand words, describing additional FBI failings in brutal detail.

WLAB aired a lengthy report from Moravia Park Drive where an unnamed BPD detective confirmed the fentanyl count had risen to twelve.

Elizabeth Pedley's paralegal called *The Mirror* asking for Dusty Rhodes. Ophelia answered the transferred call.

"Ophelia, I'm Maxine Gomez. My boss is representing Althea Ramos. We're requesting a copy of the message left on your tip line regarding the FBI's investigation of the fentanyl murders."

"I'll have to run that by Dusty and maybe the legal department. Where can I reach you?"

Gulfstream's largest aircraft, the G700, has a range of 7,500 nautical miles and can carry nineteen passengers. Under normal conditions, it requires approximately 6,250 feet of runway.

Delaware's Wilmington/New Castle Airport, aka ILG, is about seven miles from Centreville. Both its runways can accommodate the G700.

Fitzroy Adam De Burgh, his butler, valet, chef, *saucier*, *sommelier*, physician, and nurse, passed through ILG's TSA screening without incident. The Gulfstream engines were warm and ready to taxi as the group boarded.

The lightly loaded G700, tail number NAK45, lifted off runway 19 nine minutes later.

⋈ ⋈ ⋈

In Dusty's office, Ophelia relayed the request for a copy of the fentanyl call.

"Do you want me to run it by legal?"

"No, it could take weeks before they got around to answering. It's always easier to get forgiveness than blood from a stone.

"But, only give them the voice recording, *not* the originating phone number. Legal is fighting the feds, saying the number identifies our source."

⋈ ⋈ ⋈

Mitchell thought her day had gotten as bad as possible hearing the AG's requirement for her search warrant . . . until Lonnie Jerry told her about *The Mirror*'s attack.

The only flicker of good news came from the new PIS Inspector. The USPS scanners had been modified. A fentanyl package identified and isolated spared a thirteenth victim . . . for the moment anyway.

Now, another question hung like an anvil around Maddison's neck. To share this little victory with the press or not. If she did and another package got past the screening, she would spend the rest of her career running BIs on illegal aliens at the southern border.

But . . . If she got someone else in the boat, she'd have company if it sank.

A call to Director Courtemanche got a simple response. "No guts, no glory, Maddison." Up next—Dusty Rhodes.

⋈ ⋈ ⋈

"Ms. Gomez. I have a copy of the recording for you. I'll courier it to you today. What's the address?"

TWENTY-SIX

The Quantico lab processed the Bentley evidence by late morning the following day. No biometric data existed in the passenger compartment except for a thumb and index fingerprint on the back of the rearview mirror—the most frequent spot car thieves forget to clean.

A recent FBI fingerprint database addition from Washington County, MD, identified the prints as belonging to one deceased Cletis Monroe.

The trunk's examination found strands of a man's hair. DNA from a follicle did not match anything in the Combined DNA Index System.

A drug test on the hair showed 5-fluorouracil and irinotecan—common chemotherapy drugs—and fentanyl. DNA from a tiny spot of blood just to the left of the spare tire cover handle did not match Cletis'. Blood tests did show elevated levels of CA 19-9, suggesting a form of cancer, possibly pancreatic.

An examination of the envelope found in the Bentley's trunk matched those from the various crime scenes exactly. The FBI Digital Forensics Laboratory technicians traced its origin back to a likely Chinese vendor on the dark web.

⋈||⋈ ⋈||⋈ ⋈||⋈

Maddison Mitchell gave the Bureau's Public Information Office specific instructions. The PIO would announce the USPS' ability to now scan for, detect, and isolate fentanyl packages. But, *not* until being notified the preparations were in place. Next, she called *The Mirror,* asking for Dusty Rhodes.

"Ms. Rhodes, this is FBI SAIC, Maddison Mitchell. Can you spare me a few minutes?"

"I can."

Maddison shared the information she had just given the PIO. Then said, "I'm calling you to provide you with an exclusive on this story. I won't permit the PIO to release their statement until you publish it."

"And what are you expecting in return, Special Agent Mitchell?"

"A little goodwill toward our investigation."

"We're not in the amenability business, ma'am. We do, however, strongly subscribe to accuracy. I can promise you this. I will let you *comment* on what we're about to report before it goes to press. Fair enough?"

"Yes."

⋈ ⋈ ⋈

If someone fainted in Cletis Monroe's apartment, there'd be no room to fall. The FBI forensics team members there inspected every square centimeter—dusting, printing, vacuuming, and photographing—in search of more ties to the twelve murder cases. His clothes, shoes, personal hygiene items, cocaine, weed, and trash were bagged and sent to Quantico.

After almost eight hours, sealed with crime scene tape and a sign on the door reading "Crime Scene—Do Not Enter," the federal lab rats departed.

⋈ ⋈ ⋈

Elizabeth Pedley and her client sat in Assistant U.S. Attorney Calvin Sweeney's office. Hopefully, the pretrial conference could find some elasticity in the government's charges against Ms. Ramos.

"Ms. Pedley, the way to make this go as quickly as possible for your client is to have her admit to the charges, plead guilty, and beg for the court's mercy.'

"I thought . . . "

Elizabeth put her hand on her client's. "I'll speak for you, Althea." Then, looking at Sweeney, "Counselor, I'm sure that would be very convenient for your case, but we'll do that right after DOJ opens a *brothel* on Pennsylvania Avenue."

"We have your client's phone and her voice on *The Mirror*'s tip line to go with it."

"But, *do* you, Mr. Sweeney? You have *a* phone that you can't prove is my client's. Do you have an audio copy of the call to *The Mirror*? Or just the printed version?"

"We will."

"Really? I understand that the paper is fighting you on that. It seems they deem the caller's number and message are from a source and are refusing to cooperate."

⋈ ⋈ ⋈

The USPS scanners detected and isolated a second fentanyl package.

⋈ ⋈ ⋈

Julie Stephens met Wilson for lunch again at Mason's Famous Lobster Rolls in Baltimore. Afterward, in Mark Proffitt's LRI office, she gave him the latest images and fentanyl samples from the most recent MD victim.

"Can you compare this sample to the first one I brought up, Mark?" "We will certainly do that."

⋈||⋈ ⋈||⋈ ⋈||⋈

The FBI's forensic team waited outside the gates of Fitzroy Adam De Burgh's massive estate for nearly an hour for the arrival of Attorney Jefferson Bender and several staff members to monitor their search.

An inexpensive Alamo rental instead of limousines surprised Maddison Mitchell. When an associate of Gibson, Bender, and Shapiro emerged alone, surprise morphed into consternation.

"Who are you?"

The young woman didn't answer. Holding out a blue folder, she said, "This is for you." Maddison opened the document. As she read, consternation became molten anger.

Now, therefore, it is ordered by the United States District Court for the District of Delaware, upon consideration of the arguments presented by Fitzroy Adam De Burgh and for good cause shown, that the execution of the search warrant issued on the 29th Day of June 2022 for 1 Hatteras Circle, Centreville, Delaware, 19807, shall be stayed pending further order of the Court.

"You have to be *kidding* me!"

The associate smiled thinly. "Yes. Those federal judges can be *real* comedians."

⋈||⋈ ⋈||⋈ ⋈||⋈

"Ms. Rhodes' office, Olivia speaking."

"This is SAIC Mitchell. Please tell Ms. Rhodes she can publish the statement I gave her earlier."

⋈||⋈ ⋈||⋈ ⋈||⋈

The tip line audio tape arrived within hours. Maxine Gomez immediately drove it to Echo Recovery, LLC, a firm specializing in damaged audio file reclamation.

⋈||⋈ ⋈||⋈ ⋈||⋈

Maddison Mitchell tried desperately to keep her temper in check, facing Director Courtemanche. "Sir . . . it is . . . intensely *challenging* to make progress . . . on this investigation when . . . I'm handcuffed by the . . . DOJ."

"The *Constitution* handcuffed you, Maddison.

"You have flimsy circumstantial evidence against Mr. De Burgh. Quantico found *forensic* evidence linking other suspects. One dead and the other unidentified. The court's action wasn't extreme or political."

"Yes, Director. But, the court couldn't have taken the action for anyone without a fifteen-hundred dollars an hour lawyer and the AG's home number on speed dial."

"If this is too much for you, Maddison, people are waiting in the wings to take over."

Mitchell raised her hand in a "stop" motion. "I'm fine, Director. Thank you for your time."

⋈ ⋈ ⋈

Julie Stephens powered down her computer and monitor, preparing to leave the office.

As she pushed herself back from the desk, her cell phone rang. Her first thought was to ignore it, but didn't.

"Stephens."

"Julie, Mark Proffitt. Where are you?"

"Just about to leave the office. Why?"

"We need a sample of your DNA."

"You're welcome to it, Mark. But why?"

"The fentanyl sample you dropped off has an eyelash in it. We need to eliminate it being yours."

"*WOW! Okay.* When do you want it?"

"The sooner the better. Tomorrow morning, first thing?"

"I'll be there."

TWENTY-SEVEN

When she arrived, Elizabeth Pedley saw a flashing red light on her office desk phone. After unloading an armload of files, she pushed the speaker button and retrieved her messages.

The third message left the previous evening: "Ms. Pedley, this is Peter Lucas, Echo Recovery, LLC. We've finished the analysis of the tape your office sent and Ms. Ramos' sample audio. I've emailed the full report to you just now. We believe your client is a seventy-eight-point-six-two percent match to the voice on *The Mirror*'s tape.

"Please feel free to call if you have any questions or need additional information."

Elizabeth turned on her computer. As it began booting, Maxine Gomez entered, waving several printed pages.

Handing it over, she said, "This is the Recovery Echo report."

The index listed the Introduction, Methods, Analysis, Interpretation, Conclusion, and Appendix.

Most of the document would have been as understandable in Swahili as in English. Mr. Liu's expert testimony would undoubtedly be necessary if the case ever went to trial. She did a quick mental calculation.

Twenty-one-point-three-eight percent of reasonable doubt. Excellent news!

⋈⋈ ⋈⋈ ⋈⋈

Maddison Mitchell saw *The Mirror*'s story on the USPS' ability to identify and isolate the fentanyl packages. An hour later, she gave the Bureau's PIO permission to release their version.

⋈⋈ ⋈⋈ ⋈⋈

Julie Stephens arrived at LRI shortly after Mark Proffitt.

"Morning, Mark."

"Hey, Julie. Thanks for coming."

"No problem. So, you think you have something?"

"Yes, if it's not from you. Your samples are marked 'A,' 'B,' and 'C.'"

"I took 'C,' just below her waist." "Good. That's where we found the eyelash. Hopefully, it's not the victim's."

Mark washed and gloved his hands, then took two buccal swabs and rubbed the inside of Julie's cheeks with one swab on each side.

"We'll let those dry for a few minutes, Julie. How about some coffee?"

"*Yes*, I'm at least a quart low."

Judge Matthew M. McLaughlin banged his gavel, bringing the court to order.

"Good morning. Let's have introductions. Plaintiff?" "Sol Goldburg for *The Mirror*, Your Honor."

"Thank you, Mr. Goldburg.

"Defense?"

"Vincent Scarpelli, for the DOJ, Your Honor."

"Very well. So, I've read *The Mirror*'s complaint that the FBI searched the paper's phone records for a number that called their tip line without a warrant. Is that correct, Mr.

Goldburg?"

"It is, Your Honor."

"And you further claim the paper was not notified of this search before or after the search was conducted. Correct?"

"Yes, Your Honor." "Mr. Scarpelli?"

The DOJ National Security Division lawyer rose, looking far less than comfortable.

"Your Honor, the Justice Department was not required to make notification."

Judge McLaughlin looked at Scarpelli for several moments, then said, "Sir, I only know of one type of warrant with no notification requirement.

"And that would be . . ."

Scarpelli shifted his weight from one foot to the other. "A FISA warrant, Your Honor."

"That's correct, sir. Now, why would you need a FISA warrant to access the phone number of a tip line caller?"

"Your Honor is undoubtedly aware of the series of murders recently using fentanyl. We are trying to determine if these are foreign-based."

Judge McLaughlin smiled. "Where did the tip line call in question originate?"

"Windsor Mill, Maryland."

"Clearly inside the United States."

"Well, yes, Your Honor, but we didn't *know* that until . . ." ". . . *after* you deceitfully applied to the FISA court.

"I see this as yet another federal end-run around the Fourth Amendment. It is not the first time the DOJ has been caught dealing dishonestly with the FISA court.

"Upon review of the evidence presented, this court finds that the FISA warrant issued in this case was obtained unlawfully and violated the plaintiff's and, by extension, the caller's Fourth Amendment rights. Therefore, any evidence obtained from this unlawful warrant is now deemed inadmissible in court proceedings. The Department of Justice is prohibited from using any such evidence. Furthermore, all evidence obtained through the unlawful warrant must be suppressed and excluded from consideration.

"We're adjourned."

⋈||⋈ ⋈||⋈ ⋈||⋈

Proffitt returned to the lab, and Julie left for Gaithersburg. Before she arrived, Mark knew her DNA did not match the eyelash. That was the *easy* part of the lab work.

⋈||⋈ ⋈||⋈ ⋈||⋈

Elizabeth Pedley called her client. "Ms. Ramos, I have some *excellent* news."

"Yes?"

"A federal judge has ruled the FBI's access to *The Mirror*'s phone records violated their and your Fourth Amendment rights. The government can't use the information against you."

"*Oh, my God*! My prayers have been answered."

"They have, ma'am."

"And they can't come after me again, Ms. Pedley?"

"Well, they could go back to court claiming the phone number is vital to solving the murder cases. Even if they won that ridiculous argument and got a motion ordering *The Mirror* to reveal the number, I don't believe a jury would convict you. We got the voice analysis back on the tip line recording. It's only a seventy-eight-point-six-two percent match to your voice. That means there's over a twenty percent likelihood it is *not* your voice. That's a lot of reasonable doubt."

⋈||⋈ ⋈||⋈ ⋈||⋈

The task force watched Maddison Mitchell step to the whiteboard. She seemed to age just walking there.

"As you may know, our *good* friend Judge McLaughlin ruled against us in *The Mirror*'s motion. Fortunately, that doesn't impede our *snail's-pace* investigation.

"So, what do we have? Lonnie, give us a breakdown." Jerry stood and moved to the center of the room.

"Okay. We know that the fingerprint in the Bentley belongs to a dead man with at least one car theft to his credit—an Econoline Van used in a vehicle hijacking.

"A search of his apartment turned up nothing to suggest involvement in the fentanyl cases. Unless something unexpected comes to light, Mr. Cletis Monroe is a dead end."

Lonnie opened a folded piece of white paper he took from an inside jacket pocket. "Thanks to DNA forensic age estimation, the Quantico lab says the man whose blood was found in the trunk to be sixty-five to seventy-four. The sample also shows markers associated with pancreatic cancer. Hair analysis indicated chemotherapy drugs and fentanyl—likely for pain management.

"Ripley, get a DNA sample from the lab uploaded to GEDmatch, 23andMe, and Ancestry.com to look for relative matches. If so, we'll try to build a family tree.

"Fitzroy De Burgh isn't old enough to be in the primary age range to contact that disease."

Lonnie looked at an FBI agent. "Summers, find out if his father did." The agent nodded in response and made a note.

"If that's the case, then we have a stronger case to search the Delaware property."

"How do you figure that?" the ATF lead asked. "You have a car bought by a subsidiary, apparently stolen and not reported. No biometrics in it point to young De Burgh. Hair showing signs of chemo and pain management. And a blood sample indicating pancreatic cancer. If Fitz's old man had it, that's coincidental, *not* circumstantial.

"Maybe the FBI has a lower bar on PC than the rest of us, but, based on all that, we'd never expect to get a warrant without some sign of explosives in the vehicle."

Jerry smiled. "That's why you're not with the FBI."

Turning to Maddison, he said, "Anything else?"

Mitchell stepped forward. "Summers, I want an answer about the elder De Burgh by EOB today. *¿Comprende?*"

"*Sí.*"

⋈⋈ ⋈⋈ ⋈⋈

Proffitt, D'Elia, and Morgan sat in LRI's conference room.

"Okay, Mark, what do you have? Man's or woman's?"

"Yes."

Morgan and D'Elia both frowned.

Proffitt didn't wait for the follow-up question. "The sample is cross-contaminated. There is DNA from a man *and* a woman. We've separated and distinguished the woman's genetic profile using specialized techniques and software. The male sample is not complete. It's missing key genetic markers."

"Could it be used for ID?" D'Elia asked.

"Maybe for a partial match. But the ID's accuracy would be limited."

"Okay," Morgan said. "What about the woman? Could she be IDed?"

"Yes."

"*Excellent!*" Morgan said. "Great work, Mark."

"It's a team effort, boss."

"You know, Hunter, if the woman *is* the perp, that would fit the use of fentanyl," D'Elia said. "Women don't often kill violently. Poison or some other passive tool is typically a female's choice."

"That's true, Joe. But there aren't many mass murderers in the double-X-chromosome category."

D'Elia nodded in agreement. "What else, Mark?"

She's between thirty-five and fifty. Has a primarily Central European heritage. Her sample has a single nucleotide polymorphism that indicates blue eyes. She is probably not obese."

"Can you tell us anything about the man?" D'Elia asked.

"Not really. The sample could help eliminate a suspect. There isn't enough genetic data to predict his traits or characteristics.

"So, what do we do with this new evidence," Mark asked. Morgan looked at D'Elia. "Your thoughts, Joe?"

"That's a bit of a *sticky wicket*, as my Limey friends would say. The first question they'll ask is, 'How did you get the sample?'

"We don't want to hang Detective Stephens out to dry. So, we need a plausibly vague answer. Maybe 'From a member of law enforcement.'"

Morgan shook his head. "They won't buy that for long, if at all."

"I know. But maybe we can stall 'em with it for a little while. Long enough for Stephens to develop a story. Our in-house lab is certified to work on behalf of the FBI, so Mark's work shouldn't be questioned," Joe added.

"Yeah, I think I have a good reputation with Quantico."

Morgan smiled. "I'm *sure* of it."

"I guess the only thing to do is feed it to Lonnie Jerry."

⋈ ⋈ ⋈

FBI Agent Summers' search through Delaware death certificates showed Osín Darragh De Burgh's death as the result of pancreatic cancer. He updated Jerry and Mitchell.

⋈ ⋈ ⋈

Morgan updated Wilson and Stephens with the DNA results via email.

⋈ ⋈ ⋈

"Lonnie, Joe D'Elia."

"What do you have *now*, Sherlock?"

"*Careful*. A little respect might go a long way toward solving your murder cases."

Jerry didn't speak immediately. Then, in a more conciliatory tone said, "Okay, Joe. What have you got?" "A member of local LE brought a fentanyl crime scene sample to LRI's lab. "We've . . . ."

"Who?"

"Let's just leave it with what I just said now, Lonnie. The chain of custody is intact since our lab is FBI-certified. The sample is a woman's cross-contaminated with a male's.

"Our lab has separated and refined her DNA. The male's sample is incomplete. Possibly valuable for eliminating someone, but not identifying a perp." D'Elia shared Proffitt's team assessment of the female sample.

"My question, Lonnie, is where would you like us to send this information? To you, Quantico, or both?"

⋈ ⋈ ⋈

Morgan called Julie Stephens, alerting her of a need to have her facts straight, if and when the FBI started asking why she had felt the need to keep independent fentanyl samples. He assured her that LRI did not intend to divulge her information, if at all possible.

⋈ ⋈ ⋈

"How did *The Mirror* get this story, Maddison?" Director Courtemanche asked when she answered the phone.

"They got it from me, Director."

"Why on earth would you do that?"

"Sir, we've been slammed lately in virtually every media outlet for a variety of reasons, *including* the fentanyl murders. I'm trying to buy a little *ink* goodwill. I gave her an almost verbatim version of what the PIO just sent out. Nothing more."

TWENTY-EIGHT

Agent Jerry and SAIC Mitchell had to grudgingly admit that the work LRI's lab performed on the eyelash's DNA sample saved Quantico and, by extension, the investigation time. A search of the FBI managed CODIS came up empty. All the states with fentanyl fatalities did, too, except a restricted/confidential file in Delaware's DNA Data Bank.

⋈ ⋈ ⋈

Julie Stephens sat in her lieutenant's office. "Why, in Christ's name, would you do *that*?"

"I don't trust the fuckin' *feds* any more than you do, Lieu! They came here like God's gift to law enforcement and got nowhere. Maybe they'd have found what I did. Who knows? We found it and turned it over to an FBI-approved lab."

"To paraphrase an old Lone Ranger and Tonto joke, 'What you mean *we*, Detective?' You'll get tarred by the same brush as me—*us*. I learned many years ago, 'If you fuck up, make sure your boss hears it from you *first*.'"

⋈ ⋈ ⋈

According to the Rape, Abuse & Incest National Network, the largest anti-sexual violence organization in the country, Delaware ranks twenty-second for sexual assault victims' protection. One form is restricted and confidential protection of identities through DNA matching.

Since there had not been a fentanyl murder in Delaware and to comply with the state's protection laws, the DNA bank administrator refused to furnish any information without a federal court order.

⋈ ⋈ ⋈

"*Goddamn it*, Lonnie! Just submit the usual request to them through CODIS."

"We did, Maddison. They want a court order."

"What are they fucking *worried* about?"

"They're covering their asses. If the victim sues them, they can say they *had* to comply with a lawful order from the court.

"We're asking for that now. Hopefully, we'll have it by this afternoon."

"In whose court?"

"You don't want to know, Maddison."

"*Fuck me!*"

⋈|⋈ ⋈|⋈ ⋈|⋈

Morgan's intercom buzzed, and Jeannie Staron said, "Hunter, I have Judge Matthew McLaughlin's clerk on hold for you."

After pressing a button next to the red flashing light on his desk phone, he answered,

"Hunter Morgan."

"Mr. Morgan, please hold for Judge McLaughlin."

"Sure."

A few seconds later, "Mr. Morgan. I believe you've appeared before me in the past."

"I have, Your Honor. How can we assist?"

"I have an Assistant United States Attorney in my chambers asking for an order to compel the State of Delaware to release the identity of an individual whose DNA is confidential. Mr. Scarpelli tells me that the FBI's Quantico lab has not analyzed the DNA for comparison, but LRI has. He also states that LRI's lab is FBI-certified. Is that correct?"

"Yes, Your Honor, it is. Would you like documentation confirming that faxed or emailed to your clerk?"

"Yes, please."

⋈|⋈ ⋈|⋈ ⋈|⋈

"We got the court order, Maddison. I'm going to have the Delaware DNA sent to

Quantico."

"No, have it sent to LRI's lab."

"*Why?*"

"I don't want to give the defense a *spy vs. spy* argument that two labs were involved if we have to use the comparison in court."

⋈|⋈ ⋈|⋈ ⋈|⋈

Within hours of Judge McLaughlin's order being issued, the FBI made a formal request to LRI for a comparison of the female's DNA from the eyelash to that of the Delaware rape victim. An FBI agent transported the sample from the Delaware Division of Forensic Science to LRI to maintain the chain of custody.

Mark Proffitt personally supervised the samples' comparison according to specific FBI mandated guidelines and protocols. The task force and Quantico lab received the completed detailed findings report.

In Quantico, the Bureau's DNA specialists reviewed the results and concurred with LRI's conclusion—the samples were from the same individual.

⋈⋈ ⋈⋈ ⋈⋈

"Joanna Wójcik, thirty-six, is a registered nurse. At fifteen, she was raped on her way home from high school. We're running a BI on her now."

"Did they catch the perp, Lonnie?"

"No, boss. The case is still open."

"What kind of name is Wójcik?"

"Polish."

The sun's reflection off Caribbean waters made Joanna Wójcik's steel blue eyes seem to sparkle. The afternoon breeze swirled her long, almost coal-black hair.

In Joanna's case, the word "beautiful" envied "*stunning*."

TWENTY-NINE

Besides a few items in her credit report, Joanna Wójcik seemed to disappear after her Delaware driver's license renewal—age thirty-four. Once again, the FBI hit a speed bump. Their request for IRS information required a court order. Once received, there was still no joy in *Crime*ville—Ms. Wójcik hadn't filed taxes for the last four years. Nor did her social security number show employers' W-2s or 1099-MISC forms filed.

Her Truist Bank checking and money market accounts had been closed. No records showed her opening accounts anywhere else in the country. European, Asian, and offshore banks reported no accounts in her name or refused to comply with the U.S.'s Common Reporting Standard and Foreign Account Tax Compliance Act.

Only one bureaucratic crumb suggested Joanna wasn't a ghost.

⋈⋈⋈ ⋈⋈⋈ ⋈⋈⋈

AUSA Scarpelli walked into Morgan's office before Jeannie Staron could announce him. She appeared like the man's shadow in his wake.

"I'm *sorry*, Hunter! *He marched right by me.*"

"She's right, Morgan. I didn't come here to dick around with some *clerk*."

"*Executive assistant, numb nuts*!" Jeannie said, positioning herself between the two men.

"*Assistant U S Attorney* Scarpelli, Mr. Morgan. Get rid of your guard dog."

"Oh, I'd be very *cautious,* AUSA Scarpelli. My 'guard dog' is a Jujitsu black belt who can kick your fat ass back to the elevator vestibule if I snap my fingers.

"It's okay, Jeannie. I'll take it from here."

"Now, Scarpelli, just what the *fuck* do you want?"

"I have a court order here compelling you, as CEO of LRI, to tell me the source of the illegally received DNA sample."

⋈⋈⋈ ⋈⋈⋈ ⋈⋈⋈

As part of her BI, a request to the State Department for passport status—and, if valid, its number—showed Joanna Wójcik's renewal submission just after the driver's license date. The next step requested the Department of Homeland Security's U.S. Customs and Border Protection provide information on entry to or exit from the U.S. They were the only footprints in the snow of Ms. Wójcik's recent existence. Her passport had been scanned recently before boarding a flight to Grenada. Several others, including Fitzroy Adam De Burgh, were on the same aircraft.

⋈‖⋈ ⋈‖⋈ ⋈‖⋈

After scanning the order, Hunter called in the head of LRI's legal department, who confirmed its legitimacy. AUSA Scarpelli departed with Julie Stephens' name and organization.

Morgan called her immediately with a heads-up.

⋈‖⋈ ⋈‖⋈ ⋈‖⋈

While still circumstantial, the eyelash DNA and De Burgh on the same flight with Wójcik cleared the courts' PC bar. Maddison Mitchell got her warrant for the Delaware estate. Coordination with attorney Jefferson Bender and crew remained, but was quickly arranged for the following day.

⋈‖⋈ ⋈‖⋈ ⋈‖⋈

The expected small, private funeral mass for Cletis Dion Monroe at the Baltimore Basilica was not. His Excellency Archbishop William E. Lewis personally conducted the service. Naomi Monroe, Lewis' personal assistant, did not limit the gathering to family only. The resulting crowd nearly spilled out into Cathedral Street. Its sight warmed a grieving mother as much as possible on a very dark day.

Dick Schutz attended in addition to hundreds of friends, relatives, and coworkers. He didn't know how Cletis became involved in the Bugatti heist, nor did he care at this point. The memory of a bright, articulate, and funny employee overrode any past transgressions.

⋈‖⋈ ⋈‖⋈ ⋈‖⋈

Ophelia, eating lunch at her desk, as usual, searched through Facebook members associated with Airmed Pharmaceuticals. One image of Fitzroy De Burgh showed a sizable private jet behind several company employees. The fuzzy tail image read: NAK45.

Years ago, her private pilot husband told Ophelia what the number represented. She called him to ask if any public listings of registrations existed. He pointed her to a Federal Aeronautics Administration website—registry.faa.gov/aircraftinquiry.

The FAA site search returned the following for NAK45: **Owner: Miach Laboratories, LLC, Delaware, U.S.A.**

Next, a quick Google search on how to track aircraft flights listed FlightAware.com. That site's search showed the Gulfstream G700 recently departed Wilmington/New Castle Airport bound for Grenada.

🧬 🧬 🧬

When the gates to De Burgh's estate swung open for the search team and five legal observers, the FBI had more information, including the passenger manifest, crew names, flight plan, and arrival time.

Only five rooms could be searched concurrently, since each required a legal team member's observation, which slowed progress in the enormous house and surrounding outbuildings. Agents collected large numbers of specimens everywhere, often dealing with legal objections. In nearly every case, Maddison Mitchell overrode the issue, each duly noted on iPads and laptops for objections later.

The number of family photos surprised the search team. A parent's wedding day photo sat on an end table by their son's bed. In the office, another of the parents—with the woman holding an infant—sat on a corner of the desk. The opposite corner had a photo of Joanna Wójcik, identified when compared to the photo submitted with her passport renewal.

Large oil paintings of the elder De Burgh at various stages of his life were in the salon, dining room, library, and office.

After nearly fifteen hours, the search team departed with over 3,200 pieces of evidence: documents, answering machine tapes, computers, smartphones, tablets, fingerprints, hair, toothbrushes, security cameras' surveillance footage, and interviews with staff.

Standing outside the front door, Jefferson Bender called after Maddison Mitchell's departing form. "I'll be filing a formal complaint outlining the Bureau's *overreach* today with the court and *your* AG in the morning."

🧬 🧬 🧬

"The search has concluded, Mr. De Burgh."

"Thank you, Edward."

"Would you ask Ms. Wójcik to join me? And bring us gin and tonics, please." "Yes, sir. The usual, of course."

🧬 🧬 🧬

"De Burgh wasn't at the estate during the search, Lonnie."

"I know, boss. There are no FAA-registered private aircraft listing Airmed as the owner."

"We know he doesn't fly commercial, so figure it out pronto. We may need to throw the chains on Fitz."

🧬 🧬 🧬

Quantico's lab processing of the Bentley showed no valuable biometric evidence beyond that collected in Baltimore. A casual conversation between two technicians led to overlooked data.

"I don't understand how the guy stole this beast. I thought Bentley had a very sophisticated theft alarm system."

"They do. But their app *isn't*, and there are at least two YouTube video hacks on deactivating the Continental GT's. "Did you uncover the original owner?"

"Yes. An NMVTIS report shows it was sold to Miach Laboratories, LLC."

"Hey, did anyone check the GPS for travel data?"

"Let me check the log." After scanning several pages on a clipboard, he said, "No, but

I will."

⋈⋈ ⋈⋈ ⋈⋈

Bill Wilson's sister Dana Van Wyk's good fortune—the result of a relative's *mis*fortune—made a dream come true: buying a bigger house. With their second child on the way, at least one more bedroom—preferably two—would become necessary. A sizable inheritance from an uncle's estate put the detective and the Van Wyks into higher tax brackets.

Dana's realtor showed the Van Wyks nearly a dozen homes before they hit pay dirt in Hockessin, Delaware. A four-bedroom, four-and-a-half bath colonial with a three-car garage on 1.7 acres on Meadow Lark Lane. After seeing it twice, Dana and her South African husband Pieter made a full-price offer.

As the agent wrote it up, Pieter asked, "So, what are the neighbors like?"

"You really only have neighbors across the street, the Jeffersons. A lovely couple about your age. I sold them their home.

"The house to the left of yours is virtually vacant."

Pieter shook his head. "Virtually?"

"Yes, it's owned by some pharmaceutical company. Until recently, the only people you saw there were either mowing the yard or doing work inside. I thought it might be a place for company executives to stay if they were in town for an extended period. Then, according to the Jeffersons, a man who started coming every few days for several hours. Never staying overnight, though."

⋈⋈ ⋈⋈ ⋈⋈

The Quantico lab began processing the materials from De Burgh's mansion. The hair recovered in Delaware matched the woman's eyelash DNA.

⋈⋈ ⋈⋈ ⋈⋈

The Bentley's GPS data showed infrequent trips before its apparent theft. A recent regular route from the estate to Hockessin, Delaware, began weeks earlier.

THIRTY

Maddison Mitchell called a meeting of just the task force's FBI agents.

"Okay, team, here's what we know from Quantico's current analysis. The hair in the car and house are a match. Samples are identical to the DNA collected from the master bedroom and bathroom. There's a strong possibility that they belong to Joanna Wójcik. We can't confirm that until we have her DNA sample.

"No fentanyl was collected in the main house.

"There were several fentanyl-based drugs found in the Executive Cathleen Cottage. Duragesic transdermal patches for prolonged pain management.

"Actiq tablets placed under the tongue, and Subsys, a sublingual fentanyl, sprayed under the tongue. Both are for rapid relief of breakthrough pain.

"And vials of injectable fentanyl citrate for acute pain management."

Agent Summers spoke. "Why is all that in the cottage and not the main house, ma'am?" "This seven-thousand-square-foot 'cottage' would be a *very* desirable upper-middle-class home in Potomac, Maryland. The garage housed an ambulance staffed around the clock.

"Fitzroy turned it into his father's palliative care home. The cottage's size provided the twenty-four-hour doctors, nurses, aides quarters, equipment, and supplies. Short of open-heart surgery, most treatments could be accommodated there."

⋈⋈ ⋈⋈ ⋈⋈

Julie Stephens' and Bill Wilson's professional relationship had become a friendship since the fentanyl murders connected them. Julie's trips to Baltimore and frequent phone calls morphed the relationship from law enforcement professional to personal.

Wilson drove to Montgomery County for dinner. Afterward, on I-95 North, he felt an odd warmth and smiled in the dark.

⋈⋈ ⋈⋈ ⋈⋈

"So, what does the GPS data show?" the lead Quantico lab technician asked a subordinate.

"That De Burgh traveled by limo most of the time."

"Don't most rich dudes do that?"

"Yeah, probably. But the Bentley shows trips into the Baltimore area."

"Anywhere regularly?"

"Yeah, to Chateau Country in Delaware. Five-sixty Meadow Lark Lane, in Hockessin. There are some *serious* McMansions there."

"How many trips?"

"Fifteen or more."

"Where was the car stolen?"

"We don't know."

"What's the last location in the GPS?"

"Weeks later at a Ford dealership in Ohio."

"And just before that?"

"On Meadow Lark Lane."

"If it went from there to Ohio, someone heisted it in Towson."

※ ※ ※

Julie Stephens enjoyed the evening with Wilson; her daughters didn't turn their noses up like the previous, infrequent dates. But she didn't allow herself to think of Bill as anything other than a friend. Julie could be tougher than Kevlar on the job, but always a realist. A serious romantic relationship for a woman with teenage daughters didn't produce a firefly's glow, much less a spark of optimism.

※ ※ ※

The FBI began checking the owners of the homes on Meadow Lark Lane. Except for two, all were owned by private parties, most for decades. One listed for sale at 546 Meadow Lark Lane; the other, next door at 560, is owned by Miach Laboratories, LLC.

After navigating a complex trail of Delaware corporate filings, agents discovered a parent-child relationship between Airmed and Miach. The connection gave Judge McLaughlin the probable cause to promptly sign a search warrant for everything on the 1.7 acres.

※ ※ ※

Twelve Degrees North, Lance Aux Epines' western exposure offered a glorious sunset view across Prickly Bay. The glare slowly settled out of sight beyond the mansions on the Saint George peninsula. Dr. Desmond Keith, Grenada's Prime Minister, and his wife Natalie watched the spectacle with Fitzroy De Burgh and Joanna Wójcik.

The PM raised his glass of River Antoine Rum in the direction of his host. "Fitzroy, my dear friend, here is to the good life in Grenada."

"Here, here," De Burgh responded. After glancing at Joanna, he lifted his glass. "And I have a proposal to improve life here even more."

Natalie smiled, "And what might that be, sir?" "A two-billion-dollar gift." The PM chuckled. "Very funny.

"Seriously, what is it?"

"Just what I said."

Joanna nodded. "He's *earnest*, Doctor Keith," she said with a hint of a European accent.

"Well, if so, you have my *undivided* attention."

"Airmed's Wings, my philanthropic arm, will donate two hundred million dollars to Grenada's general fund this year and annually for the next nine.

"According to my research, Grenada's yearly budget is equivalent to one-point-two billion U.S. at today's exchange rate. Airmed's gift would represent a seventeen percent increase or 540 thousand Eastern Caribbean dollars for the next decade."

Dr. Keith asked himself if Fitzroy or the River Antoine Rum—known for its high alcohol content—was talking.

De Burgh saw the hesitation in the PM's eyes. "I assure you, Doctor, I'm *completely* serious."

"I am *astounded*, sir. What requirements would this endowment have?"

"None. Use the money any way you wish."

"At the risk of *equum donatum in ore spectare*, but *why*?"

Joanna smiled. Fitzroy laughed out loud. "You can look *this* gift horse in the mouth, Doctor. "I may well retire here. Grenada is, generally speaking, a safe country. If I'm to be here permanently, I want the safety of my friends, staff, and, of course, myself to be assured."

"Do you want extra police protection here? I can certainly arrange that as soon as tonight."

"That's not necessary, Doctor. My security staff is more than sufficient.

"As I imagine you know, America is a *very* litigious country. My family's pharmaceutical company ran drug tests for nearly half a century. I know of no pending litigation or investigations. However, if the authorities in America insisted on my return to face trial for *any* reason, I would expect Grenada to refuse my extradition since there is no agreement to do so."

"Do you have the authority to agree to that?"

"No."

※ ※ ※

"Maddison, we got the warrant to search the Meadow Lark Lane house. I'm setting up a team to hit it at zero-six hundred in the morning. Are you going to be there?"

"No, Lonnie, and you aren't either. That place could be a significant fentanyl threat. Send in a hazmat team first. I don't want FBI staff added to an already long list of fatalities."

THIRTY-ONE

Dana Van Wyk invited her brother to dinner.

"Pieter and I want to have friends over to celebrate the house we bought in Hockessin, Delaware. I doubt you've had a decent meal since the last time you were here. So, bring your appetite."

"*Delaware*! Is Pieter going to commute to Baltimore every day?"

"No, silly. Haven't you heard of *telecommuting*? He may have to go into the office now and then. But, there's nothing he can't do from here.

"So, dinner?"

"Not until you make me a promise."

"What?"

"That you won't ambush me with some desperate female looking for a forever relationship."

"I've *never* had a *desperate* woman here. They've *all* been attractive and bright. I just want you to have a life outside all the death and mayhem you see every day." "Well then, you'll be happy to know someone could be on the horizon."

"*What*? Who."

"A woman I met on the job."

"A civilian?"

Wilson didn't answer.

"Not a *cop*?" Disdain dripped from Dana's last word.

༄༄༄ ༄༄༄ ༄༄༄

Nary a threat met the bio-hazard-clad FBI technicians—not even the tiniest spec of fentanyl. Half a dozen clones of what looked like the Michelin Man sniffed and drug-tested their way from basement to attic. The Quantico lab wasn't much, if any, cleaner. Nor was it much better equipped.

The microscope, spectrophotometer, gas chromatography-mass spectrometer, liquid chromatography-mass spectrometer, DNA sequencer, ultraviolet-visible spectrophotometer, electrochemical analyzer, infrared spectroscope, and forensic light sources cost just under an estimated $2.6 million.

Mitchell, Jerry, and the search team stared at the equipment array, some open-mouthed. The evidence sent to Quantico consisted solely of what looked like part of a cardboard pull tab; its analysis displayed consistency with the Bentley trunk envelope.

The garage held dozens of small, compartmented storage spaces containing various analytical supplies. A refrigerator and chest freezer stored other items requiring refrigeration. The floor could have been set for dinner.

"*Jesus*, nobody is *that* clean," Maddison complained. "So far, we have a blood spot, an eyelash, hair, an envelope, and a *strip* from an envelope that's *consistent*. Precious little to hang an *indictment* on!"

"We have DNA samples from the Delaware search," Jerry said.

"Which proves nothing, Lonnie. We have nothing from the FAA?"

"Nothing registered to Airmed."

"Miach Laboratories is on the house's title. Did anyone search FAA using that name?"

"Don't know, boss. I'll check it out."

"While you're at it, Lonnie, have BI's done on all the staff members at the estate. Maybe something will turn up there."

⋈||⋈ ⋈||⋈ ⋈||⋈

Julie Stephens dodged an investigatory bullet. Her fentanyl samples' chain of evidence had been unbroken, LRI's lab certified, and its analysis valuable to the case; the verbal warning wouldn't be part of her personnel jacket.

She called Wilson. "I'm a few pounds lighter after my lieutenant chewed my ass. I'm hoping it'll grow back."

Bill laughed. "I'm sure your *derriere* will be as cute as ever."

⋈||⋈ ⋈||⋈ ⋈||⋈

"But I can make it happen," Dr. Desmond Keith told Fitzroy De Burgh. "First, we will make you a King Charles the Third subject as a citizen of Grenada through our investment program.

"I will advise our Governor-General to call the legislature into session in response to a national emergency due to the COVID-19 pandemic. We will propose a bill to accept your endowment and give you life-long Grenadian protection against repatriation to any other country.

"I won't bore you with the bill's three reading stages and committee examinations. It will be approved and sent to the Governor-General for assent. Once he does, it will become law."

Fitzroy smiled. "That's quite an effort."

"Not for two billion dollars, sir."

⋈||⋈ ⋈||⋈ ⋈||⋈

The investigations of the Delaware estate's staff members showed vanilla backgrounds for all . . . except for one. Cuban immigrant Fernando Diaz's duties at the mansion listed gardening and pool maintenance. An IRS report on his most recent tax return listed his occupation as a Miach Laboratories research scientist with an income of $164,381.

PART V
"If you want a friend in Washington, get a dog."

THIRTY-TWO

"That's one hell of a salary for a pool boy, Maddison."
"He's a 'gardener,' *too*. Let's find out what he's *growing*."

⋈⋈ ⋈⋈ ⋈⋈

Eleven miles from the De Burgh estate, the Bureau struck gold with its search warrant of Fernando Diaz's modest Westshire Drive, Catonsville, townhome. In its basement— secured with a reinforced steel door—all the materials for seven additional fentanyl packages were discovered in environmentally controlled safes. A pirated Pitney Bowes postage meter obtained via the dark web sat nearby.

Additionally, 16-gram cartridges and envelopes for several more were ready for assembly.

His computer revealed bank records for offshore accounts. Scores of transfers—all less than $10,000 to avoid IRS scrutiny—came from Swiss accounts.

Forensic cyber sleuths discovered his activities on the dark web. An order from China for fifty sets of envelopes and 16-gram cartridges loaded with fentanyl and a pharmaceutical-grade propellant for inhalation devices. The as-yet unshipped order totaled $1.25 million.

Other than children's fingerprints on the outside of the steel door, the search team discovered no biometric data in the basement.

Searching the rest of the house uncovered a shoebox with over twelve thousand dollars cash in the master bedroom closet.

⋈⋈ ⋈⋈ ⋈⋈

Within hours, an agent served a warrant for Mr. Diaz's arrest at the De Burgh estate. He asked for a lawyer before the second handcuff clicked.

An FBI helicopter flew him from just outside the gate to Baltimore for interrogation.

⋈⋈ ⋈⋈ ⋈⋈

Word reached Fitzroy De Burgh before the fed's chopper crossed the Delaware Maryland state line. Joanna Wójcik called Gibson, Bender & Shapiro for Jefferson Bender. When he came on the line, she handed the phone to Fitzroy.

"Jeff, the FBI has arrested one of my employees. He's on his way to Baltimore. Make sure he has the best representation your firm can provide, please."

"Certainly, Mr. De Burgh. On what charge?"

"I believe he's charged with possession of a schedule two narcotic with the intent to distribute, namely fentanyl."

"We're on it, sir."

"Tell him his family will be cared for *very well*, please."

"Miach Laboratories, LLC owns a Gulfstream G700, tail number NAK45, Maddison. Its last flight plan shows Wilmington to Maurice Bishop International Airport, Saint George's Parish, Grenada," Lonnie Jerry said.

Jeannie Staron buzzed Morgan. "I have a Mr. De Burgh, on line one for you." "*Really*!"

"That's who he says he is."

Morgan switched to the call. "Mr. De Burgh, Hunter Morgan here. How can I help you?" "The FBI has arrested one of my most trusted employees on drug charges. I've asked Jefferson Bender of Gibson, Bender, and Shapiro to act as his counsel. I would like to engage your organization to support his legal team."

"Mr. De Burgh, I'm sure the law firm has excellent in-house investigators."

"Certainly, but none have worked at a high level within the FBI. I believe a former executive, Mr. D'Elia, is a partner in your firm. We will pay double whatever his hourly rate is plus any expenses."

"That's very generous, sir, but LRI doesn't engage in *surge* pricing. If Joe is available, his standard rate will apply.

"Please have your staff give my executive assistant, Mrs. Staron, an email or FAX where she can send a contract."

Fernando Diaz perched on a steel chair designed to keep subjects uncomfortable with front legs two inches shorter than the back. Mitchell and Jerry occupied seats across from him.

"You know, Agent Jerry, of all the states in which Mr. Diaz murdered people, only Virginia has the death penalty."

"Yes. And any DA worth his Gucci briefcase with a moron's political insight will go for the maximum sentence. He turned the murders into a worldwide story, killing the daughter of the Speaker of the House."

"You can't talk to me until my lawyer is here."

Mitchell smiled. "We're not talking to *you*, Mr. Diaz. We're . . . "

The door opened, and Jefferson Bender, wearing a five-thousand-dollar designer suit, walked in.

"Good morning, agents. Jefferson Bender, Gibson, *Bender*, and Shapiro representing Mr. Diaz."

"My, my, Mr. Diaz. How on earth could a pool boy slash gardener afford one of the true heavyweights of the legal profession?"

"My services are just part of his benefit plan, Ms. . . . ."

"Special Agent in Charge, Maddison Mitchell."

"Ah, yes. Nice to meet you in person, Special Agent in Charge. I had a conversation with the AG this morning regarding the search of Mr. De Burgh's estate and your violations of his Fourth Amendment rights. I imagine Merrick will contact the Bureau to discuss your future.

"And who are you, sir?" Bender said to Lonnie.

"Special Agent Jerry."

"So, is this interrogation being videoed?" Maddison nodded.

"Then I'll expect a copy of it before I leave.

"I'd like a few minutes with my client agents *without* us being videoed." Jerry and Mitchell collected the documents on the table and left.

The door clanged shut. Diaz turned to Bender and started to speak. The attorney held an index finger to his lips, shaking his head.

Confused, Diaz frowned.

Bender took several minutes opening his briefcase, removing documents, then checking his cell phone voicemail and texts.

"Let's make sure they've had time to stop any recording activity. Now, exchange one of the agents' chairs for the one you're sitting on. And turn it around to face the door."

Diaz complied. Bender stood, then swapped his chair for the one Jerry had occupied, also turning away from the observation window. Picking up a yellow legal pad, he sat next to Diaz.

"That mirror behind us is one-way glass. There will be someone in there watching us all the time. I don't want anyone to be able to lip-read what we're saying. ¿*Comprende*?"

"Yes."

Bender took an iPhone from his inside jacket pocket. "I'm going to record our conversation, Fernando. Okay?"

"Yes, sir."

The lawyer started an audio recording app and set the phone on the table behind them.

"Good. Now tell me your side of the story." "I know nothing about the stuff in the basement."

"How is that *possible*, Fernando?"

"In May, a man came to my house. He said he represented a businessman who wanted to use my basement for storage and would pay me five thousand a month to do so in *cash*. I had to get all our belongings out. Once I did, my wife, kids, and I had to go out of town for at least five days. The man said he'd square it with Mr. De Burgh so I could have the time off with pay."

"What was this man's name?"

"He never told me."

"No business card?"

"No, Mr. Bender. I asked for one. He said, 'In my line of work, they're not a plus.'"

"Can you describe him?"

"A big man, over six feet. Muscular. Dark hair and eyes. He spoke with a European accent."

Bender made a quick note on his pad. "How did you get paid?"

"On the first day of each month, in an envelope in our mailbox."

"Okay, go on."

"We moved our stuff into the attic and went to Disney World for a week. When we came back, a locked steel door had replaced the original. I had no access to the basement.

"Then, in June, a different man returned. He said we needed to leave the house the following day for four hours starting at noon. I had to work, and our kids were in school until three. So, my wife went to her sister's. She picked up the kids and went to Safeway to grocery shop until after four.

"After that, the same thing happened every three or four weeks."

"Did you have any video cameras in the house or outside?"

"None inside, and you have to get approval from the association to put one up outside. I never bothered."

"And you never saw anyone after the second visit?" "No, sir. No one.

"Can you get me out of here, Mr. Bender? My wife must be going nuts at home."

"Doubtful, but I'll ask. Are you a U.S. citizen?"

"I am, and my wife and kids were born here."

"I have a powerful friend. I'll talk to him about your getting bail."

"How much will that cost? They took the cash we had."

"Mr. De Burgh told me to make sure you know your family will be treated like his family. If a bond is possible, it will be handled for you."

Joe D'Elia had LRI's in-house investigators dive deep into Fernando Diaz's past. A criminal record did not exist for the naturalized citizen. He had come from a once prominent Cuban family who still had the means to buy his exit based on falsified Canadian investment documents. Due to his Laboratories research scientist skills, the United States Mexico-Canada Agreement provided him with temporary entry and a green card. Marrying Emily accelerated his opportunity for citizenship.

By all accounts, Fernando Diaz was a hard-working model member of the American workforce.

Mitchell and Jerry laughed out loud when Jefferson Bender mentioned bail for Diaz.

THIRTY-THREE

The following morning, Joe D'Elia canvassed the Diaz family's neighborhood personally for any sightings. Few people were home during the day; some worked nights and slept. The rest had young children to tend to. No cameras had a view of the Diaz's townhouse.

LRI's investigators searched surveillance video to identify the person or persons involved. Nothing helpful could be discovered for the initial visit. The family's week in Florida showed a white box truck in the neighborhood on the first day, but it could have gone anywhere. The four-hour periods did show a 2022 black Chevrolet Tahoe. Reexamining videos showed the exact vehicle on the last day of the Disney World week. A dark plastic, semi lucent cover prevented reading its license plate.

⋈⋈ ⋈⋈ ⋈⋈

At Fernando Diaz's arraignment, the agents didn't find anything funny as their suspect walked out of court, secured by a five-million-dollar bond, a surrendered passport, an ankle monitor order, home confinement, and Fitzroy Adam De Burgh's assurance of Diaz's appearance at trial. The AG's fingerprints covered the ruling. The judge, another law school friend of Fernando's council, hadn't hurt either.

As Jefferson Bender passed Mitchell and Jerry in the gallery, he stopped, smiling into their glaring faces. "Just remember, kids. Money talks and bullshit *walks*."

⋈⋈ ⋈⋈ ⋈⋈

"Mr. Graves, Joe D'Elia here. Do you have any connections with Bentley Motors Limited?"

"Afraid not, Joe," Roger answered. "But I'd bet Dick Schutz or someone at Apex Security does. Want me to give him a call?"

⋈⋈ ⋈⋈ ⋈⋈

"Rhodes."

"Maddison Mitchell. Our PIO is going to announce the arrest of a suspect in the fentanyl murders. I will hold them off until you've had a chance to write a story."

"In exchange for what, Agent?"

"Journalistic goodwill."

"You have that already. I appreciate your call. But, just to clarify, your information won't buy a get-out-of-jail free pass."

"Understood."

"So, what are the details?"

Agent Mitchell gave Dusty the arrest basics and what the search discovered, including the shoebox full of cash. She withheld Diaz's name and family information and only identified the arrest location as Delaware. Jefferson Bender would be Diaz's counsel, and LRI had been retained to supplement Gibson, Bender, and Shapiro's investigators.

✂✂✂

Dick Schutz connected Roger Graves with Shikita Bottoms, Apex's cyber security/GEO tracking expert.

When he introduced himself, she responded, "*Bugatti Man!*"

"Well, I've been called *lots* worse."

"You're a *legend* around here, man. What can I do for ya?"

"Can LRI get a copy of the Bugatti's travel log?"

"Why do you want it?"

Graves explained the Diaz case and his connection to the car's owner. "We're trying to see if the Bugatti traveled anywhere near the defendant's home."

"Okay, I'll send you a list of the information from the cloud. Do you want it in a document or spreadsheet?"

"Spreadsheet, please."

"Give me your email address. You'll have it in fifteen minutes."

✂✂✂

Director Courtemanche could almost feel the heat radiating from Maddison Mitchell when she barged into his office.

"I need to speak to you right fucking *now*!"

"Okay, calm down and talk to me," he said, trying not to bite off his subordinate's head.

Mitchell struggled to fight off hyperventilation. "Our suspect *walked out of court* this morning! Why did you let that *happen*?"

"How long have you known me, Maddison? Have I *ever* blindsided you? If I'm going to do something, you hear it from me *before* it happens."

Some of the fire in her eyes seemed to cool. "If it wasn't you, it's the AG's doing. Why is he protecting De Burgh?"

"I don't know, but I *will* find out."

✂✂✂

Graves worked backward through the list of Bugatti destinations. The house on Meadow Lark Lane stood out as the point of theft. Numerous trips there sparked his curiosity. He requested a list of property owners in the area from LRI's investigators. Within an hour, they traced the ownership of the house at 560 to Miach and Airmed Laboratories.

Roger emailed the address to D'Elia and then called him. Finally, he updated Morgan.

⋈⋈ ⋈⋈ ⋈⋈

Dusty Rhodes called Morgan to get background on the fentanyl murderer suspect's arrest and LRI's involvement in the case.

"I can only confirm that we have been asked to assist Bender's law firm investigators.

I can't comment beyond that, Dusty."

"Well, aren't you, Mr. *Politically Correct*! 'I can only confirm . . .'

"Okay, how about a trade? I'll tell you something you probably don't know, and you do likewise." "No deal."

"There's a small article in *The New Today*, Grenada's newspaper, announcing that the country is conferring citizenship on Fitzroy Adam De Burgh due to his extensive investments there." "No deal."

"Grenada has no extradition treaty with the U.S."

"No deal."

"Fitz's subsidiary, Miach Laboratories, LLC, owns a Gulfstream G700, tail number NAK45." "Yeah?"

"Its most recent flight flew De Burgh and several staff members to Grenada. Now, you share, Morgan."

Several seconds elapsed before he spoke. "You have to promise *not* to print the suspect's name if you discover it." "Why would I do that? I'm a reporter."

"With *hopefully* a modicum of compassion in your *black* heart."

"Yeah, yeah, I know. Innocent until . . . "

"If you print a name and he's found innocent, his reputation will be permanently tarnished. So, either promise, or we're done talking."

Now, the reporter hesitated. "All right, I promise."

"Did you know the suspect got bail? No doubt put up by De Burgh."

"*No shit?*" "*Nada.*

"And De Burgh's Bugatti was stolen in Towson, near a house whose title is held by Miach Laboratories?"

"*What* Bugatti?"

"One purchased by Miach in twenty-two, stolen, and no police report ever filed."

THIRTY-FOUR

On Meadow Lark Lane, Joe D'Elia searched the blocks on both sides of the Miach Laboratory house, looking for video cameras and doorbells, noting their addresses. Only three had full or partial views of 560.

He began knocking on doors. With his Bureau retirement credentials in hand, Joe explained his investigation regarding the fentanyl murders. All three residents allowed him to search their videos of the Bugatti's travel dates.

The video doorbell across the street had an excellent view. Just after each Bugatti arrival, a black Chevy Tahoe exited one of the garage bays, departed, and did not return for several hours. Unfortunately, the video's resolution prevented D'Elia from identifying the driver or reading the Tahoe's license plate.

Another resident's video showed the Tahoe passing their home, traveling away from 560 and returning hours later.

D'Elia immediately called the investigators, requesting a search of the video near Diaz's home for a black Tahoe.

After the phone call, Joe walked across the street and up the long, curving driveway. He peered through the four small windows of each bay door, none housed vehicles.

Knowing the FBI would have processed the Bugatti and gotten the same GPS data LRI had, he called Lonnie Jerry.

"Lonnie, Joe D'Elia."

He heard a sigh before Jerry spoke. "What *now*? Your super sleuths are working for the defense. I can't talk to you."

"Maybe something to help both of us."

"You know, Joe. I'm *really* tired of your bullshit. LRI isn't about to help us! Deceive us? Yes. Help us? No fucking way!"

"Don't be so sure, Lonnie. Let me just ask you a question. Quantico must have processed the Bugatti we told you about. I'm sure they pulled its GPS data. So, you know it went to 560 Meadow Lark Lane several times.

"You must have searched the house by now."

"So, what if we did? I'm not going to share the results with you. The house doesn't fit into the Diaz case. So, you're not entitled to any exculpatory evidence."

"That's right. But the garage is a different story."

"The garage was *part of the warrant*, smart guy, but it was empty except for a refrigerator and lab supply storage."

"Not on the dates the Bugatti was there."

"What are you talking about, Joe?"

"Every time the Bugatti arrived, a black Tahoe left for several hours. When it came back, the car departed."

※ ※ ※

Dusty Rhode's article ran with information about the Bugatti's travels to Towson, something Maddison Mitchell had not divulged.

※ ※ ※

In the AG's office, Luke Courtemanche tried desperately to remain calm despite his molten core. "Sir, allowing Diaz to walk out of that courtroom undercuts our case. The fact he got bail will be all over the nation by tomorrow morning. Locally, it could well influence potential jurors. If he wasn't dangerous enough to be kept behind bars . . . maybe he's *not* guilty."

"You're not the first to register discontent over Diaz's arraignment. The Speaker of the House inserted a napalm suppository in my ass earlier. I'll give you the same response I gave Mrs. Peterson. When a multi-billionaire asks for a favor via his mega-millionaire attorney, he gets it. Those two men donate hundreds of millions to our political party every election cycle, particularly POTUS'. Who, by the way, okayed De Burgh's request.

"I told the Speaker we'd have twenty-four-seven surveillance on Diaz. Make it happen."

"*Jesus*, sir. That's a lot of manpower when he could be tucked away in the Chesapeake

Detention Facility."

"Make it *happen, Luke!*"

※ ※ ※

A black Tahoe appeared in traffic cam videos near the Diaz home every day it left the Meadow Lark Lane house. One LPR's recording resolution made it possible to read the second, sixth, and seventh characters of a Delaware license plate—M 19. A DE State Police search found nine Tahoes, two of which were black.

One belonged to a contractor in Rehoboth, the other . . . owned by a ghost. Titled initially to a Philadelphia businessman and, after repossession for non-payment, sold at auction for cash to a Marcell Ledbetter.

No such person seemed to exist. His DE driver's license had expired. Facial recognition did not find a match for his picture. Ledbetter's social security account—marked "Restricted"—had no associated IRS tax records.

The only fingerprints on file were from his 1989 separation from the Army, also marked restricted.

※ ※ ※

Several LRI investigators canvassed streets near the traffic cameras. A restaurant's security video caught the Tahoe passing. Based on the blurred, grainy image, Sasquatch could have driven it. Each video or LPR image of the vehicle showed it moving in the direction of or away from Diaz's townhouse. All video time codes were inside those of the Bugatti's arrival and departure.

※ ※ ※

"Maybe we should just let *LRI* run this case, Lonnie!"

"In all honesty, boss, as much as D'Elia pisses me off, he's given us some valuable info.

I'll never admit this to him, but it's good to have parallel probing."

"What do we know about this phantom Tahoe?"

"We're canvassing Meadow Lark Lane for residents with security cameras. That has to be where Joe spotted the SUV."

※ ※ ※

Photos of the black Tahoe were shown to the residents living near the Diaz family. One —a Helen F. Graham Cancer Center orderly— remembered the vehicle because of its windshield's hospital employee parking pass.

※ ※ ※

John Holmes, Newark, DE Homicide Detective Captain, and Morgan's friend agreed to have his Senior Detective meet D'Elia at the hospital.

※ ※ ※

Three hours later, D'Elia and Senior Detective Jimmy Fortson stood in the Vice

President of Personnel's office. Querying the parking pass database with the partial letters of the DE plate returned one entry for a black Tahoe— Margaret M. Case, a senior security officer who worked the second watch, lived in Glasgow, DE.

When Case entered the parking lot for her 4 PM to 12 PM shift, Fortson waited with an arrest warrant. Case demanded a lawyer immediately.

D'Elia followed Fortson's Ford cruiser to the Newark PD headquarters. On the way, he called Bill Wilson, inviting him to observe the interrogation.

At 220 S Main Street, waiting for Mrs. Case's attorney to arrive, D'Elia brought Fortson up to speed on the case, including De Burgh's location in Grenada and the extradition situation.

A BI on Margaret Case showed a husband—Gary R. Case, and two young children— no wants, warrants, or criminal history other than a speeding ticket eighteen months earlier, for which she paid a fine.

⋈ ⋈ ⋈

A wrecker towed the Tahoe to Newark's Forensic Services Unit. When the wrecker disconnected it, a lab technician, search warrant in hand, began processing it.

⋈ ⋈ ⋈

Department of Treasury trial Attorney Cassidy Lefevre sat beside Margaret Case.

"What have you gotten yourself into, Mrs. Case?"

"I have no idea what's going on. They arrested me when I got to the parking lot at work. I haven't *done* anything."

"Where is Gary?"

"At home, with the kids, like every other day."

"Has he been following the program's protocols?"

"Yes, he barely leaves the house except for lately." "*Lately*?"

"Gary gets stir-crazy. In the last few weeks, he started going out for a few hours to drive around and see the countryside. He was never gone long, just a few hours. He just needs to see something other than the *inside* of the house."

⋈ ⋈ ⋈

Bill Wilson arrived at the Newark PD HQs and found D'Elia.

"Hey, Joe. Thanks for your call."

"I figured this interrogation might be helpful in your McGuire case."

"It can't hurt. Who is this woman?"

D'Elia shook his head. "We don't know. I'm willing to bet she, a boyfriend or husband, is in the Witness Security Program."

"*Witness protection*?"

⋈ ⋈ ⋈

Senior Homicide Detective III Mike Lang entered the interrogation room and sat with his back to the one-way mirror. Detective II Janette Bennett joined the group in less than a minute.

As Bennett seated herself, Lang said, "Good evening, Counselor. I'm Detective Lang, and this is my partner, Detective Bennett.

"Who do we have the pleasure of working with?"

Without speaking, Cassidy Lefevre placed a business card on the table and pushed it toward Lang.

He picked it up. "Cassidy Lefevre, ESQ. Are you a lone she-wolf or with a firm?"

Lefevre seemed to bristle at the term. "I'm *independent*."

"Okay, let's get started. For the record, this conversation is being recorded.

"Mrs. Case, please acknowledge that your Miranda rights have been explained to you." "They were, but *why*?"

Bennett smiled, "Margaret, our preliminary glimpse into your past suggests you're squeaky clean. So, tell us, how did you get yourself involved in a dozen fentanyl murders?" Lefevre's reaction showed her surprise. "*WHAT! I don't know anything about any murders.*"

Lefevre said, "Why don't you tell us what evidence you have? Let's not play cat and mouse games, Detectives."

"Okay, Counselor. Mrs. Case's black Chevrolet Tahoe, Delaware tag number 9GM7K19, was parked in front of a townhouse in Catonsville, Delaware. Searching those premises found the ingredients for seven more packages, exactly like those sent to the fentanyl murder victims.

"So, why were you there, Margaret?"

"*Don't answer that,*" Lefevre snapped.

"Detective Lang, there are many reasons my client's vehicle could be there. Is that all you've got?"

"No, ma'am."

Lang described the Bentley's trips to Meadow Lark Lane, the subsequent Tahoe round trips to the Catonsville townhouse, and the arrival of fentanyl packages days later.

A wry smile curled Lefevre's lips. "That's an interesting travelogue, Detective, but it doesn't pass the '*So What?*' test."

"Here's the 'so what.' Miach Laboratories, LLC, owns the Bentley and the house at five-sixty Meadow Lark Lane.

"The Bentley contained evidence linking it to the fentanyl murders. Each of the murder victims is a child whose parent died of pancreatic cancer. Each parent participated in an Airmed drug trial to find an early test for the disease.

"Airmed Pharmaceuticals owns Miach Laboratories.

"On the occasions when the Bentley arrived at five-sixty Meadow Lark Lane, Mrs. Case's Tahoe departed for several hours. It was seen in front of the townhouse where the materials necessary to make several fentanyl murder packages were discovered." "Seen precisely where?"

"Thirty-one-forty-four Pike Street.

"When the Tahoe returned to Meadow Lark Lane from Pike Street, the Bentley departed, as did Mrs. Case's Tahoe.

"Are the dots starting to fall in place now, Ms. Lefevre?"

"Who *drove* the Bentley?"

"Undetermined at this point."

"Who *owns* the Bentley?"

"I told you, Miach Laboratories, LLC."

"LLCs *don't* drive. Who drives the car?"

"We believe it's Mr. Fitzroy Adam De Burgh, the former CEO of Airmed."

"Where's he being interrogated, Detective?"

"Mr. De Burgh is in Grenada."

"Oh! An island with no extradition treaty with the U.S."

"We're working with State," Lang lied. "They'll push that banana republic hard enough to pop out the Pope."

"I'll bet this De Burgh person can spend more money to stay there than the U.S. can offer to get him back. In the meantime, you want a notch on your gun to show you've got the case solved.

"Did you discover Mrs. Case's prints or DNA at the scene in Catonsville?" "We're still processing it," Detective Bennett answered.

"So, you have my client's vehicle in the vicinity of your drug bust, and beyond that, you don't have shit.

"Now, I'd like to speak to my client *privately*."

⋈||⋈ ⋈||⋈ ⋈||⋈

"Lonnie, Joe D'Elia."

"*Christ*, Joe, why don't you *unretire* and come back to the Bureau? At least make some decent scratch for your efforts."

"I'm making more money than The Villages' hearing aid salesman.

"Thought you'd like to know the Newark, DE police arrested a woman whose Tahoe was seen parked in front of Diaz's townhouse."

"*Who?*"

"Margaret Case. They grabbed her up earlier this afternoon. She's conferring with her attorney at headquarters."

⋈||⋈ ⋈||⋈ ⋈||⋈

"Margaret, you've got to tell me what's going on."

"I have no idea, Cassidy."

"Would Gary have any reason to be in Catonsville?"

"No. He's hardly gone out at all until lately. Gary has no friends. We can't afford any.

"I don't either. My coworkers at the hospital used to invite us to parties or drinks after work. When we declined all the time, they stopped asking.

"I can work because Gary and I met after he entered the program. No one from his old life knows me.

"He's Mister Mom. That's Gary's profession. Except for whatever he's doing for you people."

⋈||⋈ ⋈||⋈ ⋈||⋈

D'Elia introduced Wilson to Lang and Bennett.

"What's your take on Mrs. Case, Mike?"

"Too early to tell."

Bennett shook her head. "I don't know. She seemed genuinely surprised when Mike sprang the murders on her." "What does her husband do?" D'Elia asked.

"Don't know," Bennett answered. "We can't find any work history on him.

"They have a couple of young kids. Maybe he's a stay-at-home dad."

"Let's get a warrant for their townhouse and bring Mr. Case in for a chat," Lang instructed.

Bennett nodded before leaving the room.

THIRTY-FIVE

Five FBI agents stormed into the Newark PD HQs at 0300 HRS the following morning. Led by Lonnie Jerry, Gary and Margaret Chase were arrested, mirandized again, and whisked to the New Castle airport. By sunrise, the couple occupied separate interrogation rooms in Baltimore. Both demanded a lawyer.

Just before noon, Cassidy Lefevre arrived and quickly found herself in Maddison Mitchell's office. She handed the SAIC her card and said, "I want to see my clients."

"Who might they be, Ms. . . . "

"Cassidy Lefevre, just like it says on the card. Mr. and Mrs. Chase, as you very well know."

"I don't see an address on this, just a phone number. Where are you from?"

"*That's* immaterial, Agent Mitchell. Where are my clients?"

"*Special Agent in Charge,* Ms. Lefevre."

"Oh! Sorry, you can retract your claws now and take me to my clients . . . *Special Agent in Charge.* "

Mitchell pushed the intercom button on her phone. "Anneliese, ask Lonnie to join us."

"Right away."

⋈⋈ ⋈⋈ ⋈⋈

"Tell me about your little sightseeing trips, Gary."

"I just drove around, Cassidy. I had to get out of the house."

"If you bullshit me, I can't help you."

"How did your wife's Tahoe find its way in front of a townhouse with a fentanyl stash?" Case dropped his head.

"*Gary!*"

"I drove somebody there. I picked them up in Hockessin and drove them back. I *never* went in."

"Them? Who was it?" "I can't say, Cassidy."

"If you want to stay in the program, you must *tell* me, Gary."

"If I do, my wife, kids, and I are dead."

"If you don't, you're all dead anyway."

"Yeah, but the people in Hockessin *know* where I live. That means the Poles do, too.

The Mexicans may not."

"*Poles*! What have you gotten yourself into?"

"I'm *done* talking, Cassidy."

"At least tell me this. Are the Hockessin people associated with Airmed Pharmaceuticals?"

"I'm not saying anything else about *anyone*."

◄|► ◄|► ◄|►

Lonnie Jerry dropped Lefevre's business card on Mitchell's desk. "She's with Treasury's Office of General Counsel. One of the Cases is probably in WITSEC. I'd guess it's mister-mom since she's the only one working.

"You know how much clout the money changers have, Maddison. Depending on the case, we could get a male or female appendage caught in a wringer for not playing ball with them."

"*Fuck them*! I'm not going to be threatened into letting a serial killer with a dozen scalps on his belt walk."

◄|► ◄|► ◄|►

"I need to speak to my clients together, Special Agent in Charge."

"That's not possible, Ms. Lefevre. It violates protocols."

"You can't force either of them to testify against the other. So, where's the violation?"

"Either or both could be serial murderers. We will not allow them to get their stories straight, assisted by *you*."

"Are you sure that's how you want to play it?" "You have my answer, Counselor."

Cassidy Lefevre's smile dulled Mitchell's bravado a bit.

The attorney took her cell phone from a small black purse. After pressing only two keys, she put the call on speaker.

"Office of the Secretary of the Treasury, Ms. Kim, how may I help you?"

"Chi Suk, it's Cassidy. Would you tell the Secretary I'm having a problem with the

DOJ, please? I'd appreciate it if he would call the AG."

"I'll tell him right now, Cassidy. Anything else?"

"No. Thank you, Chi Suk."

◄|► ◄|► ◄|►

"What's the status, Joe?" Morgan asked.

"Don't know. The Cases are back in Baltimore at the Bureau's Field Office. I imagine

Jerry and company are sweating them pretty hard."

"Did you see any of his interview in Newark?"

"No, they'd just gotten him to HQ when the feds snatched them to the airport."

"Suppose Jerry would tell you anything?"

"I'll try. The worst he can say is, 'Go fuck yourself.'"

🧬 🧬 🧬

Sitting across the table from Cassidy Lefevre, Gary and Margaret Case held hands. She cried softly, her free hand covering her mouth. His thousand-yard stare burned a hole in the wall behind their attorney.

"Gary, tell me what you did."

"I told you. I played Uber between Meadow Lark Lane and the Diaz house." *"Who is Diaz?"*

"I don't know. The person I drove just said, 'The Diaz house.' Seven-seven-six Westshire Drive, in Catonsville."

"Did the man you took there speak with an accent?"

"Yes. British."

"And why are you worried about the Poles?"

"I can't tell you!"

"*Oh*, for *God's sake*, Gary! *Tell her*!" Margaret pulled her hand out of his and slapped his arm.

"*I can't. It'd put you and the kids at risk.*"

"We're *already* at risk. If you go to prison, you're a *dead man*, and Jamie, Michelle, and I will be sitting ducks outside WITSEC.

"*Tell her*!"

🧬 🧬 🧬

The AG's direct call to Maddison Mitchell had been short and *sour*. When Cassidy Lefevre walked into her office unannounced, the SAIC hadn't finished licking her wounds.

"So, who is this Diaz person?"

"That's none of your business, Counselor. It's part of an ongoing investigation." "Would you like to chat with the AG again, Special Agent in Charge?"

🧬 🧬 🧬

To D'Elia's surprise, Lonnie Jerry didn't explode at Joe's question.

"I appreciate your help. But I can't share anything with you."

"Just answer one question."

"What's that?"

"Are the Cases in WITSEC?"

"Why do you ask *that*?"

"The pattern of his BI and it looks like he's a stay-at-home dad." Jerry didn't answer. "Lonnie?" "Cassidy Lefevre."

"Who's that?"

THIRTY-SIX

The Department of State *wasn't* working with the Newark, DE, PD; they *were* with the
DOJ and Homeland Security's Secret Service. The US-Switzerland Tax Information Exchange Agreement allowed the IRS' discovery of a recent two-hundred-million-dollar transfer from a Swiss account to the Nation of Grenada. The sending account, one of many, tied to the Airmed Pharmaceuticals trust.

In addition to the recent announcement of Fitzroy Adam De Burgh being granted Grenadian citizenship, the conveyance raised dozens of DOJ, IRS, and SS eyebrows.

The old saying of successful people is, "It's not *what* you know; it's *who* you know," particularly in politics.

The Secretary of State, Miller Remington, knew Dr. Desmond Keith *very* well, starting with their graduate study days at Oxford. Each man admired and supported the other as they climbed the ranks of domestic and international foreign policy. Dr. Keith considered Remington one of his closest friends.

And so, when SOS Remington called the Prime Minister, Keith was pleasantly surprised.

"Miller! Good to hear from you."

"How are you, Desmond, you old war horse?"

"Very well, thank you. And you and Ronda and your family?"

"All great. Sorry, Desmond, I don't have much time today. This is a bit of a business call."

"Oh. How can I help you?"

"Grenada has recently conferred citizenship on Fitzroy De Burgh?"

"We have. Fitz has invested heavily in our country. Why?"

"You may not know about a dozen murders in the U.S. involving fentanyl."

"I'm well aware of your war on drugs."

"That's not what I'm talking about. Someone mailed small fentanyl bombs to people. When they opened the packages, the drug sprayed in their faces, killing them instantly.

"The victims are all tied indirectly to Mr. De Burgh's Airmed Pharmaceutical company."

"Indirectly?"

"Yes, Desmond. The victims were all children of Airmed drug trial patients who died of pancreatic cancer."

"Were the trials for a drug?"

"No, not specifically. Airmed was trying to find an early detection method.

"We would very much like to speak to Mr. De Burgh."

"Call him. If you don't have his number, I have it."

"We need to see him in person. We are eliminating suspects and . . ."

"*You think he's involved somehow?*"

"Of course not. It's standard police elimination protocol."

"Then just ask him to return."

"We will. I'm just giving you a courtesy call to let you know what's happening."

"I appreciate that, Miller. Is that all?"

"Just one last question. We noticed a two-hundred-million-dollar transfer from a Swiss bank to your nation."

"Yes. Fitz is providing a very generous endowment to our people."

"May I ask how *generous* he is?"

"Certainly. Two billion dollars over ten years. The transfer from Switzerland is the first installment."

※ ※ ※

Roger Graves and Morgan stood in the company canteen.

"Hunter, I've got an idea. What if we search LPRs and traffic cams near the De Burgh estate before the fentanyl murders started to see if we can identify who drives the Bentley regularly?"

"Good thought. Do it."

※ ※ ※

Gary Case took a deep breath and let it out slowly.

"Do you know what the *Pruszkow* is, Cassidy?"

"Yeah, it's Poland's version of the Mafia. Why?"

"They're a major laundromat for the Mexican Sinaloa Cartel's money."

"Okay. So . . . ?"

"They discovered I'm working with Treasury to dismantle the cartel."

"How, Gary?"

"I don't know. But that's who ordered me to start round trip service from Mockingbird Lane to Diaz's townhouse in Catonsville."

"If they're making money off the Mexican deal, why didn't they just kill you to protect their income stream, Gary?"

"That's the first question I asked myself. The *Pruszkow* knows their customer is on a wing and a prayer because of organizational infighting. Other, smaller cartels are standing in line to get access to their services. So, if they lose one, there's plenty of business in the pipeline."

"Why is there a waiting list?"

"Taking on additional cartels, like the *Jalisco* New Generation, would significantly raise their profile with the Polish authorities. The *Pruszkow* would rather make less money than face increased police attention and be caught up in a massive investigation.

"Now you're going to ask me why the Polish mafia would get involved in these murders."

"And the answer is . . . ?"

"I have *no* fucking idea. It makes absolutely no sense. But they know about me and could rat me out to the Mexicans at *any* time. So, I didn't have any bargaining power."

※ ※ ※

"Hunter, I got a name from Lonnie Jerry. Cassidy Lefevre. She's from Treasury's

General Counsel Office. More evidence that the Case family are WITSEC protectees."

"Have you passed that info on to Diaz's attorney?"

"No, I wanted to bring you up to speed first. I'll call Jefferson Bender now."

※ ※ ※

Graves called John Holmes in Newark, asking if a warrant to search DE's LPRs and street cams for the Bentley could be obtained. After the FBI big-footed their case, the Homicide Captain wasn't just *willing* but seemed almost *giddy* at the prospect.

Within a few hours, Roger and a Newark Traffic Unit member searched LPRs near the De Burgh estate via a Zoom call. They began ninety days before the first fentanyl murder. The weather had been unseasonably warm then, and hopefully, someone had used the opportunity to put the Bentley's top down.

※ ※ ※

"*Lonnie*! There's another *fucking leak* in our task force."

"What now?"

"I just got a call from that fucking ambulance chaser, Bender, asking me who *Gary Case is. And* . . . is he in the *WITSEC program*? And . . . *if so* . . . *why*?

Jerry tried not to telegraph his discomfort, glad his long-sleeved shirt would hide the goosebumps. *Fucking D'Elia!*

⋈||⋈ ⋈||⋈ ⋈||⋈

"The De Burgh residence, Calvin speaking. How may I help you?" the formal British voice said.

"This is Chi Suk Kim. I'm Executive Assistant to Secretary of State Harvey Winken. The Secretary would like to speak to Mr. De Burgh. Is he available?"

"One moment, madam."

In less than a minute, "Fitzroy De Burgh."

"Please hold for Secretary Winken, sir."

⋈||⋈ ⋈||⋈ ⋈||⋈

"Roger Graves and Newark's Traffic Unit member found several LPR and traffic camera images of the Bentley—top up and down. In the pictures showing the vehicle's interior, a woman drove. After enhancement, both photos were still too grainy for facial recognition.

Three views of the car had the top up and driver's side window down. Long, black, windblown hair could be seen.

⋈||⋈ ⋈||⋈ ⋈||⋈

"Let's talk WITSEC, Special Agent in Charge. Their placement into the program says Gary Case is extremely critical to the Treasury's Secret Service case. Have you ever been read in on it?"

"As we often say here at the Bureau, '*Fuck you!*' Lefevre."

"*Well! My, my, my*! Did they teach *that* in an annual sexual harassment seminar?

"How did Jefferson Bender react? No, wait. You'd *never* use that term with a *very influential* private attorney. Would you?" Mitchell didn't respond.

"So, here's our plan. You see, I've spoken to Mr. Bender at length. Since you've provided no evidence from the Diaz house search, Jefferson and I know you must have nothing. No prints. No DNA. That is, unless you're withholding it from Mr. Case's defense counsel. In that case, as we say in the legal profession, 'you're fucked.'

"And . . . apparently, you have no proof of who *drove* the Tahoe. So, why doesn't the

Bureau cut its losses and quit harassing our client?"

Maddison Mitchell's icy stare seemed to cool the room. If looks could kill, Cassidy Lefevre would be sporting a *toe tag*.

⋈||⋈ ⋈||⋈ ⋈||⋈

"Mr. De Burgh, thank you for taking my call."

"How can I help you, Secretary Winken?"

"Please just call me Harvey. May I call you Fitzroy?"

"Certainly, Harvey."

"Thank you. I'm sure you're aware of the fentanyl murders."

"It would be hard not to after the FBI showed up to search my Delaware home." "Yes." The word had a ring of uncertainty. "I'm aware that could have been handled far more subtly. My apologies."

"Thank you."

"I'm calling to ask you to return to the U.S. in order to provide DNA and blood samples.

"I've spoken to Desmond Keith and know you are now a Grenadian citizen. He informed me of your concern about possible litigation relating to Airmed's drug trial connection to the victims."

"That's correct, Harvey. There can be no connection to me or Airmed."

"Or Miach Laboratories?"

"No. Miach was our generic drug arm. They had no research department to speak of. Indeed, no need to run trials. The original pharmaceutical companies did those before their product releases.

"Let me ask *you* a question, Harvey."

"Go ahead."

"Why are you calling with this request? Why not the Attorney General?"

"That's fair. Merrick had every intention of doing so. I requested he let me contact you since we have no extradition agreement with Grenada. And, their recent legislative action shields you in particular."

※ ※ ※

Morgan called John Holmes in Newark. "Hey, brother. Hunter Morgan."

"What's goin' on in *Balmer*, buddy?"

"We're still working on the fentanyl murders, helping a guy's defense counsel's investigators. That's why I called. I need a favor."

"Shoot."

"You got to meet Joe D'Elia, my lead investigator. Right?"

"Roger that."

"He'd like to interview De Burgh's estate staff. Can you swing a warrant to get him in there?"

"Do morons eat Tide pods? You bet your ass I can. I'll call you when it's done."

※ ※ ※

"Have the Attorney General courier a hard copy letter bearing his signature, not some secretary's, to me. In short, clear layman's terms, it should state that I am returning of my own free will. There are no current, planned, or pending legal actions against me personally or professionally. And that I will be allowed to return to Grenada at any time of my choosing."

"Can it be FAXed to you?"

"No. It is to be hand-wet-signed *by* the AG. Fly it down."

"Can it also apply to Ms. Joanna Wójcik?"

"If you also want my nurse, she requires the same as myself. A *separate* letter, not an inclusion in mine."

THIRTY-SEVEN

A Newark homicide detective escorted Joe D'Elia and Roger Graves while they interviewed the staff members remaining at the estate in Fitzroy De Burgh's absence, with interesting results.

In the main house, an upstairs maid described the very close relationship between Darragh De Burgh and Joanna Wójcik before and *especially* after his cancer diagnosis.

"Tell me about them, please," Joe said. "How old was Osín De Burgh when he died?"

"Eighty-eight, almost eighty-nine. Before Mr. Osín got sick, Ms. Wójcik was almost his only companion. She traveled with him everywhere. He'd ask her advice on many issues.

I think Mr. Fitzroy was a little jealous of her."

"And after Osín developed cancer?"

"Mr. Osín was moved into the Executive Cathleen Cottage. She slept in the same room with him until he died. Afterward, Ms. Wójcik grieved like she'd lost *her* father."

"Was theirs a strictly platonic relationship?" The question sounded harsher than Joe intended.

"I can't personally speak to what happened in the Cottage. Other staff members told me Mr. Osín was in great pain and, during his last days, mostly unconscious."

"And before Mr. Osin's illness?"

"I'd rather not discuss that. I can't lose my job here.

"Sandy Reome, Mr. Osin's valet, might talk to you. He got fired."

"Why?"

"He got out of line. I hear he told Mr. Osín that Ms. Wójcik was just after his money. He didn't even get to collect his belongings before security escorted him off the estate. A guard packed his stuff and mailed it."

⌘⌘⌘

In the Executive Cathleen Cottage, the staff members echoed what D'Elia had already been told. Osín suffered terribly during the last six weeks of his life. Joanna Wójcik rarely left his side. By the time of his death, the woman was physically and emotionally exhausted. Racked with grief, the nurse infrequently showed herself for days on end.

When asked if Osín had been close to other employees, one staff member answered emphatically, "*Yes!*"

Just after Osín moved from the main house into the Cottage, Ms. Joanna went to New Jersey for her mother's funeral. When Mr. Fitzroy returned from his sabbatical, the Cottage became *his* home. A maid speculated he wanted to be near his father's spirit.

⋈||⋈ ⋈||⋈ ⋈||⋈

Waiting for Roger Graves to finish talking to the garage staff, D'Elia searched for and found a Sandy Reome in Bear, DE. He called, and a man answered. D'Elia introduced himself as a retired FBI Special Agent in Charge of the Boston Field Office.

"I'm in Centreville, at the De Burgh estate. Could I swing by and see you this afternoon?

I just have a couple of questions about Osín De Burgh."

"I'm leaving town in half an hour. Going away to a wedding. What are your questions?" "How close were Osín and Joanna Wójcik?"

Reome laughed. "As close as two people can get. The old man banged Joanna harder than Purdue's Big Bass Drum."

"At his age?" D'Elia said skeptically.

"His doctor brought in Viagra for daily use by the pallet load. Osín could probably have spun plates on his dick."

"Okay."

"He wasn't careful either. Knocked Joanna up. Sent her off to a very discreet abortion clinic in New Jersey for a week."

"Age didn't slow the old man down. He had an *eye* for the ladies. Marta, his nurse, was his squeeze until younger, prettier Joanna arrived. Like last year's linens, Marta was whisked off to the Cathleen Executive Cottage. But, at least, she avoided the *New Jersey* trip."

"I understand you lost your job over a comment about . . . "

"Yeah. I admired the old man. It was obvious what Joanna was up to. I felt obligated to warn him.

"As they say, 'no good deed.' I was out of there faster than a Kentucky Derby two-year-old departing the starting gate."

⋈||⋈ ⋈||⋈ ⋈||⋈

Once the documents Fitzroy De Burgh requested for himself and Joanna Wójcik were received, reviewed, and approved he gave instructions for the Gulfstream to be readied. Two hours later, he, Joanna, and the same entourage that accompanied them to Grenada departed for Wilmington/New Castle Airport.

⋈||⋈ ⋈||⋈ ⋈||⋈

According to Dusty Rhodes, her EA, Ophelia, was worth her considerable weight in *platinum* for two reasons—hindsight and *foresight*.

An example of the latter: When Fitzroy and company flew to Grenada, the rotund executive assistant set up a FlightRadar24 account and downloaded their app to her iPhone. She then created an alert for tail number NAK45—a dog barking ringtone.

The iPhone literally alerted like a drug-sniffing dog when De Burgh's Gulfstream lifted off from Maurice Bishop International Airport runway.

※ ※ ※

"They're on their way to Delaware, Maddison."

"Have techs at the airport to take their samples."

"Boss, with respect, why don't we let them get back to his estate to do that? Meeting them on the airport tarmac would suggest they're definitely suspects. I don't think that's what you want."

Anger flickered in the SAIC's eyes, then disappeared. "Yeah, you're right, Lonnie. OK. Have the techs arrive at the estate shortly after De Burgh and his squeeze get there. Give them an hour or so to get in and settled first."

※ ※ ※

Morgan organized a Zoom call with Bill Wilson, Julie Stephens remote, D'Elia, Proffitt, and himself in the Baltimore office to get everyone up to speed.

Once established, he turned it over to D'Elia, saying. "Joe, tell us what you learned in Delaware. Then we'll have Roger follow."

"We made progress in understanding the dynamics of the De Burghs.

"Joanna Wójcik was *very* close to Osín De Burgh to the extent that Fitzroy probably felt like a stepchild. She seems to have been the old man's constant companion.

"What we thought was a platonic relationship between Joanna and Osín De Burgh wasn't. According to a previous staff member, he impregnated her about the time of his cancer diagnosis. Supposedly, the pregnancy was terminated in New Jersey."

"How old was Osin?" Julie asked.

"Just short of his eighty-ninth birthday."

"Wow!" she responded. "How'd he get *anybody pregnant*?"

"Better living through chemistry.

"Anyway, Joanna took his death hard."

"Did she move on to the son afterward?" Morgan asked.

"There was no discussion of a romantic relationship between Joanna and Fitzroy. At least nothing any staff member was brave enough to bring up.

"That's what I got in a nutshell," Joe said. "Roger, your show."

"Sure. I spent my time in the garage asking about the Bentley. The lead wrench monkey told me the old man *bought* it for *Joanna*. He said Fitzroy never said anything but seemed pissed. Of course, he could have had any sports car he wanted. But, as Joe just said, it sounded like his green-eyed monster probably kicked in.

"After Osín checked out, Fitzroy began driving it occasionally. Maybe he was sending an '*under* new management' message to Ms. Wójcik."

Wilson asked, "Did she drive it at all?"

"Oh, yeah. The mechanic said she took it out all the time. Claude, the chauffeur, did as well. He took it to be serviced."

"Why wouldn't the mechanic do that?"

"The mechanic said he always made the service appointments on his day off as a kind of perk for the old guy. And, the Bentley dealership service department treated him like hired help."

⋈ ⋈ ⋈

Lonnie Jerry sat across from Gary Case, sweating like a Florida football player after an August practice session. In contrast, Cassidy Lefevre, beside him, could have just finished an Arctic stroll.

"I'm going to show you pictures of six men. I want you to tell me if one of them is the person you drove to the Diaz townhouse."

"I'm not saying anything."

"Just look at the pictures. If you don't recognize anyone, then keep your mouth shut!" "Special Agent, it's a little early to get nasty," Lefevre said, smiling.

Jerry didn't respond, placing the six-pack in front of Gary. "Pick it up and study each person carefully, *please*."

As his suspect did as instructed, Jerry watched Case's eyes closely, waiting for any speck of reaction. Nothing.

Case set the photos down, looking into Jerry's eyes, shaking his head.

"I need a verbal response for the recording, Mr. Case. Do you recognize anyone?"

"No."

Jerry nodded to a second agent standing in a corner near Cassidy. The woman moved behind the suspect.

"Come with me."

Thinking the interrogation completed, Cassidy started to rise.

"You're not done, Counselor. One more to go."

The second agent escorted Gary from the room. In less than a minute, she ushered Margaret in and seated her.

Jerry showed her the same images.

Mrs. Case didn't pick them up. "I've told you. I never went with him." "Take a look, please. Maybe you saw someone suspicious near your home." Margaret did as asked. Showed no reaction and set the photos down.

"I've never seen any of these people." "Did your husband talk about these 'drives'?"

Cassidy responded, "Asked and answered a dozen times, Special Agent. She wasn't with him and saw *no one*!"

"Did he ever say *anything* about his activities?"

"No."

"Just take a moment to think back. Any comment or complaint?"

Margaret closed her eyes for several seconds, opened them, and replied, "He said he met a man with a bit of an accent once."

⋈⋈ ⋈⋈ ⋈⋈

"Miach-AK45, New Castle Tower, wind 210 at 5 knots, cleared to land Runway 19."

"New Castle, Miach-AK45, cleared to land Runway 19. Thank you."

Miach-AK45 taxied to the terminal. As its engines wound down, the passengers deplaned, entered the building, and cleared customs.

Fitzroy and Joanna walked to the VIP entry/exit. A chauffeur held the estate limousine's rear door open closest to the terminal.

Dusty Rhodes stood between the exit and limo—a journalistic middle linebacker ready to play.

"Mr. De Burgh! I hope you had a pleasant flight."

"We did, Ms. Rhodes. Thank you."

The recognition and slight Irish brogue surprised the reporter.

"You *know* me?"

"I do. *The Baltimore Mirror* is the closest paper worth reading."

"May I ask you a few questions?"

"Would you like to ride with Ms. Wójcik and myself?" Shocked, Dusty waited for the man to laugh at the joke.

When he didn't, she said, "*Yes*, I certainly would. *Thank you*!"

Once the passengers were seated, the chauffeur closed the door and jogged behind the vehicle to his.

⋈⋈ ⋈⋈ ⋈⋈

The Cases and Cassidy Lefevre met in an interrogation room.

"Margaret, the feds have *nothing* on you. Oh, they can strut around and say you're in deep shit, but as my grandfather used to say in polite company, 'that's horse apples.' So, stick to the fact that you were not involved.

"Gary, your future isn't so rosy. These fentanyl murders have gotten international attention. The FBI's reputation in recent years has been severely damaged. They need a trophy to mount on the wall. Treasury and Justice will have a legal cage match to see where you go. Your fate depends on which department has the biggest political *dick*.

"You've got to follow my advice to your wife. Keep telling them the truth."

Gary Case looked ten years older than the day Cassidy met him. "Who do you think will win?" he asked.

"It *could* go either way. But I think a hundred thousand fentanyl deaths beats a dozen *every day* of the week."

⋈⋈ ⋈⋈ ⋈⋈

"Would you care for a drink, Ms. Rhodes?" Fitzroy asked, pulling a cut-crystal decanter with a silver "Irish Whiskey" tag from a side pocket of the limousine. "Midleton, by Jameson. The finest Irish whiskey money can buy, in *my* humble opinion."

He poured a few ounces into a crystal tumbler and offered it to Joanna, who smiled and declined.

As Fitzroy returned the decanter, Dusty said, "Yes, I've had it. My late husband Jim discovered it at the duty-free shop leaving Dublin years ago. Fortunately, his friends found it, too, while visiting our home. I think the bottles they gave him frequently over the years were more for *their* pleasure than his.

"But I need to drive back to Baltimore, so unfortunately, I must decline, Mr. De Burgh."

"No need to for the formality, Ms. Rhodes. Fitz will be fine."

"Again, thank you. I'm Dusty."

"How long has Jim been gone, if I may ask?"

"He died in two-thousand-five of liver cancer."

"I'm very sorry. Was your husband also a journalist?" "*No*. Jim *hated* reporters. He was a BPD bomb tech." "*Really*? Was this an example of opposites attracting?" "We *certainly* weren't attracted at first.

"His former brother-in-law murdered Jim's sister and three children with a car bomb. I met him when I covered the story.

"After his only other family members died, Jim fell apart. I just happened to be there to try to console him. That day was Jim's *worst* ever and the beginning of the best years of *my* life."

Joanna spoke for the first time. "I know the feeling. We lost Fitzroy's father, Osin, not long ago. A truly *amazing* man."

"Yes, I know," Dusty responded. "My condolences."

Joanna smiled. "Thank you."

Fitzroy's pleasant facial expression dimmed momentarily at his nurse's comment, but his smile returned as he asked, "So, what would you like to know, Dusty?"

🧬 🧬 🧬

Lonnie Jerry reviewed the Quantico lab biological evidence report of the material discovered at the De Burgh estate. Though thorough enough for most investigators, it didn't answer his question. He called a senior Quantico lab contact.

"Jennings."

"George, Lonnie Jerry. You too busy for a question?"

"Not from you, Brother. What is it?"

"The bio evidence from the De Burgh estate."

"Yeah?"

"Can the age of the DNA deposits recovered in the master bedroom be determined?

"It can be *estimated*, Jerry, by analyzing degradation patterns in the DNA molecules. Various factors influence deterioration. Levels of microbial activity, environmental conditions, exposure to UV light, and so on.

"Why do you ask?"

"I want to nail down the timeline for activities in that room. Can you ask your people to take another look, please?"

"Will do."

⋈⋈ ⋈⋈ ⋈⋈

"Is our conversation on the record, Fitzroy?"

"It is."

"Thank you.

"All of the fentanyl murder victims are the children of people who participated in one of Airmed's drug trials."

Fitzroy nodded. "Yes, that appears to be the case. I can offer no explanation, however."

"Is all of the data from those trials still available?"

"It is. In our archives. Would you like to review it?"

Shocked, Dusty replied, "You'd *let me*?"

"Of course. We have nothing to hide. The only caveat is that you *shall not* publish *anything* without my express written approval. I'm anticipating at *least* a dozen lawsuits as a result of these terrible murders. I don't want to add HIPAA violations to the mix.

"We'll let the FBI, or *any other* law enforcement organization do so as well. So long as they view it *locally*. I won't allow data to be removed, allowing for possible modification. There is *no* evidence of any wrongdoing in these files. I don't want it to *grow* any.

"I can assure you that neither Airmed nor any of our subsidiaries is responsible for *any* crime."

"How many people have access to the data?"

"Two. My data center manager and myself. I'll have Pawel Żyła contact you." "Thank you."

"It seems your father and you were very driven to find an early diagnosis of pancreatic cancer. Why so much interest in that particular disease?"

"Allow me a minor correction, please. We wanted to develop an early *indication* of pancreatic issues. That organ can suffer several health problems.

"Pancreatitis: inflammation of the pancreas and can be acute or chronic.

"Pancreatic cysts: Fluid-filled sacs can develop in the pancreas. Most are benign, but some may be precancerous or cancerous.

"Exocrine pancreatic insufficiency: Occurs when the pancreas does not produce enough digestive enzymes. It can lead to malabsorption of nutrients, weight loss, and other digestive issues.

"Diabetes: If the pancreas does not produce enough insulin, type 1. Or when the body becomes resistant to insulin, type 2.

"Pancreatic pseudocysts: Fluid collections that can develop in or around the pancreas after pancreatitis or abdominal trauma episodes.

"Stress in an organ is its response to challenging or threatening situations. So, Airmed's goal was never the development of a pancreatic *diagnosis*. That would have been an enormously Herculean undertaking. We merely wanted to identify *stress* in the pancreas so it could be investigated early enough and avoid lethality in the case of cancer, et al.

"Of course, in retrospect, the word '*merely*' was unattainable too.

"Now, after my *lecture*, the answer to your question. My paternal grandfather and father were taken by cancer of the pancreas. Based on his incomplete medical records, we believe my paternal *great*-grandfather was also. Our efforts were as much a quest to save the De Burgh bloodline as to benefit mankind's."

The sadness in his voice drove Joanna to place her hand on Fitzroy's.

He smiled toward her, then looked back at Dusty. "But, alas, the lineage will end with me."

Dusty shook her head and said, "You still have time, Fitzroy." "I *may* have."

Dusty smiled. "Are you screened regularly for pancreatic cancer?"

"Yes, an MRI every six months. I also have a genetic counselor on retainer."

"May I ask one last question, Fitzroy?"

"Certainly."

"Why did each of your trials require non-disclosure agreements for the participant *and* his or her family members?"

"My father was very concerned about corporate espionage, particularly from the Chinese. He wanted to ensure a successful test remained ours to donate, license, or sell as we saw fit."

⋈ǁ⋈ ⋈ǁ⋈ ⋈ǁ⋈

Citing her children's welfare and a lack of evidence, Cassidy Lefevre filed an expedited motion on behalf of Margaret Chase to be released ORO with Judge McLaughlin's clerk. Just after 4 PM, the clerk called her to the judge's chambers.

She arrived breathless to find an AUSA Scarpelli chatting with His Honor.

"Ms. Lefevre, thank you for coming on such short notice."

"No problem, Your Honor. We're anxious to reunite Mrs. Case with her children."

"Are they in the Child Protective Services system?"

"No, Your Honor. Mrs. Case's sister has them."

"Good. CPS serves a noble and valuable purpose, but it's not like being with a family member.

"I don't believe you've ever appeared before me. You're with the Department of

Treasury's Office of General Counsel."

"Yes, Your Honor."

"Very well. Let's hear your argument," McLaughlin glanced down at the motion,

"Cassidy."

"Thank you, Your Honor. Mrs. Case was completely surprised by her arrest and her husband's. She is the sole breadwinner of the family. The FBI has virtually *no* evidence against her husband and absolutely none to support any criminal activity on Margaret Chase's part.

"This family is in WITSEC due to Mr. Case's intimate knowledge of a *very* powerful and vicious Mexican drug cartel. This harassment of the Cases may destroy or damage a major Secret Service case involving fentanyl pouring into the nation. More importantly, it puts the family at risk of vicious reprisals if their location is discovered by those being investigated."

"Mr. Scarpelli, what are Mr. and Mrs. Case charged with?"

"Twelve counts each of conspiracy to commit murder and accessory to murder. Twelve counts each of obstruction of justice and racketeering, Your Honor."

"*Racketeering*! *That's ridiculous*!" Cassidy snapped far louder than she'd intended. "Easy, Ms. Lefevre," McLaughlin said calmly, leaving no doubt he was in charge.

Turning back to Scarpelli, he said, "And what evidence do you have against each individual?"

"We're still building a case, Judge McLaughlin."

"That's an excellent answer to a question I *didn't* ask you, Mr. Scarpelli. "What evidence do you have?"

"Video of the Cases' vehicle driving to and from the location of a search in which all the materials of additional fentanyl murder packages were found."

"Ms. Lefevre?"

"Your Honor, they have video of what appears to be a black Chevy Tahoe, similar to the Cases'. They have *no* evidence of *who* is driving it. The Tahoe was seized and processed by technicians from the Quantico lab. *No* forensic evidence was discovered in the vehicle.

"My clients were both shown six-packs of individuals with the FBI's *actual* suspect included. Neither recognized anyone.

"That's their *lack* of evidence, Your Honor."

"How long have they been in custody?"

Scarpelli answered. "Less than forty-eight hours, sir."

Cassidy looked at her watch. "Forty-six hours and change, by my count, Your Honor."

"Mr. Scarpelli, is Ms. Lefevre's description of your case accurate?"

"Your Honor has to understand . . . "

"No, Mr. Scarpelli. Let me stop you there. You are to have Mr. and Mrs. Case released immediately. Is that clear?"

"But . . ."

"Is . . . that . . . clear, Mr. Scarpelli?"

⋈||⋈ ⋈||⋈ ⋈||⋈

"Lonnie, George Jennings. I've got an update for you."

"Great!"

"The female's DNA samples recovered from the master bedroom were as recent as the search date.

"The male's DNA was deposited much earlier. Maybe four to five months.

"Now, keep in mind, these are *just* estimates. But I can safely tell you no man has occupied that bedroom for some time based on the evidence we collected there."

THIRTY-EIGHT

A black Ford sedan, parked on the roadside a mile from the estate, screamed FBI as De Burgh's limousine passed.

The passengers stepped out into the early evening light inside the gate at the front of the house.

Fitzroy motioned toward the open entryway. "Please come inside, Dusty. You can join us for dinner, if you like."

"Thank you, Fitzroy, but I need to return to my office and work on your story for tomorrow's edition."

"As you wish, Dusty. Your car is at the airport?"

"Yes."

De Burgh turned to the chauffeur still holding the back door open. "Claude, please run Ms. Rhodes back to the airport in one of the Mercedes."

"Certainly, sir."

"Please come inside. You can freshen up. It will take a few minutes for Claude to change vehicles."

⋈⫤⋈ ⋈⫤⋈ ⋈⫤⋈

An old saying about military combat operations is: "There's *always* ten percent that don't get the word." Some elements attack early, late, or the wrong target.

That applied to the early arrival of the FBI agent and crime technician assigned to collect De Burgh's and Wójcik's DNA. The Ford sedan rolled up behind the limo as De Burgh ushered Dusty and Joanna into the house.

A young black man approached Fitzroy. Reaching inside a jacket pocket, he removed his credentials.

"Mr. De Burgh, I'm Special Agent Bill Summers." He pointed toward his companion, "This is Crime Scene Technician Tony Grimaldi.

"We're here to collect your and Ms. Wójcik's DNA, blood, and hair samples, sir."

"Come with me then, gentlemen." Fitzroy turned toward the house. The two women had stopped. Joanna stood on the threshold, Dusty a couple of feet behind her.

The party of five entered the foyer as Claude moved the limousine to the garage.

The biological collection took less than twenty-five minutes. Grimaldi swabbed the inside of both subjects' cheeks using a separate swab for the right and left sides. Then, he took a vial of blood from their arms. Finally, he carefully collected several strands of Joanna's hair, ensuring each had a follicle attached.

The crime tech then took DNA samples from each staff member, including those brought in from the Cathleen Executive Cottage, for elimination purposes.

As Grimaldi packed the samples and equipment, Summers said, "Thank you both for your cooperation. It's appreciated."

Fitzroy nodded. Joanna turned and left the room, whispering something to a staff member. The woman followed the apparent lady of the house.

As the butler closed the door behind the feds, the woman returned with a bottle of water. "Ms. Wójcik thought you might be thirsty, ma'am."

"*Thank* you. I am."

"Claude is ready now, sir," the butler said.

"Thank you.

"Dusty, it was splendid meeting you. Claude will give you my card on your way to New Castle Airport. Safe travels."

"My time with you and Ms. Wójcik was pleasant and extremely helpful, Fitzroy. I hope the investigation into Airmed is completed quickly. Thank *you*."

⋈⋈ ⋈⋈ ⋈⋈

Grimaldi took De Burgh's and Wójcik's samples to a waiting aircraft. Once they were secured aboard, the small jet taxied to runway 19, received clearance and rolled down the runway.

⋈⋈ ⋈⋈ ⋈⋈

Studying Claude's deeply lined face in the rearview mirror, Dusty thought he might have voted in FDR's first presidential bid—1933.

The chauffeur had certainly *never* been a candidate to host a talk show. He answered questions but only *asked* one.

"Mr. De Burgh said you would give me his business card."

"Aye, Mizz Rhodes," he said, reaching into the backseat area with a pronounced brogue. Dusty took the card and studied it. The printed name surprised her: "Fitz De Burgh." It listed cell and FAX numbers but no address.

"I'm surprised at the first name listing, Claude. 'Fitz' suggests these cards are for acquaintances and friends, not business."

"Aye, they are, Madam. Master Fitz has precious little involvement in business now."

"*Master* Fitz, Claude? As in 'Master' of the estate?"

"That would be appropriate, Madam. However, I've been here since before Master Fitz was born."

"Rather informal, don't you think?"

"I never use that term officially, only in me private conversations with him. I believe he rather likes the term 'master.'"

"Why, Claude?"

"I think it reminds him of when Mr. Osín was a grand part of Master Fitz's life as a wee lad, Madam."

"Fitz took Mr. Osin's passing very hard, didn't he."

"Aye, Mizz Rhodes. Indeed, he did."

"And Ms. Wójcik did as well?"

"She as well, ma'am. I reckon harder."

"Are Fitz and Mizz Wójcik close?"

"That's not for me to say, ma'am. They are always *civil* in my presence."

"So, they don't travel together?"

"Occasionally, as in the trip to Grenada, ma'am. Otherwise, they keeps themselves to *themselves*."

"Living in the same house, I'd think they had frequent interactions."

"But they don't, Mizz Rhodes."

"Have frequent interactions?"

"Live in the same house, Madam. Master Fitz resides in the Executive Cathleen Cottage.

Has since Mr. Osin's passing, Lord rest his soul."

"Has the investigation taken a toll on them?"

"I don't reckon so, ma'am. They weren't here either time the constables came to the estate."

"*Either* time?"

"Yes, Mizz Rhodes. The FBI came and searched. Several days later, a local constable arrived with two investigators from a private Baltimore firm."

"What was the firm's name, Claude?"

"I don't know, ma'am. I didn't hear a name, only initials, 'LRI.' "In which car park did you leave your auto, Mizz Rhodes?"

※ ※ ※

The FBI reluctantly returned the Cases' Tahoe as part of Judge McLaughlin's release order. The couple drove back to Delaware in almost total silence, other than agreeing to tell the children they had been on a business trip to Baltimore. That story at least had a modicum of truth.

At the sister's home, they were greeted by adult questioning expressions and children's shrieks of joy! They stayed long enough to collect the kids' clothes, books, and games. On her way out the door, Margaret told her sibling, "I'll call you with the details later. *Thank you*!"

※ ※ ※

"Morgan! When did your people interview De Burgh's staff?"

"Where are you? Sounds like you're calling from inside a barrel."

"Driving back from Delaware. Don't avoid the question."

"Did somebody snatch LRI from under my nose, and I now work for you? We don't clear our activities with you." Morgan heard Dusty sigh.

"I'm sorry, Hunter. No, you don't owe any explanations. "I just spent time with Fitzroy and Joanna and . . . " "You're on a first-name basis with a billionaire and his nurse now?"

"I am. I met them at New Castle Airport and rode in his limousine to the estate. The FBI met them there and took blood and DNA samples and some of Joanna's hair."

"Wow! That's quite the scoop!"

"It gets better. Fitz offered to let me see Airmed's drug trial data associated with the murders. That's why I'm calling you.

"I don't have the skill, time, or patience to go through reams of data. But you do. How about we team up on this?"

Morgan didn't answer immediately, trying to hide his excitement at the prospect of assisting Diaz's defense.

"Yeah. We might be interested in that, Dusty."

"In teaming up or going through the data?"

"Both."

"*Great*! He was charming and . . . *open*. He seemed to choke up a little at the mention of his father.

"Do you know he doesn't live in the main house?"

"I did. *Fitz* moved into the Executive Cottage after a lengthy sabbatical."

"Smart ass," Dusty chuckled. "Yes, at the Brandywine Hospital for Behavioral Health in Wilmington."

"What?"

"Yes. I knew that before I met *Fitz*. Ophelia dug up that little gem."

"Well, as long as we're playing '*Did you know*?' Was there any mention of the elder De Burgh impregnating Nurse Wójcik? Or her bereavement funeral leave to New Jersey to have the pregnancy terminated?"

"*Christ*! No! How did he do *that*?"

"I imagine the usual way unless a turkey baster was involved."

"No, moron! I mean, at his *age*!"

"DuPont's old slogan." "Ah, *Vitamin V*!"

"Exactly.

"So, back to business, Hunter. LRI's staff will have to review Airmed's trial docs in

Delaware. Fitz won't allow the data to be moved."

"You know the FBI would like a crack at them, too," Morgan responded.

"I'm sure they would. Fitz said law enforcement can also examine the data with the exact location restriction.

"When I call him about your review, I'll ask if he will allow the feds' review." "Good. If Fitz agrees, please let Joe D'Elia pass the okay onto his Bureau contact."

"No can do. SAIC Maddison Mitchell has been passing me information. I need to prime that pump. But, I'll figure out how to let her know D'Elia assisted in getting Fitz's agreement."

⋈ ⋈ ⋈

Dusty's call to Fitzroy was quick and to the point. He agreed to LRI's review and the reporter's proposed communication of the same opportunity to Madison Mitchell.

THIRTY-NINE

At 1100 HRS the following morning, Attorney Jefferson Bender initiated a Zoom call with Fitzroy to discuss two issues: Fernando Diaz's case and likely individual or class action wrongful death lawsuits the Airmed Trust would likely face.

After the usual pleasantries, Fitzroy asked, "How is Fernando bearing up?"

"As well as could be expected, I think. Mr. Diaz swears he did not know of the criminal activities in the basement. I believe him.

"He asked me to tell you how grateful he is for your generous support."

"Jefferson, why did he need to take money from a stranger? He could have come to me."

"I asked him that. You gave him a job at his original salary when Airmed's business ended. Fernando couldn't ask you again after you had already been so generous."

"Why did he need more than we were paying him?"

"He's desperate to get five other family members out of Cuba. Grafting administrators demand greenbacks. They exchange them on the country's black market for many times the legal Cuban pesos rate of one CUP for one USD. I saw a report not long ago that one dollar bought 239 CUPs.

"At that rate, five thousand a month would convert to just under one-point-two million

CUPs. That could buy a lot of freedom."

"Please tell Fernando that when this is over, and he's released, we'll bring his family here."

"He'll be thrilled, Fitzroy."

"Now, what about the potential for wrongful death class action?"

"A class action suit can be brought for wrongful death. However, since the murders have been committed in multiple states, it's more likely individual suits will be filed in the victim's jurisdiction. Wrongful death claims involve complex issues that can vary in each state. So, you can imagine the complexity of bundling twelve families into a single action."

"I see."

"I have thought of how to proactively approach this exposure."

⋈ ⋈ ⋈

"I have a Ms. Rhodes on the phone for you, Special Agent Mitchell."

"Put her through."

The desk phone barely started ringing when she snatched the handset from the cradle.

"Special Agent Mitchell."

"Dusty Rhodes. I have a bit of news for you."

"Yes?"

"Joe D'Elia and I just had a conversation with Fitzroy De Burgh. Mr. De Burgh has agreed to allow the FBI to review Airmed's unredacted data trial materials. The only restriction is that all data inspections must be done at his chosen location. No data may be removed from the facility. You can take certified *copies* of any information germane to your investigations.

"If these terms are satisfactory, give me the name, number, and email address of the Bureau staff member who will coordinate this activity."

"They are acceptable, Ms. Rhodes. Thank you. Special Agent Lonnie Jerry will be our primary contact. I appreciate your assistance."

After providing Jerry's phone and email information, the call ended.

⋈ ⋈ ⋈

"I believe," Jefferson Bender said, "that a preemptive approach would be in your best interest."

"Go on," De Burgh replied.

"If you approached each family with a direct cash offer, it could minimize your exposure and simultaneously provide more compensation to each family.

"Let's say you offered one million dollars per family if they agreed not to sue. Assuming an attorney will take at least a third of a settlement in fees, with a direct payment, the family would receive an additional third of a million dollars more than going through a lawyer."

"Could we do so without admitting fault and requiring a non-disclosure agreement preventing the release of any settlement details?"

"You could set any restrictions. I'd advise against anything more than an NDA, however."

"Do you have the names of the murdered participants' family members?"

"Yes, they're listed in the charging document."

"If you approach the next of kin, would that harm Fernando's case?"

⋈ ⋈ ⋈

"I can't believe I'm going to say this, Lonnie, but I'm starting to respect D'Elia."

"I know. Every time I think he's confirmed my opinion of his being a *total* asshole, something like this makes me want to change my mind.

"Maybe . . ."

Maddison Mitchell's desk phone rang. She stabbed the speaker button. "Yes?" "The Lab's Doctor Jennings is on line two, Special Agent." "Thanks.

"Dr. J., I hope you have good news for us."

"Well . . . I have *news*. You decide if it's good or not."

"Shoot."

"Okay. First, the blood in the Bentley's trunk is the male parent of Fitzroy De Burgh." Maddison looked at Jerry, eyebrows raised. "Go on."

"The hair in the trunk belongs to Joanna Wójcik. So does the female genetic material recovered in the main house master bedroom. The male material there matches the blood in the trunk.

"Fitzroy De Burgh's DNA was not recovered in the main house. He is living in the cottage, based on the samples taken there.

"Staff members' DNA appeared randomly throughout the main house and cottage. None were a match to any crime scene evidence.

"But maybe this is the *good* news you're looking for, Maddison. Ms. Wójcik *is* a match for the eyelash recovered from the fourth Maryland crime scene."

⋈⫤⋈ ⋈⫤⋈ ⋈⫤⋈

Most defunct Airmed Pharmaceuticals office space in New Castle's Stanton Industrial Park had been sold or subleased during bankruptcy, except for the single-story data center. Five additional glowing monitors allowed the review of drug trial data in two separate rooms—two for LRI investigators and three for the feds. To scrub the enormous amount of information, LRI ran two eight-hour shifts. The Bureau's forensic team ran three. LRI's data review ended twelve hours before the FBI's.

"Nothing in the Airmed data is incriminating, Hunter," D'Elia said from Morgan's open office door. "Our people didn't find a single connection between the trials and any murder victim."

⋈⫤⋈ ⋈⫤⋈ ⋈⫤⋈

A similar conversation took place at the Bureau's Baltimore Field Office.

FORTY

Senior Associate Sharon Atkins sat across a coffee table from Kim McGuire. The attractive brunette had accepted Mrs. McGuire's offer of a cup of coffee. After a sip, she set her beautiful China cup on a coaster.

"So, how can I help you, Ms. Atkins?"

"Ma'am, I'm here to *hopefully* help *you*."

"Oh?"

"As I said, I'm with Gibson, Bender & Shapiro, the law firm representing Airmed Pharmaceuticals. Your husband's participation in one of the firm's drug trials seems to be *associated* with Roger's death."

"*Murder*," Kim said softly.

"Yes, my apologies, murder.

"Airmed's former CEO, Mr. Fitzroy De Burgh, authorized the FBI to search the companies' drug trial data for any connection between Airmed and any of the victims.

"Three FBI forensic data investigation teams worked around the clock for several days and could not make any connection between Airmed and the murder victims.

"Two independent teams from Last Resort Investigations ran a parallel investigation of the data. They could not find any connections either."

"So, why are you here?"

"As you probably know, Mrs. McGuire, hundreds of thousands of frivolous lawsuits are filed yearly. A farmer in Wisconsin puts a ladder—clearly labeled with numerous warnings—on frozen manure in March. As the temperature rises, the manure thaws. The ladder shifts, the farmer falls, breaking his arm. He sues the ladder manufacturer because no warning explicitly states, '*use on frozen manure is unsafe.*' The jury awards him seven hundred thousand dollars. On appeal, the award is reduced to two hundred thousand dollars, of which his attorney takes one-third. The farmer nets sixty-six thousand six hundred dollars for his stupidity.

"The ladder company legal fees are four hundred thousand dollars. Still less than the original seven hundred thousand dollars judgment, but a heavy cost for the lack of a 'frozen manure' warning."

"That's an interesting story, Ms. Atkins, but I'm not planning on suing Airmed."

"We're glad to hear that, ma'am. However, you lost your only child because of your husband's name being associated with Airmed. Mr. De Burgh would like to compensate you, in some small way, for the loss of your loved ones."

"Oh? How so?"

"The Airmed Trust will make a ten-million-dollar payment to you. If there are any federal, state, or local taxes, the amount will be increased so that you get the full amount."

"I don't need his money, Ms. Atkins. Roger and Ginger were well insured. I have more than enough to last me."

"Do you have nieces and nephews?"

"Yes, several of each."

"Do they need college tuition, have student loans, growing families needing more space? Ten million could buy a lot of good things for them. Or, start a memorial fund for broadcasting or communication majors in Ginger's name. At least think about the offer.

Please, don't reject it out of hand."

Kim McGuire looked down at her own coffee cup. Tear streaks glistened on her cheeks when she raised her head.

⋈||⋈ ⋈||⋈ ⋈||⋈

"Lonnie, get an arrest warrant for Joanna Wójcik. And set up another six-pack with her picture included to show Gary and Margaret Case.

"And notify his *bitch* of an attorney to get their asses in here by 9 AM tomorrow morning."

⋈||⋈ ⋈||⋈ ⋈||⋈

Driving back to D.C., Sharon Atkins' cell phone rang. She pushed the hands-free button on her Subaru Outback dash monitor. "Hello."

"Ms. Atkins, it's Kim McGuire."

"Yes, ma'am. How can I help you?"

"I've decided to accept Mr. De Burgh's offer."

"Very good. I'm still on my way to the office. I'll overnight a nondisclosure agreement when I arrive."

"Nondisclosure? I already signed one when Roger started the trial."

"Yes. This one is different. It precludes you from sharing the details of the financial settlement. Also, by signing it, in exchange for the payment, you agree not to initiate any further legal action for damages against Mr. De Burgh or any Airmed assets."

"All right."

"Oh, Mrs. McGuire, you must sign and have it notarized. I'll include the instructions in the package and a label to cover the FedEx return."

"Thank you, Ms. Atkins."

⋈||⋈ ⋈||⋈ ⋈||⋈

Kim McGuire put the wireless phone in its cradle. Opening a desk drawer, she removed a box containing business cards. As Kim added Sharon Atkins' to her collection, Bill Wilson's caught her eye. Taking it out, she dialed his number.

Wilson answered on the second ring.

"Detective, this is Kim McGuire. Have I interrupted anything?"

"Not at all, ma'am. What can I do for you?"

Kim recounted her conversations with Sharon Atkins. Then asked, "Are you familiar with this Last Resort outfit?"

"I am. I've been working with LRI on parallel investigations into the murders at the local levels. If they scrubbed the data and found nothing, you can be sure Airmed is not involved.

"And LRI's forensics lab, which is FBI certified, discovered critical evidence that may lead to arrests. They frequently assist the Bureau on cases."

"Can I get you to look at this agreement Ms. Atkins is sending me?"

"I'd be happy to. Just remember, I'm not a lawyer."

FORTY-ONE

The following morning, four FBI agents took Joanna Wójcik into custody and left the estate before Fitzroy De Burgh knew of their arrival.

⋈‖⋈ ⋈‖⋈ ⋈‖⋈

Jefferson Bender waited impatiently at the FBI Baltimore Field Office when the agents and prisoner arrived from BWI.

In an interrogation room, their backs to the observation window, the attorney said,

"Joanna, did you say anything to the agents?"

"*Ani szelestu.*"

"Sorry, my Polish is a bit rusty."

"In English, 'complete silence.'"

"Excellent. Did they read your Miranda rights?"

"Yes, right after they arrested me on twelve counts of murder in the first degree."

"According to the charging document, they found your DNA in fentanyl powder deposited on a female victim in Maryland."

"Mr. Bender, the only time I *ever* used that drug was to ease Osin's pain. I *injected* him with fentanyl citrate that came out of a *vial*.

⋈‖⋈ ⋈‖⋈ ⋈‖⋈

Cassidy Lefevre threatened to file a harassment complaint on the Case's behalf. If the Bureau wanted them to review more photos, they could . . . "Fucking well bring the sixpack to Delaware."

The response did nothing to raise Maddison Mitchell's opinion of Lefevre, but it did get the six-pack on its way.

⋈‖⋈ ⋈‖⋈ ⋈‖⋈

Wilson called Morgan and shared the discussion with Kim McGuire.

"That's one *generous hombre, amigo*," Morgan noted.

"He is *that*," Wilson agreed. "That comes out to a hundred and twenty million, if every family agrees."

"I doubt they'll all sign up. Ambulance chasers will latch onto a few, promising them a hundred million. With a strong defense showing no liability, some may end up with nothing."

"Could be.

"So, the data scrub showed nothing connecting the company, Hunter?"

"*Nada*, except all the victims' parents were in Airmed's *last* trial.

"Joe has a wild notion that someone is killing off the kids of patients so they can't pass on the pancreatic susceptibility. He believes that's why all the victims are childless. The earlier trials would have allowed more time for people to have offspring."

"That would take a *lot* of coordination and money."

"And *access* to the trial database. According to De Burgh, only he and the admin have it."

Jeannie Staron stuck her head in the door. "Mr. De Burgh is on the phone for you." Morgan nodded.

"I have to run, Bill, De Burgh is calling." "Let's talk later."

"Copy that, Bill.

Morgan pushed a button next to a blinking red light. "Mr. De Burgh, good morning."

"No, it is not, Mr. Morgan. The FBI has arrested Ms. Wójcik on multiple counts of murder and taken her to Baltimore. Jefferson Bender is there with her now. I'd like you to extend your involvement to include Joanna's defense."

"Certainly."

⋈⋈ ⋈⋈ ⋈⋈

"Ms. Wójcik, we believe we have an air-tight case against you," Maddison Mitchell said, smiling at the nurse.

Jefferson Bender responded. "Then please share it with me."

"As you wish, Counselor.

"First, Ms. Wójcik's hair in the back of her Bentley. Second, an envelope exactly like those used in twelve murders. Third, the eyelash recovered from the body of a victim. Its DNA is a match to her sample."

Bender snorted. "Okay, let's see. The Bentley is titled in the name of an Airmed subsidiary, not Ms. Wójcik. There is no way to tie the hair in the trunk to anything else there. Finally, the eyelash DNA you're so pleased about is circumstantial. My client could have known the person before death. If those things are the sum total of your case, it's weak at best.

"And, by the way. Ms. Wójcik doesn't have access to the Airmed trial database. So, how did she select the victims?"

"How would you know *that*?" Mitchell snapped. "Because Fitzroy retained LRI to assist in Diaz's and her cases. That's why they scrubbed the data parallel to your forensic snoops."

The whiff of surprise on the agent's faces caused Bender to smile.

"We'll see what the judge says at her arraignment," Lonnie Jerry said, like a kid taking his ball home. "*Don't* expect to walk her out of court *this* time."

"We *will* when the judge reviews *these*," Bender said, sliding two sheets of paper toward the feds.

⋈⋈ ⋈⋈ ⋈⋈

Neither Gary nor Margaret Case identified anyone in the latest FBI six-pack.

⋈⋈ ⋈⋈ ⋈⋈

"Ms. Rhodes, Fitz. I need your help with something."

"Oh!" The call surprised her. "What's that?"

"The FBI arrested Ms. Wójcik earlier today for the fentanyl murders."

"*What*? Why would they suspect *Joanna*?"

"I don't know. My attorney, Jefferson Bender, is with her now in Baltimore. I'm sure he'll call me soon with more information."

"How can I help, Fitz?"

De Burgh described his conversation with Secretary Winkin.

"Joanna's arrest is a violation."

"Why did you ask the Secretary of State for assurance, not the AG?"

"It *is* from the AG! Winken came to me, a friend of Desmond Keith, Grenada's PM, asking us to return to give DNA samples '*for elimination purposes only.*' I insisted that my friend, the AG, send documents to Joanna and myself, over his signature, stating we could return to Grenada at will."

"President Harry Truman famously said, 'If you want a friend in Washington, *get a dog.*'"

"Yes, your AG's word is worthless."

"Have you called *him*?"

"Suddenly, neither Winkin nor Merrick are returning my calls."

"Would you like me to share this with my readers, Fitz?"

"Yes."

"Okay, FAX or email me copies of the AG's agreements." "Yes, right away.

"I've also asked Mr. Morgan to assist Jefferson in representing Joanna. Please coordinate with LRI to see if there are additional details for her story."

⋈⋈ ⋈⋈ ⋈⋈

"Did you know the AG promised Fitzroy and Joanna get-out-of-jail-free cards if they returned to provide their DNA?"

Morgan laughed. "*Oh, no.* Merrick *welched* on a deal. *Quelle surprise!*"

"Yes, and get this, he and Fitz are supposedly old friends. The AG put in the fix to get the judge to ROR Diaz."

"I guess Joanna was a bridge too far," Morgan responded. "That says the feds didn't have anything concrete on Diaz, but think they do on Wójcik.

"Did Fitz tell you about his pay-off scheme?" Morgan asked.

"No . . ."

"One of Bender's associates offered Kim McGuire ten mil not to sue."

"That's not illegal, is it, Hunter?"

"Nope. It's a generous offer. Suppose there's no connection between Airmed and the murders. It'd undoubtedly be less expensive than twelve lawsuits, just in legal fees."

"What are the terms?" Dusty asked.

"Just to hold Airmed blameless and not disclose the amount as far as I know. Mrs. McGuire will show the document to the detective who caught her daughter's case before

she signs it. He'll update me after seeing it."

FORTY-TWO

Waiting outside the AG's office, Director Luke Courtemanche studied the signature carefully . . . and in disbelief.

"He's off the phone now, Director," the executive assistant said.

Courtemanche nodded, stood, knocked, and then opened the door.

It had just shut completely when the EA heard muffled shouting. Several seconds later, a crash and yelling.

She dialed security.

⋈||⋈ ⋈||⋈ ⋈||⋈

"Fitz, Hunter Morgan tells me you're making offers to the families of the murder victims."

A short pause preceded De Burgh's response. "I am, Dusty, and I'd appreciate it if you did not print anything."

"I won't unless and until you say it's okay. But won't your actions imply guilt?"

"I hope the offer shows compassion for the victims' families. Airmed is out of business, but that doesn't mean I'll allow its good name to be sullied."

⋈||⋈ ⋈||⋈ ⋈||⋈

An anonymous FBI leak of Joanna Wójcik's arrest led the D.C. network affiliates' 4 PM news programs. In contrast, the Baltimore affiliates carried Dusty Rhodes' *Mirror* Evening Edition story of the AG's broken promise to her. All three networks reported both stories at 6:30 PM EDT.

At 6:41 PM, POTUS called the AG for an explanation. Merrick took the call amidst others restoring his trashed office.

⋈||⋈ ⋈||⋈ ⋈||⋈

Across town, at the J. Edgar Hoover FBI Headquarters, internal Bureau security personnel escorted and assisted Luke Courtemanche in packing his office. Minutes before 7 PM, his cell rang.

"Hello."

"Director, please hold for POTUS."

"Hello, Luke."

"Hello, Mr. President."

"Have you cleaned out your office yet? I understand you require another job." Courtemanche thought that an odd thing to say. "It will be in the next few minutes, and it seems I do."

"Good. When you are packed up, take your things to the AG's office."

"Sir?"

"I want you to be my Acting AG."

"*SIR?*"

"I've been waiting for a reason to fire Merrick ever since being blackmailed into nominating the *asshole*. That *exposure* doesn't exist any longer.

"What do you say, son? You up for it?"

⋈‖⋈ ⋈‖⋈ ⋈‖⋈

Maddison Mitchell and Lonnie Jerry stepped off the elevator onto the Hoover

Building's seventh floor. The Director stood facing them, holding a large cardboard box. Two internal security members carried two more behind him. Maddison's eyes widened. "*Director*? What's going on?"

"I'm changing offices."

"To . . ."

"The DOJ."

"You didn't get fired, did you?" Jerry asked.

"Yes and *no*."

⋈‖⋈ ⋈‖⋈ ⋈‖⋈

Julie Stephens rang Morgan. "Are you sitting down?"

"As much as possible these days. Why?"

"There's a rumor that the AG just got the ax."

"*Really*. How do you know?"

"One of the feds called my LT and said the FBI Director is now the Acting AG."

"I may know why," Morgan responded, then shared the De Burgh and Wójcik documents the AG authored.

Julie laughed. "I'll bet that *would* get Merrick's dick fed onto a *wringer*!"

⋈‖⋈ ⋈‖⋈ ⋈‖⋈

An executive's firing is typically camouflaged with some vague excuse: "for health reasons," "to spend more time with family," or "to pursue other opportunities.

" POTUS didn't sugarcoat the AG's departure, stating bluntly. "I lost my confidence in him."

⋈‖⋈ ⋈‖⋈ ⋈‖⋈

The bail prediction Lonnie Jerry made regarding Joanna Wójcik became fact. De Burgh had no leverage with Merrick out of the picture as AG. Remanded, the nurse met with

Bender, various associates, and investigators in Baltimore's Federal Bureau of Prisons' Chesapeake Detention Facility.

Joanna refused to waive her right to a speedy trial at Bender's suggestion.

Gibson, Bender & Shapiro, and LRI investigators scrambled to find evidence supporting the defendant's innocence. But, proving a negative is impossible. The DOJ, on the other hand, had DNA evidence connecting her to at least one murder and inferring involvement in eleven others.

⋈||⋈ ⋈||⋈ ⋈||⋈

"You know, Mark, there's a missing link."

"In the evolution of man, or something else?" Proffitt replied, smiling. "*Hilarious*, smart ass.

"Only two people have access to the Airmed data." Proffitt nodded. "Yup."

"Can't be. *Three* people have access if De Burgh or Phillip Forge, the DBA administrator, *aren't* the killers. Have we checked out Forge?" "Yes. We found nothing to suggest his involvement."

"We need to take another look. Would searches of the database leave a date, time trail somewhere?" "They would."

Joe punched a number into his cell phone.

Seconds later, he said, "Mr. De Burgh, I'm Joe D'Elia. I'm working on Mr. Diaz and

Ms. Wójcik's cases."

"Yes. I specifically asked Mr. Morgan to assign you."

"I appreciate that.

"If we could make two more requests?"

"What do you need?"

"How long is your security video retained?"

"Eighteen months."

"Does that include the data center?"

"It does, yes."

"How about inside the staff's quarters?"

"Those as well. My father's obsession with security put virtually every inch of the estate under surveillance."

"Would you please ask your security chief to give us access to all your video surveillance data for the last six months?"

"Certainly. I'll call him now. What else do you need?"

"One last review of Airmed's trial database. *Without* your database admin's supervision."

⋈||⋈ ⋈||⋈ ⋈||⋈

Morgan answered a call from Jefferson Bender.

"Have your people come up with anything to support Ms. Wójcik's innocence?"

"Not yet, Counselor, but we're looking into every nook and cranny we can think of."

⋈❙⋈ ⋈❙⋈ ⋈❙⋈

After 1800, HRS, Proffitt, and D'Elia signed into Airmed's security system. They first searched internal data center videos starting six months before Ginger McGuire's murder.

With Airmed no longer in business, the data center's motion-activated cameras recorded nothing except occasional system maintenance and data migration. However, forty-one days before Ginger McGuire's murder, at 2341 HRS, a person entered the building, sat at a console for nearly an hour, then left. No camera angle recorded a clear image of their face.

External cameras on the property showed their arrival and departure, but poor overhead lighting prevented a clear view of the individual.

Next, Proffitt logged into the principal database administrator's ID. Mark's career began in forensic computer analytics. As he moved up the ranks and into management, the field remained a passion.

As far as Joe was concerned, the information flying by on the monitor could have been a description of the people of northern Japan written in Ainu.

Proffitt sat back and shook his head. "There *were* queries of interest erased by the primary database administrator, Joe. But *not* in our timeframe."

"What?"

"The erased queries were related to federal tax issues. Nothing about Ginger McGuire's death."

"Nothing just before she died?"

"None before *any* victim died. And, one more thing. There aren't two IDs, either. Only one *shared* between God only knows how many users."

"Can you tell who logged on?"

"No."

"What do we do then?"

"We take screenshots of all the activities to illustrate the searches, the timeframes, and the attempt to cover the tracks. Then, I'll download them to the USB thumb drive I brought.

Proffitt retraced the forensic path he'd taken initially, capturing a picture of each screen to tell the story of how the murder victims' names were collected. Finally, he plugged his thumb drive into the console.

"*Shit*!"

"What's wrong?'

"The system security is set up to prevent anyone entering malware via an external source."

D'Elia shook his head. "Now, what does that mean in *English*?"

"It means I can't copy them to this drive."

"Okay, how do we get them?"

"I'll create a subfolder in an obscure location and hide the screenshots until we can export them to LRI's system.

⋈||⋈ ⋈||⋈ ⋈||⋈

D'Elia called Fitzroy again. "Sir, can we have a list of the estate staff?
"I'd like their height, weight, and a headshot, please. It needs to include Ms. Wójcik."

Compared to their earlier searches of the usually empty data center, the estate's motion activated cameras captured a veritable mountain of video. Improved interior lighting made nearly every face identifiable.

Some live-in staff relationships quickly became apparent. A non-estate staff member made frequent visits to Marta Niemczyk's room. The staff sheet listed her as a "resident nurse," compared to Joanna Wójcik's title of "senior nurse."

"Hey, Joe! That's *Forge*!"

"You're *right*!"

D'Elia scratched his chin. "Niemczyk. Why is that name familiar?"

"Sounds Polish to me," Proffitt said.

"Yeah."

D'Elia said, "Mark, let's look for her before and after the unknown person's data center arrival and departure.

"Meanwhile, I need to call Lonnie."

FORTY-THREE

"Lonnie, Joe. Does the name Niemczyk ring a bell with you?"

"Not off the bat. Why?"

"I *know* it from somewhere but can't place it."

"Is your question related to Wójcik's defense?"

"Not that I know of. The name's just in the back of my brain somewhere."

"You sure you're not pumping me to help Wójcik?"

"Lonnie, I've *never* lied to you."

"No, but you've crowded the *batter's* box."

"Not this time, Lonnie."

"Okay. Since you've caught me in a good mood, I'll run a search."

"Yeah, I hear the DOJ is *under new management*. The former Director is acting AG.

Who's taking his spot? Maddison?"

"I *wish*. No, Luke's principal deputy for the time being."

◁▷ ◁▷ ◁▷

"Hunter, does the name Niemczyk mean anything to you?"

"She's a member of the De Burgh staff, Joe. Why?"

"Ms. Niemczyk was Osin's nurse before Joanna showed up. Looks like she's got something going with Forge, the PDBA. You might want to give Bender a call and pass that on."

"Okay."

"But my question is, had you heard the name Niemczyk in the past?"

◁▷ ◁▷ ◁▷

"Joe, Lonnie. Ryszard Niemczyk was a former deputy mayor of *Pruszkow*, Poland, accused of corruption and organized crime involvement with solid ties to the *Pruszkow* Mafia."

"*That's it*! We rounded up some *Pruszkow* people in Boston. Loan sharking, prostitution, human trafficking, and extortion.

"Do you know anything about his family?"

"No, Joe. And good luck finding any outside of Poland. You know how the EU countries lock their people's data down."

"Jefferson, Morgan here. Airmed's DBA, Phillip Forge, appears to be involved with

Marta Niemczyk, old man Osin's original nurse. It might be worth having a chat with him."

"My people are swamped, Hunter. Can one of your folks cover him?"

"Sure. I'll ask D'Elia to sweat Forge."

⋈ ⋈ ⋈

"Mr. De Burgh, I'm sorry to bother you again."

"If it helps Joanna's case, never hesitate to do so, Joe."

"While we're at it, please feel free to call me Fitz."

"Thank you. Do you know anything about Marta Niemczyk's family?"

"No. As I recall, Marta came highly recommended and attended to my father. Why?"

"We're just trying to eliminate her from our investigation."

"Is she a suspect?"

"No, sir, er . . . *Fitz*. It's just routine.

"Do you have any contacts in the State Department?"

"None that are returning my calls. What do you need from State?"

"Her birth records. That's not a trivial task in Europe."

"Europe?"

"Yes, *Pruszkow*, Poland."

"Oh. I may have a way. Give me the particulars of what you need."

⋈ ⋈ ⋈

"Joe, I called Bender. Sounds like they're balls to the wall. Can you interview Forge?"

"Roger that."

⋈ ⋈ ⋈

"Good afternoon, Desmond. How are you and Natalie?"

"Very well, Fitz. Although it seems that's not the case in Delaware."

"No. Joanna is under arrest in connection with the fentanyl murders."
"I'm sorry to hear that. Didn't you have documents that . . . " "Yes, and worthless in Joanna's case.

"That's why I'm calling. I need a favor."

"Name it."

⋈ ⋈ ⋈

D'Elia positioned a table at the estate facing a window admitting bright sunlight. Joe and Proffitt sat with their backs to it. Facing the window, Phillip Forge could not clearly see either man's face clearly.

"So, Phil. How long have you and Ms. Niemczyk been an item?" "We're *not* an item."

"Mark, don't you hate it when a subject lies to you right off the bat?"

"Yeah, it instantly destroys credibility." "I'm not *lying*."

"Phil, a gnat couldn't break wind in the mansion in private. Mr. Osín saw to that. I doubt the White House has as many security cameras. Would you like us to show you the baker's dozen videos of you entering and exiting Marta Niemczyk's room?" "I want a lawyer," Forge almost whispered.

"Do you need one, Phil?" D'Elia asked. "We're not the police."

"You said you were FBI."

"*Retired* FBI, Phil. I have no legal authority over you. So, what are you afraid of?" Forge didn't respond.

"Mark, show Phil the video."

Proffitt opened a video file on his phone and began playing it. Then turned the iPhone so Forge could watch. A date/time stamp ran in the upper left corner. The video ran for nearly a minute before Mark stopped it."

"Is that you, Phil?" D'Elia asked.

"Yes."

"Why were you working in the middle of the night?" "Running an off-site backup."

"Why?" D'Elia asked.

Proffitt answered. "If all your data is on-site and the building burns down, you are, as we say in IT business, 'fucked.'"

"*That's* why." Forge agreed.

"Why at midnight?"

"There's less traffic on the web then. The backup runs faster."

"Mark, tell Phil what we discovered in his database."

"Sure. So, you or someone masquerading *as* you ran queries in the most recent trial DB. Then tried to erase their digital footprints. We know these queries preceded the fentanyl bomb arrivals. Do you still want to play dumb and be charged with accessory to a dozen murders? Or, answer our questions?"

⋈||⋈ ⋈||⋈ ⋈||⋈

"Jefferson, D'Elia interviewed Phil Forge. He's involved with Marta Niemczyk, another De Burgh nurse. He claims she never got his ID and password for the Airmed database and couldn't have run queries to get victims' names. I think the last part is probably true. How many nurses do you know who can run sophisticated database searches? But, we ought to polygraph him. We'll run it. Just get us a court order."

"Thanks, Hunter. I'll share this with Ms. Mitchell.

"Will Forge run back and share his discussion with Niemczyk?"

"I doubt it. Joe advised him not to discuss the interview with her unless he wanted to add a dozen conspiracy counts to his charge sheet. And he reminded Forge that Virginia has the death penalty and *isn't* afraid to use it."

⋈||⋈ ⋈||⋈ ⋈||⋈

Phillip Forge's "*little*" head often controlled his actions more than the big one supporting his Florida State University baseball cap.

"What did you find, Joe?" Fitzroy asked.

"Some very interesting information. But, and no offense intended, I'd rather not share it with you now." "*Oh?*"

"That will give you what politicians love to call *plausible deniability* if you're on a witness stand.'"

"*Oh!*"

⋈||⋈ ⋈||⋈ ⋈||⋈

Staring at her desk phone speaker, Maddison Mitchell leaned back in her office chair and smiled. "Ah! The old 'third-party perpetrator evidence dodge.' I'd expect a legal thoroughbred like you to come up with something *much* more creative, Counselor." Lonnie Jerry grinned at her response to Bender's statement.

"Special Agent Mitchell, I'm just trying to keep you abreast of developments in the case. You need to look at Phillip Forge."

"*Oh*, you're *so* anxious to help us. *That's* even funnier. I won't tie up resources by plunging into a rabbit hole. We have plenty of evidence to secure Joanna Wójcik's conviction without assistance."

⋈||⋈ ⋈||⋈ ⋈||⋈

"Fitz, it's Desmond Keith. How are you bearing up?"

"As well as possible, thank you."

"Good. I won't keep you long. I just rang to tell you I have a connection with Mateusz

Morawieck." "The Polish PM?"

"The very same. I helped avoid a disastrous mix-up with Mateusz's hotel reservations last winter after he and his wife arrived on holiday. I'll let you know as soon as I hear anything."

⋈||⋈ ⋈||⋈ ⋈||⋈

Jefferson Bender filed a motion in federal court for a polygraph examination of Phillip

Forge. Judge McLaughlin heard Bender's argument for and the government's objections to the request in chambers before granting it.

FORTY-FOUR

"Is your name Phillip Adam Forge?" LRI's polygraphist asked.
"Yes."
"Are you sitting down?"
"Yes."
"Is today Tuesday?"
"Yes."
"Are you now or have you ever been in a romantic relationship with Marta Niemczyk?"
"Yes."
"Did you allow Marta Niemczyk to use your credentials to access the Airmed Pharmaceutical fentanyl trial database?"
"No."
"Did you access the Airmed Pharmaceutical fentanyl trial database on Marta Niemczyk's behalf?"
"No."
"Did you access the Airmed Pharmaceutical fentanyl trial database to search for crime victims' names?"
"No."
"Have you ever used the Airmed Pharmaceutical fentanyl trial database to find information about individuals without proper authorization?"
"No."
"Did you intend to use the information found in the Airmed Pharmaceutical fentanyl trial database to identify potential crime victims?"
"No."
"Have you shared any data from the Airmed Pharmaceutical fentanyl trial database with anyone else?"
"No."
"Have you ever lied to get out of trouble?"
"Yes."
"Was the lie you told serious in nature?"
"No."
"Have you ever stolen something in your life?"

"Yes."
"Was the theft you committed of significant value?"
"No."
"Were you ever caught or punished for the theft you admitted to?"
"No."
"Were the items you stole for personal use or benefit?"
"Yes."
"Has the theft you admitted to any connection with the current investigation?"
"No."
"Are you afraid that the polygraph test will accuse you wrongly?"
"Yes."
"Are you nervous about taking this test even though you are telling the truth?"
"Yes."
"That's the end of the test, Mr. Forge. I'll need a few minutes to score your responses. Please wait in the hall. I'll let you know when I'm finished."

⋈||⋈ ⋈||⋈ ⋈||⋈

"Prime Minister Morawieck, how are you, sir?"
"As well as one can be in the EU these hectic days. And you and your beautiful island?" "Very well, indeed.

"I appreciate your returning my call. I have a dear friend who is falsely accused of horrendous crimes in America. I know there are restrictions on the release of personal data in Poland. However, I'm wondering if a member of your staff can find the birth record of one 'Marta Niemczyk,' probably born between nineteen-eighty-seven and ninety-seven. Possibly in or around the city of *Pruszkow*."

⋈||⋈ ⋈||⋈ ⋈||⋈

"Phillip Forge passed with flying colors," the polygraphist told D'Elia via phone." "*Really?*"
"Yeah, not a single deceptive response."
"Did you ask about the Niemczyk relationship?"
"I did. Forge admitted to it. Maybe you should poly Niemczyk."
"A judge wouldn't grant it. No PC."

⋈||⋈ ⋈||⋈ ⋈||⋈

Fortunately for Gibson, Bender, and Shapiro, all the fentanyl murders occurred in states participating in the Uniform Bar Examination program. The UBE allows an attorney licensed in one state to practice in the others, with some limitations. Thus, Sharon Atkins could be the attorney presenting all the Airmed settlement offers.

The Judge brothers' widows and Professor Mendelson's parents agreed to accept the offer. Six other next-of-kin had taken it under advisement of their respective council. Two families had not responded to her calls. One victim seemed to have *no* surviving family.

※※※ ※※※ ※※※

"Prime Minister Keith, I'm Minister Morawieck's Executive Assistant. I've just emailed information to *your* EA. Please let me know if you require anything else."

※※※ ※※※ ※※※

"*Rigena Marta* Niemczyk is the daughter of *Ryszard* Niemczyk, the *Pruszkow* Mafia Don. She has a brother in New Jersey who runs a travel company. One of *Pruszkow*'s many enterprises is *human trafficking*. And get this: Brother *Czesław* is a graduate of Politechnika Warszawska, their version of MIT."

"How do you know all this, Joe? Isn't getting gold out of *Fort Knox* easier than an EU citizen's personal information?"

"It's on his H-1B Visa application. He's supposedly here working in the IT department of a Polish *sausage* company outside Philadelphia."

"A *sausage* company rates an H-1B visa candidate, Joe?"

"They claim their entire IT staff speaks *only* Polish."

"Okay, Joe. So, we know she's involved with Forge. He has access to the Airmed DB and passed his poly. The victims' names all came out of that data. Is that enough PC to get a warrant for Marta's email and phone records?"

"It better be, Hunter, 'cause it's all we've got."

"Does our assisting Joanna's counsel give us standing with the court?"

"No. The court won't allow an attorney to file those types of motions. It has to be a law enforcement agency." "Like the Wilmington, PD?" Morgan asked, smiling.

"Whichever jurisdiction the investigation took place in," D'Elia said. "Since the estate isn't within the Wilmington city limits, filing would likely be the county's responsibility."

※※※ ※※※ ※※※

Judge Matthew McLaughlin signed an expedited court order filed by the New Castle County District Attorney against Joanna Wójcik. The listed State of Delaware offenses were Unauthorized Access to Computers and Title 11, Chapter 5, Subchapter VI, Section 937: Unauthorized Access to a Computer System.

It compelled Verizon Communications Inc. to provide the records of Marta Niemczyk's cell and email communications for the past two hundred and seventy days. The order stipulated the information to be supplied within thirty-six hours. Bender's and LRI's investigators received the information with thirty hours to spare.

Further, the order authorized a tap on Marta Niemczyk's cell phone.

There were numerous emails and phone calls between Zajebisty-Travel.com and Marta

Niemczyk during the period. The phone calls intensified before Ginger McGuire's death and again a month later. Nothing incriminating appeared in the emails. They primarily consisted of family discussions and gossip, which had to be run through Polish-to-English translation programs.

The phone calls contained some curious conversations—in Polish—that made no sense. One referenced a birthday card snail-mailed to Czesław. His H-1B Visa application listed a date five months in the future.

⋈ ⋈ ⋈

Morgan, D'Elia, and Proffitt reviewed the information on a Zoom call with Bender and his lead investigator.

"If Niemczyk owns this travel company, why is it called 'Zajebisty?'"

"'Zajebisty' is a Polish slang term for 'exciting,'" Proffitt answered.

"What do Polish citizens need to visit the U.S.?" Bender asked.

D'Elia said, "Since Poland is an EU country, their citizens can use the Visa Waiver Program to visit the U.S. for up to 90 days."

"And after ninety days, Joe?" Morgan asked.

D'Elia laughed. "Probably *nothing*. The hundreds of thousands of southern and northern border incursions consume Customs and Border Protection. I'd be surprised if anyone is even *spot*-checking visitor returns."

"Then this Zajebisty Travel would be a good human trafficking conduit," Bender said. "That it would, Counselor," D'Elia confirmed.

Morgan shook his head. "So, how does any of this tie into the fentanyl murders?" he asked of no one in particular.

"It may not have anything to do with it," Proffitt said. "Joanna Wójcik replaced Marta Niemczyk as the old man's nurse. He was sleeping with Joanna, so chances are he was with Marta, too. Maybe this is a simple case of revenge."

D'Elia's eyebrows raised. "That's an interesting point. Did we see any romantic content in Marta's emails?"

Bender's investigator said, "We didn't see anything."

"Nor did we," Proffitt confirmed. "But we know one thing for sure. Marta has access to a guy with a master's degree in data management." "What's next?" Morgan asked.

"I'm going to get the Airmed security admin to let me log onto the system remotely and move the screenshots we took of the queries to our LRI system. Then you all can figure out how you want to use them."

⋈ ⋈ ⋈

Bill Wilson called Julie Stephens. "How about dinner and a movie this weekend?"

"Works for me, Billy. Let me see about getting coverage for the girls. I'll call ya back."

⋈ ⋈ ⋈

"Baltimore, we have a problem," Airmed's Senior Systems Administrator told Proffitt.

"What kind of problem?"

"The master cat is toast."

⋈║⋈ ⋈║⋈ ⋈║⋈

Morgan frowned. "Airmed's Master Cat is blown? Are there any *journeymen* cats?" D'Elia's brow furrowed like a fresh-plowed Iowa cornfield.

"Master catalog. It contains information about the locations and attributes of files on the system. Deleting it makes it impossible for the operating system to locate and access files like our screenshots of the queries."

"Can it be fixed?" D'Elia asked.

"No. It doesn't exist anymore. Whoever hacked into the system *shredded* the cat file by overwriting it multiple times with random characters or patterns to make it unrecoverable."

"So, that's it?" Morgan said.

"No, but restoring a backup will take someone with highly specialized skills and software. There's an outfit in Gaithersburg, Maryland, Washington Systems Consulting, Inc., specializing in catalog recovery. Former IBMers there bailed out the NSA recently. But even with the best and brightest, getting the drug trial database back on the air could take weeks.

"There may be a quicker way. Acronis, Inc. operates massive data centers in the U.S. The closest one to us is in Ashburn, Virginia. Airmed is going to attempt to take the latest full-system backup and restore it at Acronis. We'll be able to track the fentanyl DB queries and get new screenshots if they're successful."

⋈║⋈ ⋈║⋈ ⋈║⋈

Morgan, D'Elia and Proffitt called Fitzroy De Burgh.

Morgan started the conversation. "Fitzroy, you need to file a criminal complaint against Phillip Forge for unauthorized access, data destruction, and violation of any Delaware computer security laws immediately. If you want, I'll call John Holmes at the Wilmington Police on your behalf and ask him to charge Forge with the offenses I mentioned. We need to get him off the street today, if possible."

"Please do, Hunter. Are you worried that he will flee?"

"Like a rabbit, Fitzroy," D'Elia said. "How are the Acronis plans going?"

"Our Senior System Administrator has secured time in their Ashburn data center. He's driving down to start the restoration from the backup site this afternoon. Hopefully, he can

complete it in the next twenty-four to thirty-six hours."

FORTY-FIVE

D'Elia and John Holmes sat across the table from a visibly uncomfortable Phil Forge.

"Phil, you just couldn't keep your mouth shut," D'Elia said, slowly shaking his head.

"What?"

"You had to spill your guts to Ms. Niemczyk."

"I didn't tell Marta anything."

"So, she doesn't know about your poly test?"

"Oh, yeah. I told Marta about *that*. But just that, I took one. Nothing *else*."

"You told your girlfriend you took a *polygraph* test, and she didn't *ask* any questions."

"She asked if I was asked about her."

"And . . . *you* said?"

"That I couldn't talk about it."

"Do you realize that when you told her that, you *virtually* said, '*Yes*, they asked about *you*.'"

Forge's expression told the two men that the sun had risen behind Phil's widening, deep blue eyes.

"Let me fill you in on the situation, Phil," D'Elia said. "After your *non-*denial, Marta ran back to her brother . . . "

"Czesław?"

"You know about the brother?"

"I know *him*. Nice guy. Smart. Works for a sausage company. Marta and I drove up a couple of times." "And did you *see* Czesław at the factory?"

"No, at home."

D'Elia nodded. "That's because he *actually* runs a Polish travel agency for the *Pruszkow*, the Polish *Mafia*. Among many other activities, they run a human trafficking business. Marta has gotten you tangled up in *another* federal crime, Phil. I hope Marta was

good enough in bed to distract you when Bubba *mounts* you in the joint!" Forge looked ready to vomit.

"Here's what's going to happen, Phil." D'Elia stared at him for several seconds. "Acronis is setting up a test system in Virginia. They're going to restore the last full system backup. After they do, you're going to help Mr. Proffitt here create proof of the searches that captured the names of twelve murder victims."

"We're going to document the hacker's URL, too," Proffitt added.

⋈║⋈ ⋈║⋈ ⋈║⋈

With Joanna Wójcik's arrest, the fentanyl task force went into hibernation. Jefferson Bender's suggestion of Phillip Forge's involvement did nothing to arouse it.

He didn't call again—let the feds be surprised at trial if there ever was one.

The surveillance warrants for Marta Adamczyk's emails hadn't been particularly fruitful. The phone tap might become helpful.

Bender's law firm had several private detective firms on retainer. Two initiated twenty-four-hour surveillance. One team on Marta Niemczyk in Delaware, the other covering brother Czesław in New Jersey.

If either seemed to be about to flee, especially out of the U.S., the PI teams would make citizen's arrests.

⋈║⋈ ⋈║⋈ ⋈║⋈

In Acronis' massive Ashburn, VA, data center, a few keystrokes finished creating Airmed's test system. Their lead system administrator immediately began transferring the latest system backup, including the trial database. After nine hours and resolving several technical issues, Phil Forge logged in remotely to validate the DB's integrity. He pronounced it functional after running checksum verification, referential integrity checks, and replaying transaction logs.

Mark Proffitt took over at that point, searching for the queries used to collect the names of twelve murder victims and downloading screenshots in the process. During the searches, he discovered thirty-six additional names.

Joe D'Elia sat next to Forge, observing Proffitt's activity.

Minutes later, Forge interrupted Proffitt's actions with a phone call. "*Hey*! Look at the dates on those queries!"

"What about them?"

They were run more than *two years* ago! And notice the ID . . . *PF062001,* not *PF022022*! *Peter Fox* ran those nearly *nine months* before *I* was *hired*! He died in a motorcycle accident. That's why I'm here."

"What do the numbers stand for, Phil?" "The month and year of hire."

"I *told you I* wasn't involved!"

⋈║⋈ ⋈║⋈ ⋈║⋈

"Marta, what the hell did you and Czesław *do*?"

"Phil? Where are you?"

"In the New Castle County jail!"

"How are you calling me? Is this your one phone call?"

"No. Another inmate's letting me use the phone his girlfriend smuggled in.

"I'm being held for trial for Delaware computer crimes. They say my ID and password were used to search Airmed's database. They claim I collected the names of all those people murdered with fentanyl. I *didn't* do that."

"Why are you calling me?"

"You're the only one who could have gotten my system logon information from my iPhone. *Please*, get me out of here."

"How could I get anything from your phone, Phil? It's password protected."

"You could have opened it using my face while I *slept*."

"*No, moron*! With your *eyes closed,* the phone wouldn't *open*!"

The soft twin beeps in Forge's ear said Marta had left the building.

⋈⋈ ⋈⋈ ⋈⋈

"She's called an Uber to pick her up at the estate," the man monitoring Marta's phone tap said, alerting her surveillance team.

"Yeah, we just saw it go by."

"Don't grab her up unless it looks like she's going to squirrel." "Rabbit."

"My wife claims squirrels are more elusive."

⋈⋈ ⋈⋈ ⋈⋈

Phil Forge held D'Elia's phone out. It rang before Joe reached for it.

"D'Elia."

"Looks like you gal may be taking off. Ms. Marta called an Uber. Her detail has it in sight, heading toward New Castle Airport."

"Did she have baggage?"

"The team didn't see her get in the car. They were parked outside the estate."

"Okay. Make sure she has enough rope for a citizen's arrest to stick."

"Copy that. Will advise."

D'Elia terminated the call and looked at Forge. "I think your performance may have worked. She's in an Uber."

⋈⋈ ⋈⋈ ⋈⋈

The Uber pulled to the Avelo Airline departure's curb at the New Castle/Wilmington Airport. The surveillance team passenger took high-resolution photos of a woman exiting the car and trotting into the terminal. He set the camera down and reached for the door handle.

The driver put her hand on his left arm. "Wait. The back door's still open. He's not leaving."

New Castle/Wilmington Airport is a far cry from Chicago's O'Hare. No one responsible for security seemed interested in the idling cab or the lurking PIs.

Nearly five minutes later, Marta emerged and reentered the Uber.

ᴅᴎᴀ ᴅᴎᴀ ᴅᴎᴀ

"Marta went to the airport, Joe. She was inside for just a few minutes. Looks like she's headed back to the estate."

The Gene Pool Boy - 182

"Check Czesław's phone record. See if he got a call while Marta was inside the

terminal."

FORTY-SIX

Jefferson Bender didn't try to mask the frustration he felt. "*Jesus Fucking Christ*, Hunter. I don't know what's slicker than *Teflon*, but these people are all covered in it! We don't have shit to get Joanna off the hook and *no* prospects of finding a silver *bullet*."

"Joe and I have an idea, Counselor."

"Well, let's *hear* it!"

"We've been nibbling around the edges. Let's take a *bite* and ask Marta to take a poly." "Why would she do that?"

"She didn't run after Forge's call. *Maybe* she's *not* involved. We don't know why she went to the airport. If Marta made a phone call there, it wasn't to her brother."

"Why would she consent to a poly?"

"To prove her innocence."

"And if she tells us to fuck off?"

"Unfortunately, that wouldn't tell us anything. Marta might decline because she doesn't trust us or the test. But, if we ask her to sit for the poly, and she runs *afterward*, that would suggest something."

Bender cleared his throat. "Do it. What have we got to lose at this point? *Nothing*."

⋈⋈ ⋈⋈ ⋈⋈

"I had a great time, Bill. Thank you. Would you like to come in?"

"I'd love to, Julie, but I have a date with my nephew tomorrow morning. Dana and

Pieter is spending the day on someone's yacht, and I'm wrangling Evan. He only has two modes: one hundred percent, and *sleep*.

"Can I have a rain check?"

"You bet."

Wilson bent to kiss Julie on the cheek.

She redirected his face with two hands, kissing him full on the lips.

"*Oh!*"

"Too forward?" she asked.

"Not the *least* bit, Julie."

Encircling her in his arms, Bill pulled her toward him.

Julie's hands went behind his head, pulling his face down to hers. "Sure, you don't want to come in? The girls are at their father's."

◁|▷ ◁|▷ ◁|▷

Marta Niemczyk's phone rang as she entered her room at the estate. "Yes?"

"Ms. Niemczyk, my name is Joe D'Elia. I apologize for calling you this late." "Do I know you?"

"No, you do not. I'm working with Joanna Wójcik's attorney, Jefferson Bender."

"Why would I help her?"

"Because helping *her* might help you.

"I know Phillip Forge called you today from the Howard R. Young Correctional

Institution." "*What?*"

"Jail."

"How do you know that?"

"Phil borrowed the phone from another inmate. There is a tap on that man's phone. When the police heard Phil's conversation with you, they called the Wilmington Police, who notified Attorney Bender."

"I didn't know what Phillip was talking about."

"I *believe* you, Marta. That's why I'm calling. We'd like for you to take a polygraph test. That will prove you didn't." Niemczyk didn't respond.

"Phillip Forge is about to be charged with twelve counts of murder in the first degree. Some of the deaths took place in Virginia. He could get their *death* penalty. If you're involved, you could spend the rest of your life in prison."

"*I'm not involved!*"

"There's an *easy* way to *prove* it."

◁|▷ ◁|▷ ◁|▷

"How's *Evan wrangling* going this morning?" Julie giggled.

"*Someone* kept me up way too late last night. Fortunately, I arrived before he woke up and drank enough coffee to ward off his early attacks. But I'm fading now, thanks to *you!*"

"Oh, you poor soul! Didn't your mother warn you about women like me?"

"Fortunately, she did *not*."

◁|▷ ◁|▷ ◁|▷

In the early afternoon, Marta Niemczyk's heart rate, blood pressure, skin conductance, and respiration were ready to be monitored by LRI's polygraph equipment. "Is your name Rigena Marta Niemczyk?" the polygraphist asked.

"Yes."

"Are you sitting down?"

"Yes."
"Is today Sunday?
"Yes,"
"Are you now, or have you ever been, romantically involved with Phillip Forge?
"Yes."
"Did you recently call your brother Czesław from the New Castle, Wilmington
Airport?"
"No."
"Did you take an Uber to that airport recently?"
"Yes."

⋈||⋈ ⋈||⋈ ⋈||⋈

"We found the queries identifying the victims, boss. And, the names of about three dozen more to be *targeted*."

Morgan looked at Proffitt across his desk. "I sense a 'but' coming."

"Yeah, a *giant* but. Phil Forge's *predecessor* ran them in two-thousand-nineteen."

Joe D'Elia pulled out his notebook. "When in nineteen?"

"The beginning of August through mid-November."

D'Elia flipped back several pages and read his notes. "Then Fitzroy is off the hook. He was on his *sabbatical* in a mental institution."

"How about Marta Niemczyk?" Morgan asked.

Joe flipped more pages. "She'd been on the job for over six months."

Proffitt added, "And her poly is as clean as Forge's. One of 'em might beat the box, but two? Very unlikely. So, either they're both innocent or incredibly good.

"The date of the scans is good news for Joanna Wójcik, though," D'Elia injected. "She wasn't on the payroll until December twelfth of nineteen."

"Maybe," Morgan said. "Did you hear that Jefferson?"

On the phone in his D.C. office, Bender said, "I did. However, the feds will say, 'so what?' She may have had nothing to do with identifying victims, but the evidence points to her carrying out the murders." "Joe, when did Osín De Burgh die?"

"February of twenty. Why?"

"Could we be chasing a ghost?" Morgan asked.

"Meaning Osín set all this up before he died, Hunter?" Bender asked.

"Exactly."

Bender responded, "Well, as I suggested earlier, even if Osín planned it, he was long in his grave before the murders began."

Morgan nodded. "Yeah. Who carried on with the plan?

"Can you get a court order for Osín's phone, email, and banking records? Let's say, from six months before the queries were run up to the date of his death?" "Assuming Fitzroy doesn't object, we can try. What are you looking for?"

"A connection to anyone Osín would have no likely reason to be communicating with either via phone, web or commercially."

"Okay."

Morgan looked at Proffitt and D'Elia. "Anything else, guys?"

D'Elia nodded. "Yes, Jefferson, have you asked Joanna to take a poly?"

"I mentioned it. She didn't seem the least bit receptive to the idea."

"Do you think she's innocent?"

Bender chuckled. "I think *all* my clients are. Yes, in *her* case, I do."

"Then let's see if she's willing to prove it. We can run it. The feds never need to know the results."

"It'll be tough to keep it a secret with her in custody," Bender pointed out.

"True," D'Elia responded. "But, you're not obligated to share the results with them. If

Joanna is clean, it may help us find the perp."

FORTY-SEVEN

Two days later, Joanna Wójcik sat for a polygraph exam. Like Marta Niemczyk and Phillip Forge, she passed with flying colors.

⋈ ⋈ ⋈

"Joe, can we get a picture of Czesław Niemczyk?" Morgan asked.

"I have one from his Consular Processing Green Card application. Why?"

"Let's put it in a six-pack and have Gary Case take a look to see if he recognizes Czesław as the person he drove to Fernando Diaz's townhouse."

"Copy that. But we better connect with Case's attorney, Cassidy Lefevre, first. Based on my watching her when Margaret Case was interrogated, I'm sure Ms. Lefevre's panties will be in a bunch if we don't."

⋈ ⋈ ⋈

The usual suspects sat in Judge McLaughlin's chambers—AUSA Sergio Scarpelli and Attorney Jefferson Bender. A new addition, Fitzroy De Burgh, attended by phone. "Gentlemen, we meet again. What is the issue today?" the judge asked.

Bender explained the need for a court order for Osín De Burgh's phone, email, and banking records based on the timeframe of the database search that determined the names of the fentanyl murder victims.

AUSA objected. "Your Honor, this is merely a fishing expedition. Those records are irrelevant to the case without a clear connection to the issues."

"Mr. Bender?"

"Your Honor, as I explained, the victims were identified *before* the elder De Burgh's death. It is certainly possible he had some involvement. There is no evidence of *any* other family or staff member's involvement."

"*That's* not true, Your Honor. A member of the staff is in custody, charged with the murders," Scarpelli countered.

Bender responded. "Yes, an *innocent* woman who passed a polygraph exam without a single suggestion of deception. This request is to support her defense, Your Honor."

Scarpelli argued. "The elder De Burgh has a right to privacy, and his family's reputation is at stake."

Judge McLaughlin smiled. "Mr. Scarpelli, a first-year law student knows privacy rights rarely survive someone's death.

"Mr. De Burgh, have you been able to keep up with our conversation?"

"Yes, Your Honor. As my father's sole heir, I have no objection to releasing his records.

Proving Ms. Wójcik's innocence is paramount at this point."

"Very well. I'm granting your motion, Mr. Bender."

⋈||⋈ ⋈||⋈ ⋈||⋈

"Ms. Lefevre, Joe D'Elia. We met at the Providence PD when Margaret Case was interrogated."

"I remember, Joe. What can I do for you?"

"We have pictures of Marta Niemczyk's brother Czesław. You may remember she was Osín De Burgh's nurse before Joanna Wójcik."

"The *parade* of Poles."

D'Elia laughed. "Yes, quite. We want to show Gary Case a six-pack with Czesław's picture. We think Czesław may have been the man Gary drove to and from Mr. Diaz's home."

"Would you do this in person or online?"

"In person so we can watch Gary's reaction."

"I'll agree, but only if I'm in the room with him."

"Agreed."

⋈||⋈ ⋈||⋈ ⋈||⋈

"Fitzroy, we received Mr. Osín's phone and email records from Verizon this afternoon. His records from Wilmington Trust were transmitted to my office yesterday. I wanted to talk to you before I passed anything onto Morgan and company."

"What do they show, Jefferson?"

"We haven't yet had time to review the Verizon material thoroughly. We should have a complete picture by this time tomorrow.

"Your father's banking records show several substantial payments to Zajebisty Travel in Philadelphia. Do you have any idea why he might do that?"

"None. We don't fly commercially; our staff makes any necessary hotel or other reservations."

"Marta Niemczyk was his nurse for a time, correct?"

"She was."

"Her brother, Czesław, runs Zajebisty Travel."

"*Oh*! I did not know that."

"Would your father have had any interaction with Czesław?" "He visited his sister here a few times. They could have met." Bender didn't respond. "Jefferson, don't try to spare my feelings. My father will not return from his grave regardless of what you say."

After a deep breath and long sigh, Bender said, "Czesław has been identified as the man who set up the murder plant in Mr. Diaz's basement."

"Oh my *God*! Is *Marta* involved?"

"We don't think so at this point. Marta passed her polygraph exam with a perfect score. "There's more. Mr. Osín made a two-point-five-million-dollar payment to Ms. Aisling Coughlan in Eyeries, County Cork. Is that name familiar?"

"No."

"Are any of your family or staff from Eyeries or Cork?"

"Our chauffeur Claude MacFhionnlaoich is from Cork. I don't recall his village, though."

"So, you think my father is responsible. He was a mass *murderer*."

"Yes. We believe Mr. Osín had Peter Fox collect the names of people in the trials. We still have to figure out how the rest of the plan came together. "Did your father exhibit any strange behavior before his death?"

"He became a recluse after the final trial failed. He would lock himself in his office for hours and refuse to discuss his activities. I asked at one point if he was writing his biography. He answered, 'No, my legacy.'"

"Has your father's office been disturbed since his death?"

"No, it's precisely as it was the last time he used it. Why?"

"Can you go through it to see if you can connect the dots on his connection to Czesław and Claude?"

"I can. My father wrote in his journal faithfully every day. There are scores of them going back decades."

⋈⋈ ⋈⋈ ⋈⋈

"Hunter, I have good news and bad news. Which do you want first?" "The bad, Joe."

"Gary Case did not recognize Czesław Niemczyk."

"Okay. And . . ."

"The good news is . . . Fernando Diaz *did*."

"*No shit!*"

"Dat's da *truth,* Ruth!"

"So, Marta's brother *is* involved in setting up the manufacturing plant in Diaz's basement but *not* the distribution by whoever Gary Case *drove* to and from Diaz's place." D'Elia nodded. "Exactly."

⋈⋈ ⋈⋈ ⋈⋈

"Joe, can you get a contact in Interpol to give us some background on Aisling Coughlan in Eyeries, County Cork, on the Emerald Isle?"

"I already reached out to a buddy there. A retired *Garda Síochána* Deputy

Commissioner in Dublin. I asked him for info on Ms. Coughlan and Claude

MacFhionnlaoich, the chauffeur. We can't find a U.S. cell phone number for him."

"How does the staff communicate with him?"

"Encrypted radio. Mr. Osín was a security fanatic, hence the dozens of cameras in the estate. Fitzroy said his father trusted the 'wireless' more than phones since they were impossible to tap and had fewer dead spots.

"I asked my friend if the Garda could tell us if Claude has a local Ireland number. If he does, we can track his calls through Czesław's records.

"Ireland is five hours ahead of U.S. EDT, but I should hear something back in the morning."

"What about the two-point-five mil Ms. Coughlan received?" Morgan asked.

D'Elia nodded. "The bank records show the transfer went to the Bank of Ireland branch in Castletownbere, about twenty minutes from Eyeries, in County Cork. I asked my contact to see if Ms. Coughlan's family history shows a relationship with Mr. MacFhionnlaoich."

"Outstanding. Do we have any early results on Osín's phone traffic?"

"We do. Proffit's folks scanned the records into machine-readable files, then searched for Zajebisty Travel and Czesław's cell numbers. The old man initially had extensive phone and email communications with Zajebisty Travel, then switched to the cell number for the rest of his calls.

"Here's the clincher. The late Mr. Fox emailed the names of the first dozen victims to Czesław. A few days later, he sent the additional thirty-six names."

FORTY-EIGHT

As expected, when Joe D'Elia reached his office the following day, the blinking red message light indicated a new voicemail. An automated system sent him an email with a printout.

"Message Received At 0458 HRS From Country Code 353 1 284 7065

Joe it is grand to hear from ye, mate. Just a quick update. Aisling Coughlan is the niece of Claude MacFhionnlaoich. She is his only living blood relative. Ms. Coughlan had a daughter, Siobhán, with acute leukemia. The child was treated at Children's Hospital of Philadelphia. Mr. MacFhionnlaoich's mobile number is 353-027-586-9146. Call if you are in need of more. Cheers."

D'Elia updated Morgan quickly, then called Proffitt.

"Mark put a six-pack together that includes Claude MacFhionnlaoich, please. Then, have someone check to see if Czesław's phone received calls or dialed 353-027-586-9146.

That's an international number."

"Copy that."

⋈ ⋈ ⋈

"Hunter, do you have any past or present contacts in the Philly PD?"

"Would a retired Police Commissioner qualify, Joe?"

"Works for me. Can you get him . . ."

"*Her.*"

" . . . Her to give us a rundown of *Zajebisty* Travel's staff? If Gary Case doesn't recognize brother Czesław, maybe one of his henchmen will ring a bell."

⋈ ⋈ ⋈

"Dusty, Fitz De Burgh. Have I caught you at a bad time?"

"Not at all. It's a pleasure to hear from you."

"Thank you for that. I just wanted to let you know we've wrapped up the payments to the victims' families." "They *all* agreed?"

"They did. It wasn't easy tracking a couple of them down. Attorney Bender's firm did that; the final NDA was signed last evening."

"I'm surprised Speaker Peterson agreed. I thought she'd turn her daughter's death into a massive political outcry for a Congressional investigation and more federal oversite of the pharmaceutical industry."

De Burgh chuckled. "She was heading in that direction. We offered to create the Jasmine Peterson Pancreatic Cancer Fund—JPPCF for short. It will provide financial assistance to those afflicted with the disease and their families. It will be funded initially at twenty million dollars with another ten million donated annually for the next twenty years."

"*Two hundred twenty million dollars*? You are a *very* generous man, Fitz. I'm sure your father would be very proud of you."

"Based on the information I've received recently, I doubt that mightily."

"Can you share it with me?"

"Not at the moment, Dusty. I don't want to undercut the investigation, which appears to be coming to a close. When it is, I'll give you an exclusive and any details the police may not share."

"Am I free to write about the JPPCF's creation and the families' payments now?" "Yes, you are, Dusty.

⋈|⋈ ⋈|⋈ ⋈|⋈

Hunter Morgan and Charlotte Griffin struck up a friendship while serving on a Homeland Security Task Force following the 2015 bombing of the 16th Street Baptist Church in Birmingham, Alabama. Shortly after the group's final meeting, Charlotte became Philadelphia's first woman Police Commissioner. Following the election of a new mayor, Griffin decided to retire and form a consulting company. Philly Sleaze Stake, LLC—PSS, like LRI, became amazingly successful.

PSS already had some information on *Zajebisty* Travel, but Charlotte offered to do a deep dive into the outfit.

⋈|⋈ ⋈|⋈ ⋈|⋈

"Dusty Rhodes calling for Maddison Mitchell."

"One moment, please."

"A moment" dragged into "minutes." She was about to hang up when Mitchell answered, sounding like a long-lost sorority sister.

"*Dusty*, how *are* you?"

Surprised, said, "I'm just *fine*! How are *you*?"

"*Excellent*. How can I help you?"

"Fitzroy De Burgh has told me that Airmed's offer of ten million dollars to the families of the fentanyl murder victims' families has been completed. They all agreed to accept the offer.

"Any reaction, Maddison?"

"No, I think it's generous of Mr. De Burgh."

"So, the FBI and DOJ don't see anything questionable in the cash settlements?"

"The Bureau does not. I haven't discussed this with Acting AG Courtemanche. If he thought something was amiss, I'd have gotten some indication. Which I have not."

"And, are you aware of De Burgh's formation of the Jasmine Peterson Pancreatic Cancer Fund?"

"I was not."

"The JPPCF will provide financial aid to pancreatic cancer patients and their families with initial funding of twenty million and an additional two hundred million over the next ten years."

"Again, *very* generous."

"May I quote you on our conversation?"

"Yes, you may."

FORTY-NINE

A large file arrived in Morgan's email inbox from PSS, LLC. It contained BIs on every *Zajebisty* Travel full and part-time employee. Three men, in addition to Czesław, had various charges filed against them, including extortion, fraud, and assault without a single conviction. Somehow, victims' memories faded, or scheduling conflicts arose on trial dates.

Each man's mug shot was added to a six-pack. For a second time, Gary Case did not recognize anyone as the person he had driven to Diaz's.

Although D'Elia thought Case might be lying to protect himself and his family from the *Pruszkow*, he detected no sign of recognition in Case's eyes while scanning the six-packs.

Next, Joe slid a final photo lineup across the table before Case. His eyes lit up like a kid getting a new puppy.

Placing his finger on Claude's image, he almost shouted, "*That's him*!"

Cassidy Lefevre put her hand on Case's arm. "Are you sure?"

"You bet your sweet ass . . . " Embarrassed, he finished, "Oh, sorry. Yes, I'm *positive*."

D'Elia shook his head. "*Jesus*, Gary! You never said the guy was born before the *dinosaurs* disappeared! Knowing *that* little fact could have been helpful."

※ ※ ※

"Jefferson Bender."

"Morgan here. We've got some good news for Joanna Wójcik's case." After filling the attorney in on the identification of Claude MacFhionnlaoich as the person Case drove to the Diaz residence, he said, "Do you think the feds will at least recommend bail for her now?"

"Do we have any insight as to how the chauffeur got access to Joanna's Bentley?"

"Yes, he took it to service appointments. The dates line up with when Case says he drove.

"It looks like Claude did all of this to help his grandniece fight cancer. Unfortunately, she lost the battle. Hopefully, he'll come clean when interrogated."

"Okay. I'll call Acting Director Maddison Mitchell and share the good news."

"If you don't mind, would you let D'Elia call Jerry?"

"Casting *gluten* on the *liquid*, Hunter?"

"That's a novel way to put it, but yes."

                                    ✄✄✄ ✄✄✄ ✄✄✄

"Lonnie, I have some good news for you," D'Elia said.

"*Christ*, what *now*, Joe?"

"I think we can all button up the fentanyl cases in the next day or so."

"Yeah, how?"

D'Elia explained the most recent case developments to Special Agent Jerry, adding Bartosz Polak's name to the cast of characters.

D'Elia could hear a long sigh before Lonnie spoke.

"That's all good news from an investigatory standpoint. The bad news is now *I* get to share it with a fire-breathing dragon."

"Maybe you could slip into some Nomex underwear first."

"Maddison Mitchell eats Nomex for *breakfast*, Joe."

                                    ✄✄✄ ✄✄✄ ✄✄✄

"Fitz, Joe D'Elia."

"Joe, how are you?"

"I'm good. I have some news. Claude is the man who went to Diaz's house, apparently to collect the fentanyl bombs and mail them."

"*God*! Of all the people I'd have suspected . . ."

"It doesn't appear he did it out of greed, Fitz. Your father sent a sizable sum to Ireland for Claude's niece. Her daughter was battling cancer."

"How is she?"

"She died several weeks ago."

"Anyway, Claude will be arrested in the next few hours. I just didn't want you to be surprised."

                                    ✄✄✄ ✄✄✄ ✄✄✄

"Maddison, don't get pissed over what I'm about to say. It's good news."

"Yes?"

"Marta Niemczyk's brother Czesław was identified as the man who approached Diaz wanting to rent his basement.

"De Burgh's chauffeur, Claude MacFhionnlaoich, is the man Case drove to and from the Diaz residence."

"Who did *that*?" "D'Elia and company."

"*FFFFFFFFFFFFFUCK*!"

"Like I said, it's good news, Maddison."

"Yes, and makes the Bureau look like *Barney fucking Fife* on his *worst* day!

"Get a warrant out for Czesław Niemczyk and bring him down here ASAP. And pick up MacF . . . *whatever the fuck* his name is. I want an *agent* to verify that ID *immediately*, if not sooner!"

FIFTY

With Czesław and Claude in custody the following morning, Fitzroy's secretary scheduled a Zoom call for one PM with Jefferson Bender, Morgan, Cassidy Lefevre, Maddison Mitchell, and their appropriate staff members. The Acting FBI Director accepted . . . *reluctantly*.

With all joined on the call, Fitz opened the meeting. He sat behind an enormous desk framed by stacks of books on each side. As the camera zoomed in, the volumes appeared identical in size and color.

"Good afternoon. I know there are a lot of questions remaining before the fentanyl investigation can be closed. I hope to answer some of them on this call.

"In a conversation with Jefferson a few days ago, he asked if my father's office had been disturbed since his death. And if not, would I try to unravel the mysteries around his involvement in the case.

Gesturing toward the two stacks of books, Fitzroy said, "These are my father's journals." He took a volume from one of the piles, showing it to the camera. Zooming closer revealed gold leaf lettering on the 8" X 11" black leather cover.

Osín Darragh De Burgh
2019 --

"These are the records of his life. They hold many answers and even more questions. I have had copies made of all of these and will ship them overnight to the FBI, defense attorneys, and LRI.

"In a conversation I had with Hunter Morgan at the beginning of this nightmare, he related something I believe is proven by my father's actions. Mr. Morgan said he learned a valuable lesson during his first tour in Vietnam. 'People are *never more dangerous* than when they feel they have *nothing* left to lose.'

"We knew our last trial did not appear promising early on. Yet, we continued with it, hoping for some tiny positive shred to build on. It did not materialize. I saw something in my father's face that day for the first time . . . defeat.

"No, *more* than simple defeat. The *soul-crushing* realization that your life-long dream is *impossible*. He was never the same.

"I know what I've read in this last journal wasn't written by the man Osín Darragh De Burgh was for the vast majority of his life—caring, honorable, generous. But, enough of a preamble."

Fitzroy set the volume down on the desk, looked at it for several seconds, then faced the camera again.

"In two-thousand-nineteen, my father made the acquaintance of Czesław Niemczyk through his sister Marta. He saw something dark and mysterious in Mr. Niemczyk. They talked about the drug trial that had just closed.

"Czesław said, '*Kto nie ryzykuje, ten nie ma.*' 'He who does not take risks, will not have.'

"And, '*Nie ma rzeczy niemożliwych.*' 'There are no impossible things.'

"My father began believing *any* small impact on pancreatic cancer would be *far* more preferable than doing *nothing*. And, it's obvious, reading his own words, that he agreed with Niccolò Machiavelli. 'The *end* justifies the *means*.'

"One *small* contribution could be preventing the descendants of pancreatic cancer victims from passing on genetic death sentences. If the victims' children had not procreated, the BRCA1 and BRCA2 genes, their accomplice PALB2, and the CDKN2A, KRAS, and TP53 genes would not put future generations at risk. Of course, this eugenics theory ignored that future partners carrying these genes would erase any short-term benefits."

Fitzroy paused for a sip of water.

D'Elia asked, "Fitz, how did Mr. Osín know the genetic makeup of the cancer victims?"

"We had done genetic workup of every trial member before allowing them to participate."

"Thanks. Please continue."

"He discussed his theory with Czesław Niemczyk, who my father thought *very* bright. Among Czesław's various business interests is the distribution of illicit drugs, including fentanyl. Although the primary ingredients and precursors used in the synthesis of fentanyl are not publicly disclosed, not only did Czesław know what they were, he could provide them.

"We built the laboratory on Meadow Lark Lane in case something caused the Airmed or Miach facilities to become inoperable. The most joyous times in my father's life revolved around chemistry. He produced the practically pure fentanyl by himself."

Maddison Mitchell interrupted, "We had our forensic team do an in-depth analysis of Meadow Lark Lane and found no trace of anything, let alone fentanyl."

"Once he felt he had enough fentanyl for his plan, he sent in three industrial cleaning companies in succession. I imagine one would have sufficed, but he believed in overkill." Fitzroy shook his head. "That was a *poor* choice of words. Forgive me, please.

"On one of the visits before my father died, he and Czesław discussed the latter's going to Fernando Diaz's home with an offer to rent his basement. They knew . . . " "Why Diaz?" Maddison Mitchell asked.

"I was about to tell you, Acting Director.

"Czesław and my father knew Mr. Diaz's desperation to get family members out of Cuba and would not be likely to turn the funds down. Additionally, as an employee, if necessary, the threat of losing a very lucrative *gardening* position would keep Mr. Diaz in line."

Cassidy Lefevre asked, "How did the chauffeur become involved with Mr. Case?"

"Patience, Counselor, I'll get to Mr. Case in due course.

"In order to keep the plan compartmentalized, a second party needed to package the fentanyl dispensers into the envelopes that would ultimately murder the targeted offspring. That was the job of a Czesław loyal associate, one Bartosz Polak."

The attendees heard paper rustling as Morgan thumbed through Charlotte Griffin's list of Zajebisty Travel employees. Finding Polak listed, he nodded silently to D'Elia and

Proffitt.

"Mr. Polak left the assembled weapons for a third party to pick up and mail. At the same time, on one visit, he placed an order with the Chinese company to replenish the stock of dispensers and envelopes.

"Now, on to your client, Ms. Lefevre.

"Once again, Mr. Case's story is also about *leverage*. Czesław, through his *Pruszkow* connections, knew of Mr. Case's involvement in a drug cartel's prosecution. The murder plan needed the weapons moved out of Diaz's home. Mr. Case couldn't refuse if he wanted his family to survive.

"Siobhán, Claude MacFhionnlaoich's grandniece, had cancer and faced certain death if she couldn't escape the clutches of the United Kingdom's National Health Service. Again, they leveraged Claude into risking his freedom to save Siobhán and kept the *compartments* secure with yet another new team member.

"The two-and-a-half million-dollar *gift* sent to Aisling Coughlan was large enough to pay the UK's burdensome taxes and leave sufficient funds for travel and America's best treatment. As a result, Siobhán is a happy, healthy young lady today.

"Questions?"

"Mr. De Burgh, Mark Proffitt. Did Czesław destroy the system catalog?"

"I don't *know*, but I suspect so. That happened well after my father's death. I take his words in these journals as what lawyers call 'his dying declaration.'

"Czesław is described as being highly trained in computer science."

"Yes, a master's in data management," Proffitt confirmed.

Jefferson Bender asked, "Is there any indication Marta Niemczyk was involved in any way?"

"No, my father mentions that he and Czesław purposely kept her in the dark to protect her going forward. I believe Mr. D'Elia calls it '*plausible* deniability.'"

"I have a question," Morgan said. "How did they know the prospective victims had no children?"

"Simple detective work. They checked to see if the children lived at the addresses listed in the applications to join the study. If they did, searches of birth announcements, certificates, and social media were done. If they were not at the listed address, paid online background investigations could usually provide current addresses and if children were involved."

"Were any mistakes made," Cassidy Lefevre asked.

"There were not," D'Elia answered for Fitzroy.

"Fitz," Joe continued, "any indication of how the unused envelope was left in the Bentley's trunk, or 'boot' as you call it?"

"No, that happened after my father's death. I suspect when Claude collected several of the bombs, he inadvertently picked the envelope up as well. He had to have mailed the murder weapons before the Bentley was stolen. Somehow, the envelope was never removed. Thank *God* for small mercies."

"You're happy it was discovered?" Maddison Mitchell asked.

"I am indeed."

"But your father's reputation? He'll now be known for his final act, not his pharmaceutical career." Madison responded.

"That is very true. To the world, Father will be infamous as a mass murderer. But Airmed and Miach Laboratories are his legacy. Their innovation and drive to solve common and deadly problems made the world a better place for tens of millions of patients.

I would rather one man's reputation be sullied than the exemplary efforts of generations.

EPILOGUE

The Pennsylvania State Police arrested Czesław Niemczyk on one of his rare visits to the Polish Sausage factory. Since a PA citizen was among the murder victims, the Keystone State's Attorney General refused to turn the prisoner over to the feds. Czesław refused to cooperate with the prosecution or take a plea bargain. He was tried and sentenced to life in a maximum-security facility. Ninety-four days later, a Graterford State Correctional Institution Correction Officer discovered Czesław's cold body in a shower. He had been shanked in both kidneys.

Delaware authorities turned Claude MacFhionnlaoich over for federal prosecution, saving DE the time and cost of incarceration and a trial. He died of a heart attack while awaiting the trial to begin.

The FBI stormed the *Zajebisty* Travel office. Computers and other electronics, including stand-alone hard drives and cell phones, were confiscated and sent to Quantico for analysis. Lab technicians discovered a wealth of information about the *Pruszkow* crime organization and Czesław's *hacking* tracks to shred Airmed's master catalog. Working with INTERPOL, several dozen Poles were arrested and prosecuted on both sides of the Atlantic for human trafficking, money laundering, drug manufacturing, and distribution.

Seventy-one young women were discovered in *Zajebisty* leased properties in and around Philadelphia. The names of hundreds of others, provided by lab Quantico technicians, kicked off attempts to locate and free them.

Marta Niemczyk had an innocent reason for her Uber trip to Wilmington/New Castle Airport—picking up her cousin. Inside, she discovered the flight had been canceled and returned to the De Burgh estate.

Maddison Mitchell became the FBI Director, with Lonnie Jerry as her *aide-de-camp*. Within six months, Lonnie decided to retire. He returned to the Bureau as a contractor teaching Investigative Techniques in Quantico.

Luke Courtemanche passed muster with the Senate Judiciary Committee to become the Attorney General. He initiated several sweeping changes to streamline his organization.

Julie Stephens and Bill Wilson married six months later. They lived in their respective homes until Bill's retirement, after which he moved to Montgomery County.

How the *Pruszkow* mob connected Gary Case's involvement with the Sinaloa Cartel's prosecution remains unanswered. But, taking no chances, Gary, Margaret, and the Case children disappeared overnight.

Gary's testimony of the cartel's intricate workings resulted in warrants being issued for eleven high-ranking members. The Mexican government refused to extradite them. Each man died in a variety of odd accidents within six months, temporarily crippling the organization.

Dozens of FBI agents and Federal Marshalls raided numerous U. S.-based cartel front companies, confiscating hundreds of millions in cash and cryptocurrencies. Cash smuggling operators were picked off, yielding millions in various currencies, with the majority in dollars. The seized computers and external hard drives provided troves of additional data to further eviscerate the Sinaloa Cartel.

Joanna Wójcik, Marta Niemczyk, and Phillip Forge were cleared of any involvement in the case.

Aisling Coughlan was not required to return any of the money contributed by Osín Darragh De Burgh.

Dusty Rhodes wrote a series of articles outlining the fentanyl murder victims, Osín Darragh De Burgh's and Czesław Niemczyk's relationship, and Fitzroy's complete transparency in solving the case. She received her third Pulitzer Prize.

The End

GLOSSARY

140	Sergeant for the sector or squad
2100	The original phone extension for the homicide is still in use to identify that department.
ACES	Auto Crimes Enforcement Section
AG	Attorney General
AI	Artificial Intelligence
BBB	Better Business Bureau
BI	Background Investigation
Big-Foot	Take Over
BPD	Baltimore Police Department
BWI	Baltimore Washington International
CBP	Customs and Border Protection
CDC	Centers For Disease Control
CDS	Controlled Dangerous Substance
CODIS	Combined DNA Index System
CR	County Road
DBA	Data Base Analyst
DFL	FBI Digital Forensics Laboratory
DMV	Department of Motor Vehicles
DNA	Deoxyribonucleic Acid
DOA	Dead On Arrival
DOJ	Department Of Justice
EDT	Eastern Daylight Time
EOB	End Of Business
EU	European Union
FCI	Federal Correctional Institution
FCPD	Fairfax County Police Department
FISA	Foreign Intelligence Surveillance Act
Garga	Ireland's Police Force
HIPAA	Health Insurance Portability and Accountability Act
HIT	Auto Theft/Heist Interdiction Team
ILG	Wilmington/New Castle Airport
IMPD	Indianapolis Metropolitan Police Department
IP	Internet Protocol (internet address)
IT	Information Technology

KGA	"Dispatch" or "Communications" KGA comes from an old BPD call sign—KGA410. It is used to refer to dispatchers—KGA.
Lateral	A dual transmission to dispatch and another officer
LE	Law Enforcement
LPR	License Plate Reader
LRI	Last Resort Investigations
MC	Montgomery County
MCAC	Maryland Coordination and Analysis Center
MCP	Maryland County Police
MCPD	Montgomery County Police Department
ME	Medical Examiner
MO	Method of Operation
Morbus Hepatitis	Latin for Liver Ailment
MPCTC	Maryland Police Correctional Training Commission
MRE	Meals Ready to Eat
MSP	Maryland State Police
Multi-GNSS	Global Navigation Satellite System
NCB	National Central Bureaus
NCIC	National Crime Information Center
NMVTIS	National Motor Vehicle Title Information System
NOK	Next Of Kin
OCME	Office of the Chief Medical Examiner
OED	Oxford English Dictionary
PC	Probable Cause
PDBA	Primary Database Administrator
Perp(s)	Perpetrator(s)
PIO	Public Information Office
PM	Prime Minister
POTUS	President Of The United States
PPCT	Pressure Point Control Tactics
ROR	Released on Own Recognizance
RTK	Real-Time Kinematic Positioning
SAIC	Special Agent in Charge
SOS	Secretary of State
SS	Secret Service

SWAT	Special Weapons And Tactics
URL	Uniform Resource Locator
USMC	Uncle Sam's Misguided Children
USPS	United States Postal System
WITSEC	Witness Security Program

ACKNOWLEDGEMENTS

Thank you to my friends who allowed their names to be used as characters.

- *DENISE FERRUCCI*, my wife, is the **light** of my life. She has supported me in ways too numerous to list. Denise is **always** there to love and encourage me over and over. Her loyalty, generosity, and compassion **know no bounds**. **Thank You**!

- *DON HEALY* has been a friend and invaluable source of information for my last four books. He is now enjoying retirement with his wife, Gisela, in suburban Baltimore.

I introduced myself to the following Baltimore or Maryland Law Enforcement organization members through Don. If he didn't know the answer to my question, he recommended a subject matter expert. None of my work, starting with and after *High Order*, would have been remotely as technically accurate without Don's involvement.

- The late *JOSEPH A. COSTANTINI* was Don's first introduction. At the time, Joe was Baltimore's Lead Bomb Technician. It didn't take long for Joe to become a dear friend. He provided technical assistance until the very end of his life. Joe was a fantastic man: brilliant, knowledgeable, funny, and courageous. We miss Joe *every day*.

- *PAUL DAVIS* has been a valuable friend for nearly two decades. His knowledge of police tactics, procedures, and policies made *The Gene Pool Boy* and my earlier law enforcement-related novels far more crisp and understandable to readers. Paul, like Don and Joe, is a treasured friend and collaborator.

- *ROBERT STANTON*, retired Chief of Detectives of Baltimore's Homicide Unit's eight squads, answered endless questions about the makeup and internal workings of the organization he led. His knowledge of the origins of various BPD terms and radio call signs never ceases to amaze me.

- *RANA DELLAROCCO* is the Chief of Science and Evidence for the Baltimore Police Department's Forensic Science and Evidence Services Division—aka the Crime Lab. Like all mentioned above, Rana answered my questions about evidence collection and processing. Her detailed descriptions of their lab activities made *The Gene Pool Boy* a far more accurate story than it would have been otherwise. Rana was yet another **great** resource through Don Healy.

- *TAD WILSON* is a man who has turned piles of my words into formatted manuscripts without breaking a sweat. I have to believe that process doesn't happen—at least in the case of my work—without his uttering numerous expletives. Tad knows *more* about Microsoft Word than Bill Gates' crew. A true Word virtuoso and **dear** friend, if ever there was one!

- *BARBARA CARLSON* has been correcting and editing my work since the early 21st century. After her incredible work in finding my scores of stupid spelling errors—and laughing with me over them—Barbara continues to amaze me. Each time I think she's reached the pinnacle of perfection; Barbara proves I wasn't patient enough.

ABOUT THE AUTHOR

I grew up in East Texas, about halfway between Houston and Dallas. By the time I was 18, I found myself on the wrong side of the law in Chicago. A judge told me I could either go to the Illinois State license plate factory or provide him with proof of my enlistment in any branch of America's Armed Forces. I left the courthouse, turned right, found an Army Recruiting Station a few blocks away. In the 60s, if you could fog up a mirror the Army would take you.

Not long afterward, in early 1964, I found myself in the Republic of South Vietnam as a member of the Military Assistance Command – Vietnam with approximately 18,000 other Americans. I spent the year mostly north of Saigon in Pleiku, Ban Me Thout, and finally as part of the team supporting the Vietnamese Military Academy in Dalat.

After returning to "The World," I was assigned to Ft. Bragg, North Carolina. There I learned that the Army believed it was much easier to send successful "advisors" back to Vietnam than it was to make new ones, with "success" being defined as "survival." I probably misled the Army into thinking that was OK, when I reenlisted for six more years and skipped a "Vietnam Orientation," foolishly thinking that I'd learned more in a year than I could in an hour.

My second tour in the RVN went in the opposite direction. The Mekong Delta was my home that year, mostly in Bac Lieu Province assigned to the 21st Army Republic of Vietnam. By 1966 the U.S. build-up in Vietnam was in full swing with Marine and Army units operating in unit strength, mostly north of Saigon.

Once again I returned to Ft. Bragg and spent a year there before being sent to Italy in 1968. Italy was a whole lot more livable than MAC-V. Again, there was a "Vietnam Orientation" and since I hadn't cracked the code yet, I skipped it. In '69 . . . you guessed it, I received orders to return to MAC-V. Note to self . . .

During '69 and '70, I returned to the Mekong Delta and Bac Lieu Province. This time I was assigned to Civil Operations and Revolutionary Development Support Team 20.

By then, the war was going through the "Vietnamization" stage, a euphemism for "pulling-out," which turned over more and more of the support and combat operations to indigenous personnel. However, MAC-V advisors continued to do what they had since becoming America's first ante in Vietnam: train the troops, then accompany them on combat operations. Organized directly under General William C. Westmoreland, CORDS consisted of a civil-military structure designed to pacify their areas of operation by training the local populations into Regional and Popular Forces military organizations and improving the government's responsiveness. The latter consisted of various CIA Rural Development organizations working to dig wells, build schools, and provide remote medical assistance.

In 1970 I returned to Ft. Gordon, Georgia, where I attended every Vietnam Orientation scheduled. But alas, in early 1972 I received orders for . . . Yup! However, I had less than 90 days until my reenlistment was up, and once I pointed out to a crusty old warrant officer at personnel that I had no intention to "re-up," the orders were canceled.

In 1974, I finally learned that you could make more with your mind than you can with your back. I went to school, got a degree, and was hired by IBM. It's a long way from the bib overalls of Carlisle, Texas, to the three-piece suits of IBM and even farther from the Mekong Delta to "The World." Life was great . . . and I was miserable. The VA's Vietnam Vet Outreach program was my salvation. Not for what it did for me, but rather for what it told me to do for myself . . . write.

And I did, about all the things I couldn't talk about. That was the genesis of ___No Survivors___, my Vietnam novel. It's based on real people and events during my three tours in Vietnam and is dedicated to the more than 58,000 names on The Wall, their families, friends, and all veterans.

In appreciation for all that my fellow veterans have done for me, and in recognition of the fact that well over 150,000 veterans are homeless on the street every night, I donate 50% of the royalties from ___No Survivors___ to various veterans' support organizations.

High Order, my second novel, is based on actual Baltimore Bomb Squad cases. Again, the characters are drawn based on the bomb technicians, patrolmen, and detectives I met while doing research for *High Order*.

My son Brian and his cousin Matthew man the "Thin Blue Line" in Colorado and Texas. In tribute to my family's involvement and the many members of the Baltimore City and Baltimore Country police forces and bomb squads who assisted in the writing of *High Order*, 50% of the royalties are donated to various state and local police support organizations.

Primary Candidates, my third novel, is available in hardcover, paperback, and e-book formats. In writing *High Order*, I made many contacts and good friends in the law enforcement community.

The current situation in the U.S. Department of Veterans Affairs shows that veterans are seriously under-supported. Thankfully, there are many excellent private groups stepping in to assist our brothers and sisters in arms.

Since many in law enforcement and current and recent members of the military were so critical to the creation of *Primary Candidates*, I am donating 50% of the royalties to various law enforcement and veterans' support groups.

The Immaculate Infection is now available. Iran's Revolutionary Guard Corps has been ready to strike the Yankees for some time. They want retribution for crushing international sanctions and the destruction of Iran's major oil refinery and a shipping terminal on Kharg Island. The Supreme Leader has refused to approve the attacks. But after America kills the country's most iconic general, millions of Iranians screaming for revenge cannot be ignored. The Ayatollah greenlights the three-phase plan unleashing devastation dwarfing 9/11.

As with my other works, 50% of my royalties are donated to our Veterans and First Responders.

If you enjoy these books, please don't lend them.

I wish you well!

Mike Sutton

Life member of

- *Vietnam Veterans of America*
- *American Legion*
- *Combat Infantrymen's Association*
- *Disabled American Veterans*
- *Veterans of Foreign Wars*
- *VetFriends*
- *Vietnam Veterans of America*

For more information about Mike Sutton's life and career, visit him at: https://mksutton.com/about-mike-sutton/ .

One Last Thing . . .

If you enjoyed this book or found it useful, please take a moment to post a review on Amazon. Enter https://www.amazon.com/Mike-Sutton/e/B001KI9TP8/ref=ntt_dp_epwbk_0 into your computer's internet browser, and it will take you to this book's review link on Amazon.

I read all reviews personally and use what I learn to improve the book, so please take a moment to help me improve your reading experience. It will make my books better and give you the satisfaction of knowing that you have made a difference for all my readers! Thanks for your continuing support!

Made in the USA
Columbia, SC
25 January 2025

d6f630fa-658a-4c4b-afec-3fd21d5aed4bR01